PRAISE FOR ROSEMARY RAWLINS

"A riveting and heart-rending account of one young woman's ordeal during the Cambodian genocide."

— WILLIAM J. DUIKER, SCHOLAR AND AUTHOR OF *HO CHI MINH, A LIFE*

"A young Cambodian girl's life is upended by the brutality of war in this novel...

The author artfully contrasts the beautifully simple life the Sangs once enjoyed with the ghastly one paradoxically imposed by utopian rhetoric. This is a poignant emotional drama as well as an astute exploration of a sad period in Cambodian history.

A heartbreakingly touching tale, historically intelligent and emotionally devastating."

— *KIRKUS REVIEW*

"A poignant story with a 'voice' that will draw you in.

First, the evocative writing. So few writers have the ability to write in a voice that is not their own but is the voice of their protagonist who is from an entirely different place, time, and culture. Rosemary Rawlins has this ability. Next, the story itself; the love, graciousness, and gentleness of a family and people subjected to evil that most readers will be almost unable to imagine. This beautifully told story will help you to imagine it. Then there is the education, almost effortless for the reader, that this story offers. Please take this gift in both hands, and when you have read it, share it with your world."

— JENNI OGDEN, AUTHOR OF *A DROP IN THE OCEAN*

"All My Silent Years is *elemental, direct, raw, intimate, and transformative. A story that* grips you and carries you directly into the beauty and tragedy of a hidden corner of contemporary history. The consequences of what happened in Cambodia in the 1970s are still unfolding. Thanks to Rosemary Rawlins' intimately detailed story of how an idyllic Buddhist family was upended by remote and corrupt national interests, we are pained at what was lost, and awestruck at what has been reborn."

— JONATHAN MARCUS, AUTHOR OF *EVERYTHING IS
HAPPENING AT ONCE*

"True history, yes—but perhaps just as important, a book I couldn't put down. A story that grabbed me from the start."

"Imagine what it must have been like to grow up as a child amidst the tragic upheaval of the Cambodian Civil War. In this exhaustively researched but deeply felt first novel, Rosemary Rawlins brilliantly evokes the lived experience of a young girl, Sokha, whose peaceful, rural childhood falls to the upheaval of the killing fields. This is what it must have been like to see your family torn apart, your home destroyed, your dreams turned to nightmares. Yet through it all, this remarkable heroine survives with one goal, to reclaim her loved ones and find a place they can call home. "

"Heartfelt. A moving story about a young Cambodian girl caught up in the violence of the Khmer Rouge (Pol Pot) regime. I especially enjoyed specific details about life in Cambodia and learning some of the history of the time period (mostly the 1970s). Now I'm curious to read more about America's involvement in Cambodia around the time that the Vietnam War ended."

ALL MY SILENT YEARS

A NOVEL

ROSEMARY RAWLINS

Arkonn!
Rosemary Rawlins

RARECOMPOSITIONS

All My Silent Years
a novel
by Rosemary Rawlins
Published by Rare Compositions, LLC
Nags Head, NC
© 2019 Rare Compositions, LLC
rosemaryrawlins.com

Publisher's Note:

This book is dedicated to the extraordinary woman who inspired the character of Sokha.
She wishes to remain anonymous.

GLOSSARY

Angkor: City
Angkar: "Higher organization"
Ba: Pa (slang for father)
Bong: Slang for male or female person of older or similar age, affectionate
Chlop: Khmer Rouge militia spies, often young children
Cyclo: A pedal-powered rickshaw (cycle rickshaw)
Kampuchea: Kingdom of Cambodia
Khmer: Native Cambodian or language of Cambodia
Khmer Rouge: "Red Khmer" or Communist Cambodian
Krama: Traditional Cambodian garment with many uses: scarf, bandanna, to cover face, or sling to carry children
Kru Khmer: Traditional Khmer medicine practitioner
Mea: Ma (slang for mother, pronounced May)
Preah: *God* or *King or as adjective: sacred* or *holy*
Sampeah: A Cambodian greeting. Palms pressed together. The more respect intended, the higher the hands are held, from chest high (for friends) to forehead level when praying to God or sacred statues
Stupa: A mound-like structure containing relics. A place to

meditate. Serves as a Buddhist shrine. Ashes of the deceased may lie within the stupa along with offerings of food for the dead for their transition to a reincarnated life.

Wat: Temple. Angkor Wat means Temple City.

Vossagga: Letting go of clinging and craving. Relinquishing.

HISTORICAL CONTEXT

The Angkor Empire of Southeast Asia began in 802 CE and flourished until it sprawled across modern-day Thailand, Cambodia, South Vietnam, and Laos; but conflicts carved up the kingdom until Thailand ended the Angkor period in 1431 CE.

A subsequent annexation upset Cambodia in the late 1600s when Vietnam gained control of the Mekong Delta, cutting off Cambodia's access to the South China Sea. The loss of this treasure trove fueled successive conflicts and generations of anger and hate.

Fearing the eventual takeover of Cambodia, the French stepped in as a protectorate in 1867, and added their footprint to architecture and education.

In this land of turmoil, Prince Norodom Sihanouk won Cambodia's independence in 1953.

In this land of crumbling temples, where farmers and fisherman worked dawn to dusk while kings were seen as divine gods on earth, Sokha was born.

In this land of two seasons—the dry, sunny season and the wet monsoon season—a patchwork of green rice fields flourished as Sokha grew.

In this land imbued with animism, where rocks and trees vibrate with helpful or vengeful spirits called the Neak Ta who must be appeased, Sokha prayed.

In Cambodia—Kampuchea—the land of the Khmer people, history is long and memories are steeped in the anger and violence of warlords and kings.

In the northwestern province of Battambang, amid beauty and strife, Sokha's story begins.

1

Davi Sang
April 1964-1965

Davi Sang labored beneath the shade of fragrant fruit trees in a country laboring through contractions of its own.

The dry season is ending. I sense the southwest monsoon season coming. May is only weeks away, and I must be ready to help sow the first rice seeds for the long growing season. Hurry, child. Come into this world so I can get started.

Walking, squatting, and holding her swollen belly, Davi noticed every detail of her home. She scanned the stilted house raised ten feet high by eight thick, round pillars, not the mere sticks most farm families used to support their homes—Boran would not have that—and she noticed, as if for the first time, the fine texture of the tropical hardwood walls topped by a roof of red clay tile, her husband's statement against the blue sky. *Here we will stay. No traveling for you, little one.* She'd had enough of moving place to place with Boran's army posts, and although the farm required heavy hands-on work, Davi was suited to it. Acres and acres of fruit trees and rice fields brought sustenance and stability. Davi felt something akin to love for this land and all it produced for her family. A strong cramp interrupted her thoughts, and Davi crouched.

"Focus on what you see, not on the pain. Look around you," the midwife said. Davi's womb pulled the energy from every limb, making her legs feel wobbly. She felt the pressure of a hand squeeze her shoulder. "Walk. Walking helps," the midwife continued. Davi stood and managed a few steps to the ceramic bowl of water sitting on a tall tree stump and dipped her fingers in the cool water to wet her lips before she looked up. Colorful shapes of damp laundry hung from a rope tied between two mango trees. A chicken scratched the dirt for her chicks, who competed for exposed bugs. *Good mothers, those chickens*, Davi thought.

Finally, feeling ready, Davi padded over to the wood platform beneath the house where her oldest daughter had placed a woven mat and cotton sheet, and she pushed. Within an hour, Sokha Sang slid into the midwife's hands.

"It's another girl!" the midwife said. Once she checked and wiped the slippery baby clean, she handed the child to her mother. "She's strong and healthy like you."

Still panting, Davi snipped a piece of Sokha's hair from the top of her head to detach any bad luck that lingered from a former life, and she tied a holy red string to the infant's arm to keep the mother of the baby's past life from visiting her. Once done, she laid back down with a sigh of relief. She had brought a third daughter into the world.

Through a fog of exhaustion, Davi saw her husband approach. Boran had a way of walking, his shoulders wide, never hunched. His figure blurred from the steam of the boiling pot on the fire. Davi heard his deep voice before she dozed off. She had meant to remind him to pay the midwife well so she would not have to be her servant in the next world, but the penetrating warmth from the heated rock resting on her belly lulled her into oblivion, a peacefulness she had not known for months.

Upon waking, her thoughts flew to her new daughter. "Where is she?" she mumbled, still drowsy.

"I have her," said Mali. "I'm right here." The baby's head rested in the crook of Mali's arm, eyes squeezing and opening as if trying to adjust to the light. Mali rocked her instinctively, her gaze fixed on her new sister's face.

Davi turned her head. *Look how competently Mali holds an infant, and how young and beautiful she looks! Why have I not looked more closely at her lately? She's fifteen, almost old enough to marry.* The thought jolted her. She looked again at Mali's thick black hair framing her round face—her straight eyebrows over warm, maternal eyes.

"She's perfect, Mea," Mali said, now smiling at Davi. She bent and handed the baby to her mother. "And look, Aunt Ary and Uncle Keo brought us dinner. Fish Amok, and I have made rice enough for a few days."

"They were here? I missed them?"

"You were up all last night. They did not want to wake you and didn't stay long," Mali said. She lifted a bamboo tray of eight banana-leaf baskets filled with fish and spiced noni leaf. "Look, no cooking tonight, and Uncle Keo brought his clay pot for steaming with turmeric for your skin. He said you must keep warm for a few days to regain your strength."

"My sister is always cooking and has been smart to collect the seeds of herbs that have grown scarce. It's the secret to her special meals," Davi said.

Mali nodded in agreement and held the tray to her nose for a whiff.

"I'm glad I gently suggested we settle this land near my

sister's farm," Davi said. "Had I insisted, Ba would never have done it. Men like to know they are making the decisions in the family," she said with an instructive tone. "Sisters should stick together if they can. It makes for a happier life."

"And now I have another sister," Mali said. "A gift."

Davi lifted Sokha to eye level as if the baby could stand on air, and she stared into the glinting dark pools of her newborn's eyes. "So you have been the one kicking me all through the dry season! I'm your Mea, and I already know a few things about you. You have a lot of energy," she said. Sokha fussed, and Davi attached the baby to her breast.

"She's going to be a good eater," Davi said. When Sokha drank her fill and drifted off to sleep, Davi asked, "Should we introduce her to her other sister?"

"Jah, I'll get her. She's been keeping away—a little scared of what might be happening to you—but there's been plenty to distract her, especially that new stray puppy."

Davi gave Mali a warning look. "Cows, pigs, chickens, ducks, and roosters. Do we not feed enough animals already?"

Mali shrugged and smiled, knowing that if Chantou really wanted the puppy, she would have it. Her father thought caring for animals was good training for children.

The four-year-old ran across the yard and stopped short when she saw her mother propped on pillows holding the baby. A little black puppy chased behind her. "Chantou! Come meet your new sister," Davi said.

Chantou hesitated, her forehead creased with worry.

"Come, but not too close," Mali said and held her arm in front of Chantou to keep her from touching the baby with her grubby hands. But before she saw it coming, the four-year-old sneezed in the baby's face, and Sokha wailed making Chantou jump.

Mali and Davi laughed. "Your first shower!" Mali said.

Davi wiped away the mist from Sokha's glistening cheek and soothed the baby as Mali pulled Chantou into her lap.

"Thank-you, Mali, for taking care of everything while I slept," Davi said. "You will make an attentive mother someday."

Mali pressed her hands together as if in prayer and bowed her head, unable to repress her proud smile.

2

General Boran Sang

Boran saw the stern look of concentration on his wife's face. Davi was on the hunt for Sokha, the child who walked before one year of age and now ran after any bug, bird or butterfly. She didn't mean to hide, but her diminutive size made her invisible in the tall grass and the shadow of trees. Boran made excuses for the child. *I've grown soft. Maybe I was too hard on Mali and Chantou when I was younger and always on my way to a meeting. Sokha's determination amuses me; she's got a soldier's focus and a warrior's will.*

Boran chuckled to himself, and decided he was getting old, but ever since marrying Davi, his second wife, he'd settled into the kind of domestic life he never imagined he'd live. The army had been everything to him; the country had been his first priority. He wanted Cambodia to grow in stature, to increase trade with the west, to expand and prosper, *but lately, with all this unrest....*

The word *unrest* sparked an explosion of frustration in his head. He bit his bottom lip and winced. *I thought retiring and moving away from the border was enough to protect Davi and the girls, but have I miscalculated? The Mekong bombings are driving villagers here, illegal rice trades are causing arrests, and communist rebels are attacking Lon Nol's army. It seems I've failed.* His negative thoughts made him scowl. *Stop thinking. This does no good!* He thought of his wife's words: *You must calm yourself. Stop looking ahead.*

He remembered he had an assignment at that moment. He was supposed to get something from Keo. What was it? *Yes, medicine for Chantou. I'd better go now before Davi chastises me!*

Boran hiked over to his brother-in-law's farm and found Keo standing near the outer edge of his property. "I have come to talk to you, and you appear as if waiting for me," he called out in a friendly voice to disguise his angst. He pressed his palms together in greeting.

"What brings you here, General?" Keo asked, performing the sampeah in return.

"Not a general anymore," Boran chuckled. "Just a farmer and concerned father. Davi sent me, but I wanted to talk anyway."

"What does your tireless wife need? She never asks for anything."

"It's not for her, it's for Chantou. She has some kind of hives on her arms, red bumps—some of it oozing, may be infected. Davi says you make a salve that might help. I've come to see if I could trouble you for some." He handed Keo a small sack of red chili peppers. "For Ary, from her sister." Keo nodded and started walking toward the house. "What do you hear when you travel to the villages?" Boran asked as the men walked side by side.

"The news is grim," Keo said. "Our own people are fighting each other. I had enough sick people to cure before all this violence began."

"Yes. So I've heard." Boran put his arm out signaling Keo to stop walking, and the two men stood in a shaded banana grove, a distance from the house. At this hour of the day, the heat came alive, visible, like waves in the air. "Have you heard talk of bombs dropping inside our country?" he asked.

"Yes, near Kampong Cham," Keo said, his sculpted face clouded with concern. "America's war with Vietnam is spilling over the border."

"I've heard the same. Prince Sihanouk will not be able to keep us neutral if he allows the Viet Cong to use our land to rest and resupply. The Americans won't stand for it."

"What about your General? Lon Nol? He's Prime Minister now. When you worked with him in the army, wasn't he supportive of accepting America's help?"

"Lon Nol certainly sides with the Americans, as do I. But, he *serves* Prince Sihanouk who does not trust the Americans. Sihanouk keeps giving in to the Vietnamese for fear they'll invade us if we aggravate them."

"Ah! Prince Sihanouk walks a perilous path if he thinks he can keep China, Hanoi, and the U.S. equally content. It can't be done. He has to pick a side and stick with it," Keo said.

"He's trying to play all sides, but he can't even control the communists in our own country. He thinks the Khmer Worker's Party is a ragged bunch of rebels, but they are recruiting young men and boys all over here." Boran paused and scratched his lip.

"I know. He dismisses them, calls them the Khmer Rouge. I don't understand the Prince. Sometimes, I think he cares more about films and French food than our welfare."

Boran nodded in agreement and scowled. "Hah! You are right. The government is now in charge of buying and collecting all rice, so farmers can't profit from sales to the Vietnamese. And people are fleeing the Mekong area, but they have to live somewhere. As usual, Sihanouk has left Lon Nol to deal with angry villagers, and now they have killed two soldiers and attacked the police station." Boran took a deep breath and blew out his exasperation.

"At least our families are safe here."

"No one is safe, Keo. Not until this fighting ends will anyone be safe."

A look of dread crossed Keo's face. "Enough of all this. Let me find that salve for Chantou. We don't want her hives to get infected." The two men walked over to Keo's house where Boran accepted a container. "Put a small amount of this on Chantou's bites a few times a day, and tell her not to scratch or her Uncle Keo will give her some bitter medicine to swallow."

Boran chuckled. "She knows you are too kind to do that to her. She'd never believe me. And do you really expect a six-year-old not to scratch an itch? What kind of healer are you?"

Keo laughed and nodded his head in agreement.

"Chantou's a good girl, but a nervous one," Boran said. "I sometimes think she's so sensitive that she feels *my* tension crawling on her skin." Boran held up the container. "Thank you for this medicine and for listening to an old general complain." He turned and started walking back to his farm, deep in thought.

"Next time, bring me some good news!" Keo shouted after him in a jovial voice.

Boran did not turn around but walked back home as beads of sweat formed on and below his nose. When he licked his lips, a sore inside his top lip that was only beginning to show, started stinging. He had meant to ask Keo about the irritating ulcer that had formed in the last week. *Next time*, he thought.

On his thirty-minute walk home, Boran could not shake the image of radicals venturing on his farm demanding food and shelter. His rice paddies and fruit trees could attract hungry communist soldiers making trouble in the jungles around the Thai border.

He decided to dig a foxhole just in case.

3

Keo
The Samlaut Uprising

Arooster crowed, and Keo stirred as the early morning breeze from the open window and front door carried a welcome coolness to his skin. He opened his eyes, and the first thing he saw was Ary's nightdress hanging on a peg. The thought of her pulling it over her head, of her honey-colored skin, aroused him, and he smiled. A pile of freshly laundered towels and school uniforms lay folded on the chest at the foot of their wooden bed. His own black pants and white button-down shirt dangled from a hanger on a nail like a headless ghost across the room.

I long to stay in bed and not do what I must do today. The fresh scent of jasmine rice wafted through the door. *Ary is already cooking breakfast; her feet so light, she didn't wake me.*

Keo dressed and padded across the house to descend the twelve steps that led to the packed dirt below the house where a pile of different-sized sandals blocked his way. *Why can't people keep their own shoes in their own spot, and why can't Ary ever throw out the old ones? Must she pile them up like a termite mound?* Using his toes, he sorted the shoes and slipped his feet into the largest black sandals with a grunt.

"Shhh" Ary whispered as she peeled garlic. Their only son still slept on a hammock in the yard. Ary's face begged for a few more moments of peace. Keo nodded and walked to the clay cistern where a blue plastic cup floated on the rainwater. He scooped some up, swished, and spit the water out on the roots of the mango tree. The second cup, he swallowed, cool water sliding down his throat, easing the dryness caused by night. He must have slept with his mouth open again. Ary had said, "You looked like an old man who saw a ghost!" and laughed at her own joke. He did not find her humor funny. *You look like that too, sometimes, but I would never tell you,* he thought. Still, he loved the sound of her laugh. From the cistern, he padded underneath the house and plucked a small banana from the bunch hanging by a nail on the stilt and poured a cup of tea to carry on his walk.

Squatting over her mortar and pestle, Ary continued to crush fresh garlic, ginger, and onion to add to the morning's rice porridge, as Keo began his daily walk past the pond and the mango trees, past the yucca plants, and through the tall grass, until he reached the majestic sugar palm tree that had shaded his land for fifty years. After placing the tea and banana before the miniature spirit house he built beneath the tree, he knelt in prayer. *To the spirits of the land, I pray for protection and offer tea and fruit for your enjoyment. Please bless our soil with fertility, watch over this family, and bless the spirits of my ancestors.*

Finishing his prayer, he sat back on his heels and meditated, losing track of time and place until a slight breeze called him back. Straightening his unusually tall Khmer spine, he raised his arms above his head to stretch. Exhaling as he lowered his arms, he imagined all of his troublesome thoughts being pushed aside, so he could perform his work with pure intention, without judgment.

Turning back toward the house, he saw Ary's aluminum rice pot resting on three boulders above her cook fire and heard the chirping voice of Chhay as they gathered to eat. *I'll be sad when his voice goes deep, and he's no longer a child. He's getting to the age where bad influences could intrude—propaganda and guns, a bad mix for young boys.* His thoughts turned to Boran who had approached him to see if he could help the wounded near Samlaut where fierce fighting between Lon Nol's soldiers and the villagers had erupted. Boran had expressed hope that Lon Nol's troops would defeat the communist rebels for good.

Keo wondered why Boran left his high-ranking job with the government. He was only about fifty, and he still talked about politics and the military all the time. *Does Boran know more than he says aloud? Where is all this leading? My ride to Samlaut will be here soon. I best get moving.*

As Keo walked back to the house deep in thought, a young voice called, "Ba!" and a tall, lanky boy ran to greet him. Chhay still wore the willing eyes of a child. He was a miracle because Ary had suffered three miscarriages before she carried him full term. Keo never lost his sense of wonder over Chhay's existence, over the boy's facial features that resembled his own. Despite all his troublesome thoughts, Keo's lips spread into a smile, and his mind eased as he joined his family for breakfast.

Cross-legged, on the bamboo platform below the house, Keo ate his bowl of creamy rice porridge and sipped a cup of Moringa tea, hoping it would help his stiff ankle.

Ary broke the silence. "Must you travel so far today?"

Keo heard the strain in her voice. "I'm only traveling to the outskirts of Samlaut. Besides, I'll be on a motorbike with another Kru Khmer. The trip will be faster than traveling by oxcart."

"Be careful. You could be in danger."

Keo did not like her threatening tone of voice. "We'll be back before dark. I'll be treating government forces. They'll look out for us."

"Just come home!" Ary said with uncharacteristic force.

Keo forced a laugh for his son. "Of course I will." He set down his bowl and threw Ary a scowl of disapproval, for these matters should not be discussed in front of children. He took a second to consciously clear his anger and turned his attention to Chhay, who seemed oblivious to the whole interaction. The boy was busy scraping every last grain of rice from his bowl. "Make sure you finish your chores before going to school," Keo said to Chhay. "And obey your mother while I'm away."

Chhay responded with a nod.

Ary touched Keo's shoulder, and he felt her raw fear. A look of apology crossed her face. Keo rubbed her fingers in return. "I must get ready now," he said.

His words prompted Chhay to jump up, but before he dashed to the washbowl to rinse his hands, he stopped.

"Ba," he said, "Later, can we fish together? After school? When you get home?"

"I will try, but I can't promise I'll be back in time. Now go get some eggs for your mother and take the cows out in the field before you walk to the temple with your cousins." Keo watched as Chhay bowed in obedience. *I wonder how long he will so easily obey the orders of his father,* Keo thought. *I must begin teaching him to look after himself and his mother in case anything happens when I'm not around.*

Keo stood planted in prayer as Chhay splashed water on his hands, as he ran on coltish legs to the chicken coop. *Preah Buddha, send us your peace, so the monsoons of madness surrounding our country soften to showers that nourish instead of destroy.*

4

Battambang, Cambodia
1968

Sokha watched her younger sister, Kunthea, sitting on a soft cloth on the ground; she looked like she might topple over any minute. Although she'd been captivated by the baby's impossibly small crescent fingernails and pink poking tongue a year ago when she was born, she grew bored with her because Kunthea could not run or play any games. Sokha rose on her bare feet ready to bolt, but Mea pulled her back. "Stay right here," she said.

A muted booming sound echoed in the distance. Sokha wanted to go to the pond and play. She didn't want to sit in the dark hole again when the loud noises grew near. Her father had spent days digging the shelter on the highest point of the farm. Chest deep on Ba, the hole was barely visible once he pulled the bamboo roof covered in foliage over the top. *It's sticky, shadowy, and stinky down there,* Sokha thought. She gave her mother a mournful look.

"We don't have to hide in the hole yet," Mea said. "But you

cannot run off and do as you please all the time. I need to know where you are. Here is some cloth. Hold it for me, and make yourself useful." Davi worked her needle through the fabric. "Remember that you're a girl, not a monkey."

Sokha lit up. "Look Mea, I am a monkey!" she cried and rolled around on the ground.

Davi's eyes flashed a warning. "No, you are a young girl, and you have to stop running around and tearing your skirt. Now sit up." Sokha squirmed away and stood before her mother, her eyes daring Mea to scold her.

Mea huffed. "Proper girls do not go running or climbing or splashing into the pond. You must learn to sit still like Chantou if you want to go to school."

As morning's dim light brightened into a ball of white-hot sun burning in a cloudless sky, three men dressed in long saffron robes approached the farm. Their bare feet, covered in dust, made them look like floating ghosts drifting across the grass. Davi looked down at Sokha before the men approached. "Remember to hold your hands as high as your eyebrows for a proper sampeah to show respect for their holiness," she whispered and pressed her hands together as if in prayer.

The young monks advanced and held out their bowls for a food offering. Sokha steepled her dimpled hands and dipped her head along with her mother. The monks nodded in appreciation, and Davi scooped small servings of rice into their outstretched bowls, mindful not to touch the monks.

After accepting their offering of rice, the monks offered a blessing, turned, and continued on their mission, snaking down the street, their robes leaving puffs of dust behind them as they faded in the distance.

Sokha saw Ba striding toward her mother, and instinctively glanced up at Mea for guidance. Understanding what her mother expected, she pressed her hands together at the nose level and bowed her head slightly, remembering the respect required for a parent. The greeting earned her a warm smile and paternal nod. She returned Ba's approval with a broad-faced grin.

"Boran, another family has come asking to help in the rice field," Mea reported. Ba nodded in acknowledgment, his lips flattening in a frown at the news. *Is he angry?* Sokha stood tall, stretching her spine as high as she could in his shadow. When his mood grew dark—and she could never predict when—his voice made her quake. She listened intently to Ba, for she knew he had earned great respect.

"Sokha, take the cows and lead them to the field. I will be watching you," he said. "Come at once if I call you."

"I will, Ba!" she said and offered a quick and clumsy sampeah before sprinting off, remembering the time her father had lifted her high enough to touch the white cow's ears.

On her way, she glanced at the stretch of road where she saw lines of weary people trudging along the wide path between her land and the Buddhist temple. Mothers carried babies while children carried small sacks. She had asked her mother the day before, "Who are they?"

"Just people from other villages," Mea had said.

"What are they carrying?"

"A little food."

"Why? Are they all going to school like Chantou?"

"No, they are walking to a new village, Sokha." Her tone of voice announced that she was done answering questions, but Sokha wanted to know more.

Turning her attention to the largest cow, the one she had named "Cow," she padded along the damp grass. "Hello. You look pretty today. Are you hungry?" she asked, as she crouched and crept closer to the large animal. She stood listening as if the animal would talk back, but she heard only the buzz of flies that loved to swarm on Cow's back. While examining the animal's underbelly and moving her eyes up to scan the cow's thick, white neck and long face, the sound of an anguished female voice flew to her ears, and Sokha swung around to see Mea and Ba speaking to a distressed young woman in the road. In the brief exchange, the woman cried out, and her mother and father listened. After a few minutes, Mea called over to Mali, and she joined them holding a bag. Mea took it and handed the woman what looked like a sack of rice. For a moment, Sokha felt a rush of sadness and curiosity, but her thoughts changed instantly when the cow beside her let out a moan that made her jump again.

Her heart raced. "You didn't scare me," she said, catching her breath. "You are my favorite, and you can lead the others," she said. She took hold of Cow's rope and said, "Come, you will find more grass over here, and I can get you some rice straw." Several other cows followed in single file behind her, making her feel like a leader, like Ba. Everyone listened to Ba and did what he said.

It was March, near the end of the dry season crop, and the harvest would soon begin. Davi and Mali had woven mats from coconut leaf, and those mats would soon be covered with rice to be dried in the sun. After a day or two, several cows would be put to work threshing. They would trample the rice over and over again. Once done, the grains would be separated from the straw, ready to be cleaned by winnowing. This was Sokha's favorite part, watching Mea and Mali hold their large round baskets. They would throw the rice up into the air, and glinting white particles would rain back down into the basket. They never dropped a single grain. But this was only the short season harvest and would not be so big. The long rice-growing season would begin in May when the monsoons would drench the paddies for months from May to November.

Watching her special Cow eat made Sokha hungry, so she picked a long strand of grass for herself. One bite and she spit it out. "Why do you eat that?" she asked her friend. Cow swished her long thin tail in response. "Your tail looks like a streamer!" she said and began to daydream about her favorite time of year —the New Year. Her mind conjured up the party that would spiral through three or four days of festivity. The Buddhist temple would overflow with foods and sweets of every kind. *Mea is sewing my new dress. I can't wait to dance, and then Mali's getting married! Two parties!*

Sokha twirled around. She tried to talk to Cow about how excited she was, but tired of the unresponsive animal quickly and walked past her mother's gardens: patches of sweet potato, corn, cabbage, yucca, maize, cucumber, sugarcane, and kabocha squash. She strolled past the pond and the chickens that roamed the yard delighting in the way they scattered as she passed, dragging a long stick behind her. She thought about what Mea had told her. "Mali is nineteen, all grown up, so she and Rotha will be like your Ba and me, a couple, and they will make a family of their own."

Sokha didn't know much about Rotha, but she guessed Mali liked him, or she wouldn't marry him. Or maybe Mali just wanted to ride his motorbike. She recalled her mother telling Mali, "Remember the Chbab Srey teachings. Be respectful of your husband. Serve him well and keep the flame of the relationship alive. Otherwise, it will burn you." Sokha had asked, "Who will burn you?" and her mother and sister had laughed. She did not understand grownups.

She spotted her favorite climbing tree with curving low limbs and began to climb.

"Be careful!" called Mea as Sokha grabbed a branch and stepped up on a high root to reach the next level. There she sat, feeling tall, feeling the flutter of leaves on her skin, the feeling she liked most in the world: to be outside, high up, seeing every-thing—as tall as Ba. The thought of him made her remember that she should check on the cows again before she made her father mad. Once she led the animals back toward the house, her stomach rumbled, and she ran toward the cooking area. Mea saw her running and pressed her palms out to signal: *slow down!* "A proper Khmer girl walks softly and slowly," she said.

Davi sat on the wooden platform shredding banana flower to season the soup while Mali cut sour mango, and Chantou mixed a bowl of chili and salt spiked with sugar for dipping. Chantou stuck her pointer finger in the mix and held it to Mali's lips.

"Good?" Chantou asked.

"Needs more sugar," Mali said. "These mangos are *sour!*" The girls giggled.

Sokha felt left out and wanted to help cook. *Chantou gets to do everything: wear the blue uniform, go to school, and come home at midday to cook.* As her sisters and mother bantered, she crept close to the fire to watch the mudfish cook in a pot on a bed of lemongrass.

Mea's voice stopped her short. "How many times must I tell you to be careful, Sokha!" she scolded. "Come. Sit quietly and wait."

"But I want to help, too," Sokha complained.

"We'll go searching for vegetables for Nom Banh Chok this afternoon. It's good to be helpful, but you must be patient and learn *how* to be helpful."

Ba approached and put his hand on Sokha's back. "Come sit," he said, his expression soft. Soon the rest of her family gath-ered around a large bowl of rice, roasted fish, vegetable soup, and sour mango. Davi served Ba first, and then the sisters, oldest to youngest.

Sokha ate quickly so she'd have time to play with Chantou while Mea nursed Kunthea and showered the baby with sniff kisses. Mali cleaned up the lunch mess, throwing scraps in the compost heap.

"Chantou, come play with me!" Sokha called. Sitting on the ground in a dry patch of dirt, Sokha poured a cup of water to make clay. She formed a little pan and set it in the sun to dry. Chantou sat beside her and shaped a tiny pot. "Tell me about school," Sokha begged her older sister.

"Yesterday, a boy arrived late to class, and the monk whipped him with a switch on his skinny legs, and he was not allowed to cry," Chantou said.

"I don't want to go to school if the monks do that," Sokha said, wincing. She twirled another piece of clay in her fingers to make a snakehead fish. "I would make Ba hit the monk back!"

"No! Ba would never do that. You must always do as the monks tell you. They are nice most of the time. They teach us many things and tell us stories. If you are on time and you sit quietly and listen, the monks won't bother you. But knowing you, you can't do that, can you?" she said, teasing.

"Oh, yes I can!" Sokha said. After a few moments, Ba called out. "There's work to be done, and school is starting again soon, Chantou. Hurry along."

"Look, I made a little duck for you," Chantou said. She handed the damp figure to her younger sister, picked up her school sack, and started walking back to the temple for afternoon classes. "I'll see you later!" she said. Sokha held her gooey gift and ran to show her mother.

Davi nodded in admiration. "Let's put him in this sunny spot to dry out," Mea said, smiling at the excitement on Sokha's face. "You will soon be five, and you will wear the school uniform, too, Sokha. I'll be making you a blue skirt with a white shirt. Do you want that?"

"Jah! I will be good at school. I will never get whipped," Sokha said, placing her duck on the flat rock her mother pointed out, but in her mind, she wasn't so sure. It was hard to be good all the time. Mea glanced at her sideways.

"Did your sister tell you stories about monks?" Sokha nodded her head furiously as she looked into her mother's eyes. "Don't let her upset you. Just listen, work hard, and obey, and you will find that the monks are wise, and if you pay attention, they will teach you to be wise, too."

As the sky darkened, the family donned sandals and followed the dirt path that divided the rice fields between the house and the temple. They filled their buckets from the temple pond, hanging them on bamboo rods balanced across their shoulders to carry the sloshing water home. Sokha, too young to lug water, kicked pebbles along the way.

"Sokha! Come. Walk with me and stop chasing stones. Sokha ran to her mother, who walked beside Ba.

Boran cleared his throat and spoke in the direction of his youngest girls. "Did you ever hear the story of the girl who was told to fetch firewood for her mother?" he asked.

Sokha and Chantou shook their heads no.

"The girl walked off with her small bucket of water for refreshment and went searching for wood as the sky grew cloudy and dark. She knew rain would soon fall, and she knew the rainwater would be clear and cold, so she dumped her warm water out. She waited, but no rain came. She grew thirsty and stayed thirsty because she trusted the sky too much. You must never trust anyone or anything too much. You see?"

"Jah!" Chantou said. But Sokha wasn't sure.

"I trust you, Ba—and Mea, and my sisters. Is that okay?"

"Of course, we are family. I'm only telling you that sometimes strangers or things look different than they really are, and you should be careful.

While Sokha puzzled the story out, her mother interrupted her thoughts. "Sokha, would you like to go to the market with me tomorrow?" she asked.

Sokha nodded, and her eyes brightened.

"We will buy enough fabric for two skirts," Mea said.

"Can we buy some longan fruit?" Sokha asked. "Chantou said they look like dragon's eyes, but they are sweet and juicy!"

"Yes, if I can talk the price down, I'll get some," Mea said. For the rest of the way home, Sokha's mother sang a song she made up. She sang quietly to herself as Sokha listened and let her mother's voice fill her ears with music.

The next day, Sokha kept thinking about school and wondered if she would like it.

"The school day starts with prayer," Chantou had told her. "At temple, we sit on the floor and pray. We bow after each song. After that, we have lessons, and we must write the words the monk teaches us." She paused a moment, then bowed her head and whispered, "I saw a student playing around when he was supposed to be silent, and the monk made him kneel on jackfruit! His knees were all dented later on."

"Ow!" Sokha cried. "That's like kneeling on needles! Mea says they won't do that to me!"

"I only tell you for your own good, so you will not get in trouble," Chantou said. "Sometimes you think you can do anything you like, but you can't at school."

Sokha thought of the monks that visited Mea for alms. The stories her sister told her did not sound like the peaceful monks she knew. She would search their faces for mean spirits in the morning when they came to collect their rice.

What could be more cruel than making someone kneel on jackfruit?

5

Battambang

S okha asked her mother once again, "Where are all those people going?"

"Don't concern yourself with others, Sokha. They go where they go for their own reasons," Mea said. Bedraggled strangers trudged past the farm, and when she walked with her family to collect water, she saw small families slumped over each other on the ground sleeping or propped against trees staring ahead at nothing. Mea nudged her when she stared.

By late August, Sokha hardly ever saw her father in the yard, and when she did, he touched his lip in a way that made him look nervous. He and Keo often talked on the shady side of the house, whispering to one another as if they were making secret plans. Sokha listened when she dawdled nearby and heard words that didn't make sense. Curious, she lingered near the corner of the house as still as a stalking cat.

"Hmm," she heard Uncle Keo say. "Stop talking for a minute. Your mouth is looking worse. You must be careful with your hot soup and not pick at the sore." He stepped back with a look of concern on his face.

Boran's voice took on a snarling tone as he spoke of things that made no sense to her. Sokha sank deeper into the weeds. *Maybe I should not be here.* She heard her mother's steps as she climbed down the stairs of the house to collect dry laundry. She could not move now.

Uncle Keo leaned toward Ba. "Boran, it is not good for you to get upset like this." Squinting his eyes, Keo looked closely at Ba's mouth. "Are you using the salve I gave you?" he asked.

"I am."

"And?"

"It helps a little, but there's an ulcer on the inside, and it's hard to eat, so I can't manage food very well." After an awkward silence, Boran shook his head from side to side as if shooing off his personal complaints like flying insects. "Stop fussing over me, Keo."

Ba's eyes darted over to Sokha who had crept closer to avoid Mea's eyes.

"Don't you have chores to do?" he asked. "Didn't Mea ask you to go collect basil for dinner?"

Sokha looked at the ground and then at her father. As she turned to leave, she paused and saw Uncle Keo pull a small bottle out of his pocket and hand it to Ba. "I have prepared Sra thnam for you. Drink it. There should be three doses here. It will help your appetite and give you energy," he said. "And you must stop thinking about what could or might happen. Calming your mind will help your body heal."

Uncle Keo unexpectedly laughed. "I suppose I should stop asking you questions about the war if I want you to feel better! Right?"

Ba laughed out loud. "Yes, Keo, it's all your fault."

Hearing the two men laugh, Sokha let out the breath she'd

been holding. She wanted to make up for her laziness, for upsetting her father.

"Ba! Uncle Keo!" She stopped and performed a perfect Sampeah. "I promise to do my chores right away, but I start school tomorrow, and Mea has finished my uniform. I wanted to show it to you. Do you want to see it?"

"Of course, and soon," Uncle Keo said, looking down at her eager face. His face radiated sincerity. "But I'm afraid I must return home now. Your Aunt Ary will be waiting for me. Enjoy your first class tomorrow.

"And Boran," he said, bowing with palms together, "I leave you with my blessing and Ary's affection for Davi and your girls." Boran returned the gesture, and after his brother-in-law walked away, he looked down at Sokha and shook his head.

"You never give up, do you?" he said. Sokha took her father's hand, eager for his approval. "Please, Ba. I'll show you!"

"I will come. But then you must work quickly," he said.

The following morning, Sokha buttoned her white shirt and pulled on her navy skirt. *Do I look the way I should? Will the monks be nice? Will I get whipped?* Her worries dissolved at school as she melted into the meditative story her teacher told:

"Listen carefully to *The Lotus Story:* it tells how the Buddha rose to enlightenment," said the young monk in his tranquil voice. "Imagine you are a lotus seed buried in a dark and muddy pond, yet you don't feel discouraged. Instead, you begin your journey upward toward the sun and air through the muck and grime. You grow strong roots below as you strive to reach the surface of the pond, and you push past the darkness and the obstacles in your way as you grow taller and taller, the warm sun drawing you all the way up to the surface of the pond. Your stem grows sturdy, and a bud forms on top. And then, one day, you bloom into a beautiful flower, your delicate white petals opening to the world. Out of sheer determination, you have pushed out of the mud to become a thing of beauty and delight, just as the Buddha was able to acquire the splendor of enlightenment once he had overcome life's suffering."

Sokha envisioned herself as the lotus seed over and over again. The lesson ended with one of her favorite mantras. In her lyrical voice, she recited with her classmates:

I am well.

I am happy.

We are well.

We are happy.

Do no wrong actions.

Do as much good as you can.

Purify your mind.

On her way home, she walked with Chantou. "What does purify mean?" she asked.

"It means 'to clean,'" Chantou said.

"How can I clean my mind?"

"By blocking out questions. Impossible for you!" she laughed.

"Is not," Sokha said.

"Shhh! Listen." An explosion echoed in the distance. "Let's get home quickly."

At the house, Ba stood calling them with his hands to join the family in the hole in the ground. Gun pops and thumping sounds grew closer, yet Sokha's parents appeared calm.

"We will all be safe here," Ba said. Mea snuggled Kunthea in her lap. Sokha leaned into Mae's shoulder and felt Chantou's knees touching her own. She smelled stale breath and sweat in the cramped space and clutched her book bag close to her chest.

"No talking," Ba whispered. Sokha closed her eyes as her good-natured mind filled up with wishes. *I can't wait to climb out of this hole and go back to school tomorrow. I can't wait to see my new dress. I can't wait for the New Year party. I can't wait....*

In the following weeks, Sokha noticed that Ba no longer stood outside in the damp morning air surveying his land and announcing what needed to be done. The sore on his lip grew into a bulging tumor, and his commanding voice thinned to a raspy whisper. The less her father appeared, the more her mother seemed to be everywhere at once. Mea flitted from job to job, feeding the animals, scrubbing the clothes, and cooking the soup. She directed workers in the rice field and around the gardens. At meals, she prompted Ba, "Drink this broth. Just a little more," using the same voice she used to encourage baby Kunthea.

As Mea tended to Ba's lip with homemade balms from Uncle Keo, no words were exchanged. Pungent salves that tickled Sokha's nose were applied, but Ba continued to lose weight, and some days he did not go outside at all. He didn't complain, but he separated himself and no longer looked like the vigorous father she knew. When she asked her mother if anything was wrong, Mea told her, "It's just the way things are right now."

Uncle Keo visited most evenings, sitting with Ba away from the girls while Aunt Ary talked with Mea. Sokha had never seen Aunt Ary look so serious, the lines on her forehead creased over her straight eyebrows.

"Sit for fifteen minutes, Davi. You have been working too hard. I have cool lemongrass tea for us to sip. Please rest a bit." Sokha saw her mother's back stiffen in resistance, but she complied, and the two women sat quietly together, Mea clutching her cup of tea so tight, it looked as if she could crush it.

~

Soon after Sokha turned six, she returned home from school
with Chantou on her lunch break and did not see her mother
outside. Chantou ran up the stairs while Sokha stayed below to
grab some sweet tamarind for a snack in the cooking area, and
there sat Mali with Kunthea in her lap, a surprise, since Mali
now lived in Battambang city with her new husband, Rotha.

"Mali!" Sokha shouted with a smile. She ran to her oldest
sister and noticed she looked grim. "I'm glad you came! Can you
stay for dinner?" she asked as she peeled her tamarind pod.

"I'll be here for a few days," Mali said. "Mea sent for us—to
help."

"Rotha's here, too? To help? With what?" Mali didn't answer.
She looked up the stairs at the doorway with hollow eyes and
continued to rock Kunthea.

A sting of danger shot through Sokha's body. She threw her
snack down and started up the stairs. Before she reached the top
step, her mother appeared in the doorway, her face pinched in a
way Sokha had never seen. "I need to talk to you out here," Mea
said. "Go down. I'm coming. Chantou, come along," she said
over her shoulder.

Down in the cooking spot, Sokha sat suspended in slow
motion, watching her mother's hand on the wood rail as she
descended the staircase, gripping and letting go, her feet
touching each step as if feeling for a solid surface below, as if she
might fall. Chantou followed behind, her eyes cast down. At the
foot of the stairs, Mea looked gravely at her daughters, "All of
you, please sit. I need to tell you something."

The girls arranged themselves on the wood platform in the
shade beneath the house as Sokha searched her mother's face
for clues about what happened.

"What I have to tell you may be hard to accept, but this is the
way of life. Your father had cancer on his lip that caused him
pain, and now his pain is gone. Your father died today. He will

soon transition to a new life." Sokha had never seen a dead person, only a dead chicken, a dead bug. *What does this mean?*

"The monks will help us take care of things, but you must know that your father was a good man, and so we will honor him."

"Where is he?" Sokha asked. "I want to see him." *Why don't Mea's calm words match her face? She looks like she's about to cry.*

"Sokha, you will not see your father again in the way you think of him," Mea said. "He's gone. He looks like he's asleep, but he will never wake up. Not in this life."

Chantou wept and leaned into Mali and Kunthea. Sokha ran to her mother's side, and Mea gathered her in her arms. After a few moments, Mea spoke.

"There is much to do, and we can't sit around. Sokha, go check the animals. They need water and rice straw. Mali and I will make plans." Sokha walked away but turned and circled her way back around the house to listen. *What plans?*

Wanting to know more, she curled into herself behind the outhouse and listened carefully as Mea and Mali spoke in hushed voices.

"I think your father killed himself with poison."

"Mea! Why?" Mali's voice shook.

"The pain was too great," Mea said. Sokha gasped loud enough for her mother and sister to hear, and her gasp turned into sobs.

"Come here! Right now, Sokha," Mea ordered.

Sokha ran and faced her mother. Anger filled her chest and surged up her throat. Turning in fury, she yelled at her mother, "No! You're lying! Ba wouldn't do that. Why would he leave us like that?"

"Hush! Do not say this to anyone else," Mea said, holding Sokha's shoulders. "I did not want you to hear this, but Ba had his sickness for a long time. It wasn't just his lip, there was sickness inside his body that you couldn't see, and it hurt him terribly. He has been suffering, but now he can transition to another life, a better life."

Sokha stared up at her mother's face as Mea's whole body and expression changed as if she had morphed from an eagle protecting its young to one with talons out. She felt her mother's fingers dig into her shoulders. "You must not hide and listen to others. You are too curious for someone your age." She let go of Sokha and stepped back. "We will *not* speak of this again."

Sokha didn't understand why her mother suddenly went pale—as if speaking these last words drew all the life out of her. She didn't know why she must never speak of her father's death or how it happened. Her small frame trembled with grief. *Ba was a great general in the army; he was always the strong one. How could he be gone?*

Davi turned her attention to her eldest daughter. "Mali, we must notify the monks. Ba did not die with a monk beside him to calm his soul, and their prayers will help his spirit rest." Sokha slumped to the ground and cried as Mali walked away.

"Sokha, all of life is impermanent. Nothing lasts forever. The good news is that there is rebirth. Let us pay our respects to the Neak Ta. Come," Mea said, still standing. Sokha pressed her palms to her eyes and slowly rose to her feet as her mother called her sisters.

Chantou and Kunthea came quickly. *Where had they been?* Sokha wondered. *Why can't I be like them—in the right place—where I should be?* Davi instructed Chantou to pour a small cup of tea and instructed the girls to choose an offering of food to serve to the tutelary spirits that protected their land. She then led her daughters to the family shrine, the Neak Ta, marked by a pile of mounded stones beneath a prolific mango tree near the house. Sokha recalled her father leaving food and trinkets for this spirit tree each morning and realized her mother knew exactly what to do.

Before the stones, Davi placed Boran's treasured walking stick so they would recognize him, and she added a wooden bowl of fruit and rice as gifts of appeasement. Chantou handed her the cup of tea, and Davi poured the first drops into the ground for the Neak Ta to savor as she and her daughters knelt and prayed to the spirits to bless their father and the land he loved.

Within an hour, the monks assembled on the farm to chant, Sokha wondered about the questions the monks had posed to her mother. "Have you cleansed your mind of anger and dread?" the eldest monk asked. Davi had nodded in agreement, her face serene.

Sokha wondered if Mea was telling the truth, for she didn't know what dread was, but she felt anger for all she couldn't understand.

Sokha's mind swirled with questions. What would happen next? What would be done with Ba? And she heard her mother ask Aunt Ary questions of her own. "Who will supervise the workers in the rice fields? Who will guard the farm? Who will be our eyes and ears without Boran?"

"You have us. You have Rotha and Mali," Aunt Ary said.

"But they don't live here anymore. They are hours away in Battambang city." *You have me, too, Mea. You have me and Chantou and Kunthea,* Sokha thought. *Why do you forget us?*

"There is much to do," Davi said.

Ary soothed her, and taking her hand, she said, "Come, we must prepare his body."

Davi turned to Sokha. "Please be helpful. We can't forget our chores, no matter how hard they are to do today," she said. Mea gave Sokha a penetrating look and turned toward the steps of the house with Ary.

"But what are they doing?" Sokha asked Mali as they disappeared into the house. "They must wash Ba's body. I need to go help them. Please go help Chantou."

Chantou looked after Kunthea as she gathered fruit while Sokha sulked.

"I'll go take care of Cow," she said. Taking Cow's rope, she led her to a stump next to a tree, stood on it, and mounted Cow's back. Cow let her settle there and rub her bony spine. Sokha's legs felt Cow's warm hide radiate peace and security through her limbs and up into her chest.

Ba sent me to you because he knew I loved you, she whispered to Cow. Ba is gone. Did you know that? Ba is gone," she said as if convincing herself.

From a distance, Sokha saw Uncle Keo and Rotha standing on the upper deck of her house. Each hung a white flag on the top of the railing post. As it fluttered in the breeze, Sokha noticed an image on the flags that she could not see clearly. Once hung, the two men entered the doorway and disappeared. Soon after, they carried Ba's fully dressed body down the steps and lifted him into a plain wooden coffin opened at the top.

Sokha led Cow back toward the house, let go of the rope, and ran to see the box that held her father, but she hesitated before looking. "What did you hang on the house?" she asked Rotha.

"It's a crocodile flag," he said. Sokha looked confused. "It's a sign to all who visit here that someone has died because long ago, King Chan Reachea's daughter was eaten by a crocodile. The king made sure the animal was found. His daughter's body was recovered, and he built a temple and stupa to remember her. It's a tradition."

Sokha gazed up and saw that the outline of a crocodile had been drawn on the white flags. Now, everyone would know her father was dead. Suddenly, she felt the courage to walk forward and look inside the coffin set under the trees.

A body laid fully dressed, the only flesh showing, a pair of hands. His face was covered with a white cloth and tealeaves were sprinkled all around him. "Is this Ba?" Sokha asked, unsure.

She looked to her mother, tears fogging her eyes, and Davi reached for her. Sokha pressed her face into her mother's soft belly and felt Mea's strong arms enfold her for several stretched moments before she heard Chantou speak.

"I don't feel good. My stomach hurts," she said.

Mea loosened her grip. Mali and Chantou stood nearby wiping tears. Kunthea sat in Aunt Ary's lap on the house steps. Sokha's cousin stood off to the side.

Ary answered Chantou. "I have something I can give you that will help," she said.

Chantou leaned into her older sister, weeping.

"We will have visitors, and the monks will pray for Ba for three days to guide him on his way," Mea said. "Ba is gone from us but not dead. This is Samsara. The cycle of life."

Sokha watched as Rotha and Uncle Keo lifted a lid onto the coffin, sealing him off, the way she sealed off her mind from too much sorrow to take in.

"Girls, we must prepare ourselves for the funeral," Davi called.

Sokha sat as still as the Buddha statue while the attending monk shaved her head to signify the shedding of vanity and the severing of ties between her deceased father and the living. As her strands piled into shiny black nests beneath her, she tried not to cry. *Pieces of myself are falling to the ground.*

Mali stood alongside her mother. The two women rubbed

their hands together and on their clothing as if trying to erase a scent. Their somber faces created a sharp contrast to Chantou's cheerful one as she sang in a whispery voice and bounced Kunthea on her lap to humor the child until it was her turn to be shaved. When, at last, Kunthea's head gleamed as smooth as a river stone, Davi picked up the child and carried her to the house as her other daughters followed. Inside, they helped each other sort through traditional white funeral clothing.

For the next two days, the family joined several monks as they sat on woven mats and chanted prayers by Boran's body. Villagers came and watched and offered food with their condolences. On the third day, the family dressed carefully.

Sokha smoothed out the fabric on Kunthea's white shirt as they stood in formation with the funeral procession. She signaled to her little sister to follow as Boran's body was carried to the temple grounds. One by one, mourners from the village fell in line behind the family.

As if choreographed, a crowd began to congregate in honor of General Boran Sang. Robed monks placed his body on a raised bed of sticks on a patch of land between the house and the temple, and a monk lit the fire to set Boran's soul free from bondage as his family and others stood to witness the cremation. Sokha listened to the loud crackling fire as it sizzled and popped, interrupting the rhythmic voices of the chanting monks.

Earth returns to earth.
Fire returns to fire.
Wind returns to wind.
Water returns to water....

Their chants lulled her into a trance as she stood in witness with her family. Every few minutes, she turned her head to check on her mother. Davi's stiff spine and her stoic expression froze as friends whispered words of reassurance that the monks were aiding the release of good energy from Boran's body.

Sokha's nerves stung at the sight of her mother's strained face, but she composed herself by imitating the posture and behavior of her older sisters. *I would rather be whipped by monks than have my mother look at me the way she did today. I will stand still. I won't speak.*

Sokha waited and watched the rising white smoke swirl to gray plumes. The sizzling sparks sounded like vibrant bits of Ba's personality piercing her ears—his vigor, his courage, his vigilance. At first, she felt as if her legs would give way from the collective weight of the seriousness that permeated the proceedings, but as the minutes passed, and the air thickened with smoke, the energy inside her swelled with a need to explode.

When General Sang's body had completely burned, the monks completed their funeral prayers, placed his ashes in an urn, and tied the urn off with white string so no evil spirits could escape. His remains were placed on a shelf in the temple in accordance with tradition.

Finally, the family began walking home, and the crowd dispersed. As she put one foot in front of the other, she felt the tension ease out of her muscles, and looking once more into the sky, she saw the last wisp of smoke wither and disappear.

From mid-May to September, the downpours of the southwest monsoon felt like the release of unshed tears for Sokha as she tried and tried to be grown up, to make her mother proud, and be a help during the long rice-growing season. For the first time in her young life, the rain felt dreary, and the clouds looked like ghosts as they sped across the sky blocking out the sun. Ba was no longer with her, and yet he was everywhere—in the shadows, in the puddles, and high up in the branches of the big mango tree.

6

Davi

1970

avi thought of Boran every moment. She spoke to
him in her mind. *At ten years of age, Chantou is the
oldest child on the farm. She senses every danger around
her, but it's six-year-old Sokha who frightens me because she does not
see danger anywhere and will do anything to satisfy her curiosity.*

"Sokha, please keep your eyes on Kunthea and don't let her
wander too far," Davi called. Sokha possessed a sturdy build, an
athletic body, unlike her two older sisters. She could carry heavy
objects and lift dead tree limbs at her young age. *She would have
made a wonderful son, strong and brave* Davi once thought, but
silenced herself. *She's a girl, even if she'd rather play like a boy.*

Davi's mind surged with all the things that needed doing.
*Watch over Kunthea when the girls are at school, oversee the rice crop
and gardens, harvest the fruit trees, carry water for washing, mend
the clothes, and cook the meals. Someone must help care for the
animals—how did we grow to have a dozen cows? I'll need Ary's and*

Mali's help to start training Chantou and Sokha in as many chores as possible, and I'll need to take on more help in exchange for food.

A series of rainstorms had kept Keo and Ary away, and she grew increasingly anxious, but today, the clouds dispersed. Davi saw Keo from a distance in her peripheral vision, her senses on high alert. "Keo!" she called. "Over here!" She'd been turning over wet soil in the full sun of her garden, even though the air felt no different than the steam rising from the soup pot. The skies had poured thick ropes of rain in sudden bursts for the past three days, and Davi deftly plucked out the weeds that had sprung up with the sun's return.

As Keo strode across the yard, she wiped her dirty hands on the cloth she kept in her pocket and stood upright to offer the sampeah.

"Hello, Davi! You look like you could use a break," Keo called. Davi's chin-length hair clung to her neck as perspiration dripped from her temple. She pushed the wet hair away.

"Come, let's talk," Keo said. The two walked toward the meal platform under the house, where Davi scooped a cup of water from the cistern for Keo.

"You are taking time away from your family to check on us. I appreciate it, Keo," she said, handing the cup to him.

"I know you well, Davi. I'm here to give you rest. You'd never stop working if I didn't show up," he said. "Let's sit."

"How is my sister?"

"Ary is well. She said she hopes to see you tomorrow and bring you some of the new teas we have been mixing. How have you been managing the laborers on the farm?"

"They work, but I think they worked longer and with more energy when Boran was in charge," she said. "The rice is growing well, but we are not weeding fast enough."

"I'll check on them before I go and offer them my gentle

advice," Keo said with a smile. But I come with some serious news, I'm afraid."

"No, not politics...."

"I know. I hate to speak of this with you, but with Boran not here—well, you must know. There has been rioting in Phnom Penh."

"There's been fighting everywhere for years, and Phnom Penh is far away, so..."

"The embassies have been ransacked, and Lon Nol has taken over the government. There's been a coup. Prince Sihanouk is no longer in power."

Davi sucked in her breath. "Has he been killed?"

"No, he's in China. He'd been traveling, as usual. Lon Nol and Sirik Matak have taken over the government."

"Why? Lon Nol's the Prime Minister. I thought he and Sihanouk were on the same side!"

"Lon Nol has been furious with Sihanouk for allowing the Viet Cong to hide in our borderlands where the Americans are forced to bomb them. He finally took matters into his own hands. Boran would approve." Davi nodded as if Boran's approval reassured her.

Keo continued, "Lon Nol is kicking out the Vietnamese. He always believed that Prince Sihanouk let them get away with too much. The good news is that the Americans are backing Lon Nol, and so are the South Vietnamese."

"This sounds hopeful. Maybe it will all be over soon?" Davi felt lightheaded.

"There's more. Even though Prince Sihanouk is out of the country, he's turning people against Lon Nol through radio announcements from Beijing. He has the Chinese on his side. What I really wanted to tell you is to be very careful because Prince Sihanouk has the support of a lot of people. It seems unbelievable, but he's giving his support to the Khmer Rouge in retaliation against Lon Nol."

"The Khmer Rouge? He made fun of them. He never liked them!"

"Yes, but he's lost power, and to regain it, he's decided to join forces with them. Most of the farmers around here are backing the Prince, too. So don't mention that Boran was a General with Lon Nol to anyone who works for you or visits the farm. You never know who you are talking to."

"I see," Davi said. Although she thought of Boran night and day, she rarely said his name. She never talked to a soul about politics either. It was not supposed to be her concern. She didn't want to worry her family. She didn't want to know these things! *I'm so tired of angry people with nothing to do but fight. I just want to live my life!* Davi closed her eyes, and an image rose in her mind: Americans, Viet Cong, Chinese, and Khmer Rouge soldiers twisting into violent tendrils like the Banyan tree, ensnaring her until she disappeared like a speck into the center of a tangled web of invaders. A sudden burst of overwhelming fear gripped her, and the color drained from her face.

"Davi, try not to dwell on this, but promise me you will bring the girls to my farm at once if you feel threatened. I told Boran I would watch over you, and I will."

Davi did not like knowing that violence surrounded her. She was beginning to feel suspicious of everyone—the very complaint she held against Boran.

Two weeks later, Keo stopped by with a worried frown clouding his typically cheerful face. "I must speak to your mother alone," he said when the girls ran to greet him. Davi's face turned ashen.

Chantou picked up the cue. "Sokha, let's take Kunthea to the pond and gather water lily stems for dinner," she said. Sokha didn't move.

"Sokha, go with Chantou," Davi coaxed. "I won't be long." Sokha bowed with her hands pressed together and ran after her two sisters.

"I know you are carrying great burdens right now, Davi," Keo began. "I don't want to alarm you too much, but the situation is dire." Davi could see that Keo measured his words carefully. "Hundreds of Vietnamese men were killed in Churi Changwar —some call it a slaughter—by Lon Nol's troops. People all over the country are condemning it, and although the attack was far away, there will be revenge killings. The violence could break out anywhere. Conditions are unpredictable. I came to warn you," he said.

Davi stared at Keo. *What do you mean? What do you expect me to do? I am not a soldier. I cannot hold all this at once!* She had feared this moment, and still, she didn't have a plan. She scolded herself for hiding in the gardens, for working night and day as if she could make all this trouble disappear if she just stayed busy enough. Keo straightened his shoulders. "Maybe it's time to leave the farm, to live in the city, closer to Rotha. He is young and strong, and Mali can be a big help to you," he said. "Are you listening, Davi?"

Lost in thought, Davi squeezed her eyes shut. She put her hand to her mouth, opened her eyes, and looked over at her three young daughters framed by the placid pond, the azure sky set perfectly in the background. Sokha stared back at her as if she knew her every thought. *That child sees everything and cannot be contained.* This fleeting thought made a chill run down her back. Davi could not bring herself to speak but nodded her assent to Keo.

"I am nearby if you need me," he said, and paused, his voice choked with emotion. "I can have Chhay come stay with you if you wish. He's only fourteen, but he can run and get me if you should..."

"No. No, Keo. Let your son stay at home. Let me think. I have two good families helping out here most days. One of the young men is trustworthy, I think. I could send him if trouble arose."

"The offer is there. And we will check on you as much as we can," Keo said. "Now, can we talk about more important things like finding some star apple for Ary and Chhay? I'd like to take a few leaves to make a rheumatism infusion, too." Davi nodded and walked the farm with him while he collected his fruit and samples, and they circled around to the house before he left. Although Keo kept the conversation light, Davi could hardly control the flutter in her chest.

"Stay well, Davi. We're here if you need us," Keo said before he turned to leave.

Davi watched him walk away, and then she climbed the steps to her empty house. She needed a few minutes to sit and breathe, to slow her heartbeat, to still the loud screams inside her mind. *Where are you, Boran? Why aren't you here to help me? I need you!*

7

Sokha
Early 1970-1972

Sokha noticed changes in her family. Mea looked worn
out and haggard, and Chantou worried out loud about
the strangers walking near their home. Sokha took it all
in and remained quiet, still trying hard not to cause any more
trouble for Mea.

A strange man yelled from the dirt path to Davi, "Hey, I hear
you need a man in the house over there! Come here! I'm your
man."

"Mea, why do you let him yell at you like that?" Sokha asked,
breaking her own rule. She could no longer stand it.

"I will not answer," Davi said. "His words are like dead leaves
twisting and turning in the air, Sokha. They fall lifelessly to the
ground—they mean nothing."

It meant something to Sokha, and she wanted to punch that
man. *That's what Ba would do!* She kicked some dirt and turned
her back on the man in the road. Too young to discern intentions, she sensed the violation. She knew Mea missed her father.

She watched her mother gaze out over the rice fields, her face a mask of grief until she snapped out of it and threw herself into farm work. Occasionally, with her ears wide open, Sokha heard Mea cry at night beyond the curtain that separated their sleeping mats. She fought the urge to climb in with her and offer comfort, but she stopped herself, sensing her mother's dignity and knowing how her mother detested weakness.

Come morning, Sokha looked at Mea, unaware that her eyes were glassing over with fury and tears for not being able to help.

"What is it, Sokha?" Mea asked.

"Nothing." Sokha looked at the ground and struggled to calm down.

"Mali and Rotha should be here soon," Mea said to lighten the mood.

"Rotha, too?"

"Jah. He's a good husband. He doesn't want Mali to hurt herself on his motorbike, so he took a little time off work to carry her here."

Soon the rumble of the motor and a cloud of dust marked their arrival. Mali hopped off the bike, excited to see her family. After she hugged everyone and picked up Kunthea for a squeeze, Sokha blurted out, "Mali, men are yelling at Mea from the street."

"Sokha," Mea said. "That's enough." Mali's face grew concerned, and she exchanged knowing glances with Rotha.

"It's nothing—just desperate people. They mean no harm," Davi said. "Come, let's eat. I have lunch ready for you."

"I need to check something on this bike," Rotha said. "I'll be there soon. Go start."

Mali handed Kunthea off to Sokha. "You look like you've grown two inches in two weeks!" she said.

Sokha beamed at her older sister. "Mea is teaching me to sew and make soup!" she said.

Mali nodded her approval and turned her attention to her mother. "Living here alone with the girls is unsafe. You are unprotected with people straying onto your property. What if someone tries something?" she asked.

"As soon as I can be sure that the farm is in good hands with people I trust, we will come and join you in the city," Davi said.

Panic rose in Sokha. *Leave home? What is she talking about?*

"More and more people are homeless and hungry and begging for food! Soon you will have none left for yourself," Mali said. "People are desperate. Please try to leave soon. Besides, I have good news. Rotha and I are going to have a baby, and I'd love to have you with me."

Davi threw her arms around Mali. "I'm happy for you. Your first child," she said.

"Jah, and another one to feed. I could use your help in the city, Mea."

"We're moving?" Sokha asked.

"Not right now. Let's eat. No more talk of this," Mea said. Sokha didn't believe it. *Mea would never leave the farm. She's just making Mali feel better by saying it.*

Halfway through Sokha's seventh year, she sat in a circle with her sisters at dinner eating mudfish, snails, and rice when her mother announced, "We are ready to move to the city to live with Mali and Rotha."

Sokha stuck her chopsticks in her rice, stopped eating, and swallowed hard.

"In the city, we will blend in. No one will care that we're alone without Ba. It will be better for all of us," she said. Chantou cut off another piece of fish. Kunthea held her bowl out for more rice and nudged it toward her mother.

"Mea! But what if we don't want to go?" Sokha cried. Chantou glanced up; a worried look crossed her face—the look she wore when Sokha spoke out of turn, when she behaved improperly and upset Mea.

"It's no longer safe here for us," Davi said. "There are things happening that you do not understand. Think of this as a new start."

"I don't want a new start! We can't leave the farm. This is our home. How can we just leave it? Who will take care of the animals?" Sokha cried. She wiped the tears across her cheeks and gave a snort that made everyone gape at her.

In a firm voice, Davi said, "Uncle Keo, Aunt Ary, and Chhay will be moving to the city, too. If Uncle Keo doesn't feel safe, I don't either."

Sokha sulked and looked away from her mother. "I won't go," she said. Chantou put her bowl down to watch her sister and mother clash. Sokha saw her sister go pale, and it gave her pause, so she hung her head low in deference.

"Here's the truth!" Davi said. "You *will* go. There are soldiers with guns nearby. We are at war, and we must go to the city until it ends. We have two good families to manage the rice fields and animals while we are away. We plan to return someday, but it's not safe here anymore."

"But...Mea!" Sokha cried.

"There are some things in life you cannot change, Sokha. We have no choice right now. We must leave, and I will need your help and cooperation. Now eat your meal. It's not every day we have snails. I thought we'd celebrate."

"Celebrate?" Sokha said. With tears streaming down her cheeks, Sokha stared at her mother in defiance before she put her bowl down, rose on her agile legs, bowed a weak sampeah, and ran off to bawl with her friend, Cow.

"I'll never leave you," she said to the animal standing before her. "I'll hide in the grass, and I'll stay here. No one can make me leave! None of this would have happened if Ba didn't die!" When she finished sobbing, she leaned her forehead against Cow's warm body while stroking the animal's side. The docile beast accepted all of Sokha's despair.

During the next week, Mea spent all of her extra time with a young couple that often helped in exchange for food. "We promise to keep the property in good order until you can return," said the young man, and Sokha felt a flash of anger toward him. *Who are you to take my farm?*

"We will be leaving within days. Time to get ready," Davi announced soon after.

Sokha bit back her voice. *This is my home! You can't make me go!* But inside, she knew there was nothing she could do to make everyone understand that they should stay.

Within hours, they were forced to flee to the foxhole by the sound of gunfire dangerously near. "This is why we are leaving," Mea said mournfully as she huddled in the dark hole with her three daughters.

"Jah, but we are safe here. No one's ever hurt us," Sokha muttered.

"We can't take chances," Mea said. "Now hush. No more talking."

On moving day, the family gathered their clothes, some pots, a store of rice, a rolled-up rug, and a few personal items. Davi tucked the only photo she had of Boran inside her pocket and pressed her hand against it.

After a long look back, the gloomy families walked alongside their belongings stuffed in an old ox cart. Rotha also pulled a cart attached to his motorcycle and sped ahead of them. "Don't despair," Keo said to the bunch. "This may soon be over, and we could be back again as if it never happened."

The quiet caravan walked past rice paddies and farms,

across short rickety bridges, and through thicket-lined paths, and after four hours of trekking, they saw taller homes, majestic palms, and spired stupas surrounding an elaborate pagoda near bustling streets and markets. Sokha's melancholy gave way to awe and wonder. A little further on, they entered an older, run-down section of the city, and that's where Davi paused to find the exact address.

As their cart rolled up in front of the hovel that Mali and Rotha rented—a one-room house on street level—Sokha winced. Her shoulders sagged at the sight of this dilapidated structure—*we are a poor family now. There's no land here.* Instead, they paid a landlord to live in an ugly shack on the street with no shaded kitchen area. Loud popping noises made her jump, motorcycles revved, brakes squealed, and cars sped across the road. She remembered the melodic sound of chirping crickets, humming insects, and croaking frogs. She remembered the feel of mud between her toes in the rice field, the cool breeze that rustled the leaves of the tree she loved to climb, and she knew she did not belong in the city.

"Everything is so cramped. There's no space," Sokha complained to Mali, who started to feel more like a second mother to her than a sister.

"Give it time," Mali said in her silky voice before turning her attention to Davi, who looked more out of place than Sokha. "Come, Mea, it's not too complicated here. I'll show you where the temple is," she said as she guided her mother around the streets like a hesitant child. Sokha followed. "Look, there are many interesting statues around the pagoda and school," Mali said in an animated voice.

"Statues cannot teach a child anything," Davi replied.

Sokha wanted to complain to her mother about the new house, but she didn't dare, for fear of adding to her misery over losing Ba and the farm. Besides, Davi had reminded Sokha in the past that it was not proper to complain. She remembered her mother's words: "You must accept the way things are and make peace with your own discomfort as the holy monks have taught you." In spite of her mother's advice, she knew that Mea felt as unhappy and out of place as she did because she no longer hummed her songs.

Then, one day, she heard proof. Sokha caught Davi groaning to Mali when she thought Sokha wasn't listening. "I'd rather labor all day in the fields than push stale food on strangers for an hour," she said. "I liked growing my own food." Sokha had never before heard her mother complain about anything.

Davi had boiled sweet potatoes to sell at the markets. In the early evening, she returned home with unsold leftovers. "I had no luck selling these sweet potatoes today," she moaned. Setting the basket down, she stared at the vegetables in disgust. When Sokha greeted her with a heartfelt smile, Davi averted her eyes and barely acknowledged her.

"It's okay, Mea," Sokha said.

Davi continued to stare at her unsold wares. Slowly, a blush of shame rose in her cheeks, and Sokha felt her mother's helplessness seep out into the room.

"Don't worry, Mea. We'll have more for dinner," Sokha said. But when everyone gathered for the evening meal, her mother barely touched her food before giving most of her portion to Kunthea who always wanted more because she was growing. Sokha stared at her mother. *Is she still sad that Ba died or does she just hate the city? Is she mad at me?*

"I'm letting you all down," Davi said. "I don't like asking for money. It's degrading." Chantou looked as if she'd burst into tears at her mother's words.

Rotha spoke up. "No work is degrading. Not in these times. We are all working for our family, and we appreciate your help."

"Living here is an adjustment," Mali added. She touched her

pregnant belly. "I need you here. Thank you for trying, Mea," she said.

"Tomorrow will be better!" Sokha said. Her enthusiasm made everyone laugh and begin moving about to clean up after the meal.

Davi enrolled Sokha in classes at the city temple because she was not yet eight years old, but she enrolled Chantou in the public school. Sokha had to get used to the ways of the new Pagoda and didn't know any of her fellow students. Her house did not feel like home. The air in the city smelled like rotting garbage on hot days when the trash sat outside for too long. When Sokha complained to Mali, she insisted, "You will get used to it."

Most of the things Mali told Sokha, she believed. This, she did not.

With every passing month, Sokha saw her mother sink deeper into misery until Mea's body began to resemble her mood, sinking into itself, the jaundiced skin of her face sagging into a permanent expression of sorrow.

As the New Year flipped to 1972, Sokha turned eight, and her mother enrolled her in the same public school that Chantou attended. Sokha felt a wave of relief, and while she had felt out of place in the temple as the new student, the public school made her gape in awe. The grounds swarmed with blue and white uniforms. The spacious campus was comprised of four long rectangular buildings set in a square with a large courtyard in the middle. A tangle of scooters and bicycles filled up one corner.

Chantou pointed the way before she ran off with her friends to class. "I'll meet you at lunchtime, right here," she said.

Sokha felt the school swallow her, and struggled to find her way. Her temple schools had all been one large room. Fully furnished and decorated, this school could not have been more unlike the temple. Students sat at desks in modern classrooms, and there were no prayers!

On her first day, the teacher announced, "Nails must be clean, hair must be combed, clothes should not be stained, and girls must wear a long enough skirt, or they will be sent home."

"Let me check that skirt," Chantou said to Sokha on the morning of Sokha's second day of public school. She pulled on the hem to make it look longer. "Don't let it slide up or you'll be in trouble. Isn't it nice that we can walk home for lunch again like we did on the farm?"

"Jah, but I wish we had money for fish from the food cart! Two of my friends eat there every day," Sokha said.

"You're never satisfied. Always wanting more!" Chantou chided, and Sokha smirked. Within a few weeks, Sokha began to bring a snack to school so she could spend time with her new friends at lunch and recess. She usually brought whatever her mother and sister were selling at the market along with a handful of rice wrapped in banana leaf. If she was lucky enough to get a fried banana before going to school, that kept her full most of the day.

One afternoon, Sokha and Chantou found a scribbled note at home after school telling them to run to the clinic to meet the family. "Mali must have had her baby!" Chantou said, and off they flew.

To Sokha, six-pound Vibol appeared like magic. He was an unnamed entity in Mali's belly only hours before, then suddenly a fully formed human. The first time Sokha saw him, she was reminded of the awe she felt when Kunthea was born, only this time, it was her sister becoming a mother! She watched Mali hold her newborn son and smile at Rotha. Mali looked tired with her hair disheveled, and her brow still beaded with sweat. As Mali handed the infant to Mea, Davi's mouth rounded in cooing sounds, and her face radiated maternal love. For the first time in weeks, Sokha saw her mother smile. Looking around the room, Sokha felt a swell of love for all the people gathered to celebrate the newest member of the family.

A few weeks following Vibol's birth, Rotha announced, "Mali and I have found a better place to live. It's close by, so you can stay in your school," he said, looking at Sokha and Chantou. "You'll have a longer walk every day, but the house is bigger with some trees around it," he said, and that made Sokha grin.

In a rare burst of energy, Davi helped her daughters pack up their belongings and even found the strength to carry her treasured rice pot filled with utensils on moving day. Sokha ran up and down the outside stairs at the new house, delighted to be living in an elevated home with more space. Time and time again, she volunteered to carry possessions up the steps, for the pure joy of ascending them.

"I have a gift for you," Mali said to Sokha as they unpacked baskets together. Mali pulled out an hourglass-shaped object, metal on the bottom and glass on the top. "It's a kerosene lamp. Now you can see after dark. But don't stay up too late reading or you won't get up in time to collect water from the distribution center. That's still your job!" she said with a jab and a smile.

Although it took willpower, Sokha tried not to stay up too late studying. Right before dawn, she rose with Chantou and padded out to the street. They carried buckets across their shoulders on a bamboo pole and walked a half-mile away to collect water for the family's cooking and washing. "The sky looks like fire!" Chantou whispered.

Sokha counted five colors in the sunrise: pink, purple, red, orange, and yellow. "Like a painting I saw at the market," she said.

A gradual sense of ease settled on Sokha. The new lamp, the stilted house, and Vibol's baby antics cheered her, but she noticed that these changes brought little solace to Mea.

"Mea, the sun is rising. It's time to wake up," Sokha said in the morning. Davi rolled over to go back to sleep. When Sokha and her sisters returned with water, Mea murmured groggily from her bed, holding her stomach. When Chantou and Sokha left for school, her mother had not roused as usual to prepare food for selling in the city.

Keo, who had settled in a house several blocks away with his family, visited and suggested an herbal tea for Davi that might improve her stomach cramps, but Davi didn't get up to greet him. Instead, she spoke to him in whispering tones lying flat on her sleeping mat.

She's getting like Ba, Sokha thought. Her mind returned again and again to the sickness that pained her father, even when she told her mind to stop thinking.

_____

8

City of Battambang

E very time Sokha came home; she heard radio voices talking in the house that Davi seldom left. Unable to work, Davi listened to newscasts all day on Rotha's old radio. She then proceeded to relay grisly details about land-mines hidden in the country that blew up from a misplaced footstep, of villages being leveled, of farms and homes replaced by smoldering craters in the ground. Rotha snapped the radio off and told her to read. He dropped a book on her pallet: *The Teachings of the Buddha*.

At breakfast one morning, Davi spoke in a haunting tone. "The Khmer Rouge have taken most of the countryside," she moaned. "Cambodia is disappearing."

"You're scaring us, Mea," Chantou said. "What are you talking about?"

Mali echoed her. "You upset yourself listening to the radio. You must concentrate on getting better. We are safe here in the city."

She misses the farm, Sokha thought. "I learned a new song

today at school. Do you want to hear it?" she asked. Mea didn't answer. Her face remained expressionless.

If music won't work, gifts might help. Sokha had no money for gifts, but she searched her mind for something that Mea might like. Finally, she found a smooth stone shaped like a fish.

"Look, Mea. It's for you. Feel it," she said, handing the stone to her mother. Davi sat on her mat and leaned against the wall. She took the stone and rubbed it between her pointer finger and thumb. A slight smile creased her eyes.

"My outdoor girl," she whispered. "You found a gem." Mea's eyes held love, and Sokha soaked it up.

Davi lay sick for months, and she grew angry. "Prince Sihanouk is traveling with the Khmer Rouge and encouraging them. How could he side with them?" she grunted. "Boran would be stomping in disgust!"

"That's it," Rotha said and took the radio away. "I don't like doing this, but you are sick, and your anger is making you more sick. I'll find Uncle Keo. Maybe he will know what to do."

Mali glanced sideways at her sisters, and no one spoke of their mother's outbursts. Instead, they worked harder to cover her chores. Mali worked many hours selling vegetables and fruits. One morning she prepared a tray of fried bananas. As she placed the tray on top of her head to leave the house, she asked Sokha, "Would you like to help me sell door-to-door after school today? Uncle Keo gave me two branches of longan to sell that he got in trade. We could get a good price for them. No one can find longan anymore."

"Jah," Sokha said. "But I'd rather eat it myself!" Mali chuckled. "Has Rotha left for the hospital early to water his cabbages?" Sokha asked.

"Jah! He did. I'm glad he got permission from the hospital to use that little strip of land as his personal garden, since he's right there all day. He's getting five riel now. His cabbages are the best around. I better go before it gets too hot. See you later."

Sokha smiled at her sister's bright face. Mali had turned out to be right. The city was not as awful as she had feared, even though it seemed to be getting more crowded by the day. Sokha grabbed a small container of rice as she left the house with a growing sense of admiration for Mali.

After school, as she prepared to help her sister, Sokha chatted with her unresponsive mother. For the first time, she noticed that Mea's stomach stuck out like the belly of a pregnant woman. "I'll look for another stone for you while I'm out. Okay?" she said. Mea nodded lazily.

While walking to school, Sokha finally asked Chantou, "What is wrong with Mea's stomach?"

"I don't know, but it might be a tumor," she said.

Sokha stopped walking and looked at her sister. "Does it hurt her like it hurt Ba?"

"No. At least Mali said it doesn't," Chantou said. She turned her face from her sister. "There's nothing we can do. It's just the way it is, and Mea has calmed down since we took the radio away. Let's go, or we'll be late for the flag going up."

Sokha stuck close to the comfort of her sister's side as they made their way to the school courtyard. How could her sister ignore this? It was clear to Sokha that her mother was fading away and yet everyone in the house went about the day as usual. Perhaps Mea had been right when she told Sokha that her mind was greedy, always wanting to know what others knew. Perhaps she should be more like her sisters and just pay attention to what she needed to do.

When Mea's whole body swelled, Mali took her to the hospital where she slept for a day or two. Mali tried to stay with her as much as possible, and her sisters visited later in the afternoon. "What is her illness?" she asked the doctor. "What can we do?"

"I'm sorry, but we can't seem to find anything to treat. Take her home and let her rest," the doctor suggested. "We don't have enough beds to keep her here."

Mali grimaced. "Thank you for your *help*," she said with a half-hearted sampeah. Sokha stood by listening and took the doctor's advice as a sign of hope. *There's nothing to treat—isn't that a good thing? Mea is just sad.* She helped Chantou support her mother out to the sidewalk while Mali flagged a cyclo to carry Mea home.

Within days, it grew clear that no amount of rest would cure Davi, and she could not babysit Vibol because she was too sick to pull her body off the sleeping mat.

At nine-years-old, Sokha stayed in the house most evenings to watch her nephew and younger sister while Mali and Chantou worked extra hours. Recently, she'd fought battles of her own. When Kunthea cried and finally confessed that some girls had been bullying her outside the temple school, Sokha paid a visit to the girls.

"Which ones," Sokha asked. Kunthea pointed to the leader. Sokha strode over to three seven-year-old girls walking away from school on the dirt path. She stood a full head taller with wide shoulders and muscular legs. In a flash, she pulled the leader's crisp white collar and snarled, "See this girl?" She pointed to Kunthea. "She is my sister; she's only six! You are older than she is and should know better! If you insult her or hurt her, you will deal with me! Hands off my sister! All of you! Do you understand?"

When she jerked her hand away, the girls nodded quickly and scattered away. Sokha felt a wave of self-satisfaction. Kunthea thanked her profusely and said, "I never saw a girl as tough as you!"

"They deserved it," Sokha said. "Tell me if they bother you again."

In the evening, while Mali, Chantou, and Rotha still worked, Sokha raised her mother's head to sip water and kept Kunthea and Vibol busy by showing them how to make figures out of clay from the road, mixing her tears with water and the dusty earth.

Sokha was born in the year of the Dragon, in the element of Wood. She had been told that Wood Dragons possess magical powers and uncommon strength—that they are capable of soaring to the highest heavenly heights—but on this day, Sokha had no magic. She could not bring Mea back to life.

Davi Sang died in her sleep on a morning like every other. When Mali brought her a bowl of noodle soup for breakfast, she found her body cold and called the family together before they all rushed off to school and work. Sokha told herself she should have paid more attention to Mea, she should have read to her, rubbed her back as her mother rubbed hers when she was a child. She had meant to but seemed to have so many other things to do. *"My outdoor child."* The words repeated in her mind. Her mother had looked at her with pride that day.

Once again, white flags were hung on the house, and the family gathered with the monks. Rotha and Keo built a simple coffin with donated scraps of wood, and the monks came to the house and chanted for two days.

"There are a lot of funerals this week," the head monk said. "Two days is enough." So Mali and her sisters gave as much as they could to the Neak Ta outside their door. Food had grown scarce as the city grew overcrowded.

"Surely, Mea was a good person and will be rewarded. She

worked harder than anyone when she could and gave up the farm to keep us all safe," Mali said.

If a person is born in the same lunar year as someone who dies, Buddhist custom prohibits that person from attending the cremation. Sokha was born in the same lunar year as her mother. Mali and Ary had prepared Mea's body for cremation before everyone departed in a procession to the temple grounds, carrying Mea in a box above their heads. Before they left, Chantou whispered to Sokha, "I wish I could stay here with you. I do not want to watch this," and the two girls cried in each other's arms.

Sokha stood above in the doorway of the stilted house and watched her family disappear around the corner as they walked two-by-two behind the casket.

I am nine years old and have no parents. Sokha walked from her own sleeping area to Mali and Rotha's sleeping area and beyond where she saw Mea's sleeping mat rolled up against the wall. She walked to the pantry where root vegetables sat in baskets and herbs hung from nails along the wall, where the large wooden mortar and pestle still smelled of pounded garlic. She walked in circles around the house, agitated and feeling left out.

Finally, she stood before Mea's sleeping mat and stared. After a few minutes, she unrolled it, fell to the floor in the dim light, and cried out for her mother. Once the tears cleared, she sat up, closed her eyes, and did as Mali suggested. "Remember Mea as she was when she lived on the farm with Ba. That's who she really was. Not a sick old woman in the city."

Relaxing her shoulders and breathing evenly as the monks instructed, she heard her mother singing to her, even as she carried heavy buckets of water. She saw her mother sharing food with strangers; she saw her offer a sampeah, and the curve of her spine as she bent her strong back in all her chores:

washing clothes, weeding, planting. She remembered how her mother tended Ba. "You were right to move us to the city," she whispered. "I'm sorry I was mean to you about leaving the farm." *May your next life be rich with blessings and comfort. May your next life be filled with children who love you as much as I love you.*

A few hours later, Sokha's family returned to the house after the cremation, and the atmosphere changed from a silent cave to a buzzing hive of food preparation and chattering. Sokha could not help remembering her mother's words after her Ba died: "There is a rebirth."

Uncle Keo spoke in riddles like the monks. Sokha asked him, "If Mea will be reborn, why can't I see her again?"

"What begins must end. The hardest part is letting go."

She glanced over at Mali, her oldest sister.

"Are you our mother now?" she asked.

"I'll never replace Mea," she said. "But I'll always care for you."

9

City of Battambang
April 13, 1975

On the first day of the New Year celebration, the girls woke up early, eager to clean the house. Sokha shook the rugs and mats out and placed them back perfectly on the floor that Chantou had just swept. Kunthea wiped every surface of the house clean. Mali supervised and gathered items to bring for the long day ahead—the celebration of Moha Songkran – the welcoming of angels to the New Year.

Rotha held Vibol to keep him from getting in the way of the busy women; and once declared clean, Mali lit a candle and a stick of homemade incense to welcome the New Year angel into their home.

"We're done," she said. "Let's collect our food."

"Yes, it's time to go. Already the street is filling up," Rotha said.

Sokha's body tingled with excitement as she strolled to the temple with her family along with groups of eager neighbors.

Festive clothes and food were scarce, but everyone needed a holiday.

Colorful streamers greeted them along the way, and as they grew closer, they saw the temple entrance marked with a lush garland of coconut leaves and flowers. Inside, candles glowed around the Buddha statue at the White Elephant Pagoda, Wat Tahm-rai-saw.

"The White Elephant is a happy sign," Mali said to her sisters, "because the Buddha's mother saw a white elephant in her dreams the night before her son was born." Before entering the temple, they all removed their shoes and left them by the entrance. Inside, monks sat in rows, their ochre garments pooling on the floor as they recited prayers. Rotha lit a stick of agar wood incense before the Buddha statue.

The girls added to the line of dishes set before the monks to be blessed. Mali and Kunthea brought bowls of rice. Chantou offered a cabbage dish, and Sokha presented two roasted sweet potatoes as thanks to the Buddha for his teachings. Sitting on the floor with their feet tucked beneath them, they listened to the hypnotic sound of monks chanting and inhaled the heady scent of Khmer spices. After paying their respects, they gathered their shoes and entered the temple courtyard.

"Look! Can we try?" Sokha asked as she stepped out onto the loud, brilliant street. Apples hung down on strings from the branches of a tree, and several young boys were making onlookers screech with delight as they tried to take a bite out of the dangling fruit with their hands behind their backs. The apples kept spinning and swinging in the air. Sokha picked a spot and tried. The apple shot away from her.

"Try jumping," a familiar voice said.

"Uncle Keo!" Sokha cried. "You should try it!" Keo shook his head, and Sokha sprang up, but she could not get a bite and gave up laughing. She stepped away to give Chhay a turn and stamped her foot in mock protest when he got a bite on the first try. Goodnatured like his father, he flashed her a sympathetic smile.

"I want to play hide-the-scarf," Chantou shouted. Sokha chased her to fight for a spot in the game. For lunch, the whole extended family chose a spot beneath a shady tree and savored festival food. By the end of the day, Sokha collapsed with exhaustion.

Before sunrise on the second day of the New Year, Sokha woke up in a somber mood. Chantou slept beside her, so she quietly uncovered the stack of colorful flags tied to sticks that she and Kunthea helped make for Mali, Rotha, Uncle Keo, and Aunt Ary. Chantou had scavenged scraps of material and helped her sisters arrange them into captivating combinations. Picking one up, she imagined her mother sewing, her smooth face concentrating on every stitch.

"Will this be enough to thank them for Vanabot?" she asked her sister.

"It's all we have," Chantou said. "They won't expect anything. Watch, you'll see."

Sokha heard someone else waking up and quickly wrapped the flags again.

An hour later, after their morning meal, Chantou spoke: "Because we honor you for all you have done for us, we made these for you!" Sokha lifted a square of paper and Kunthea unwrapped it as if opening a present. She could not keep from squealing with delight as she selected one flag for each of her elders and handed them out.

Mali accepted her blue and red flag—the traditional Khmer flag colors—and waved it with pride. "What a surprise! How did you manage it? Just look at these!" she said. Rotha waved his banner, so the fabric tickled Kunthea's cheek, and she laughed.

"These are lovely," Ary said. Keo studied his flag with the

attention one might give a textbook. He checked the stitching and patterns up close and nodded his approval.

Music echoed on the streets throughout the day as traditional dancers entertained crowds near the temple grounds. Outside on the street, others joined in the dancing to the swell of the bamboo flute, xylophone, and barrel drums. Mali smiled easily as she waved her homemade flag and twirled. As the ring of dancers grew wider and wider, Sokha noticed how gracefully Chantou moved to the music. Her back arched, her knees bent, and her fingers curved backward. Her arms snaked up around her face as her body moved like a serpent in one fluid motion. *Even her fingers seem to dance,* Sokha thought.

Sokha began to imitate her sister. She kicked off her sandals, but when she tried to curl her toes, she tripped. She laughed out loud at her clumsiness. "Bong, how do you do that?" she asked.

Chantou pulled her aside and explained. "Concentrate on the hands first. The movements are symbols. See my fingers? This first gesture is a tree," she said. Sokha copied the gesture.

"Next, there are leaves, flowers, and fruit, and when the fruit drops, a new tree grows. We repeat the cycle of life—the seed, bloom, death, and rebirth." Chantou went through the motions, and Sokha mimicked. After a few tries, she had a general idea. "Come, let's dance again, bong," Chantou said.

Sokha followed her sister in the dance circle and began to feel her hand gestures transforming her into something other than a young girl. She could not get her elbow to look like Chantou's, but as her hands stretched, she felt her ten separate fingers, each distinct and able to move in ways that gave different impressions.

Watching Chantou, Sokha observed a kind of beauty in her sister she hadn't noticed before. Dancing made Chantou relax and glow. Sokha wanted to feel the same but felt herself concentrating on the gestures too much to be fluid. Chantou glanced over her shoulder at her and smiled. She gave the slightest nod of approval, and Sokha continued dancing until the music stopped.

As the sun retreated, a dedication ceremony for departed ancestors who had moved on to a new life began, and Sokha wondered about her parents and reincarnation. *Who are you now? Are you happy?* Outside on the temple grounds, mounds of sand, stupas in remembrance of the dead, grew taller and wider as people added handfuls of sand to them. *I'm not the only one who has lost someone I love* thought Sokha as she opened her palm and released the sand. *Look how high the piles grow!* Her ears filled with the sound of monks conferring blessings on the spirits of the departed and on the living who remembered them.

"One more day!" Chantou said to Sokha as they made their way back home.

"I wish it would never end. I love the music and all the food. And no one gets in trouble!" Sokha said.

"Not even you!" Chantou chided.

"Don't forget the flowers!" Mali called as she grabbed up Vibol to leave for the temple in the morning. Sokha, Chantou, and Kunthea each held a paper flower they had made to help decorate the Buddha statue. Thgnai Loeung Sak marked the first day of the New Year symbolizing a new beginning. Monks blessed the stupas that were formed the day before, and Sokha and her family joined in washing the statues of the temple with leaves dampened in perfumed water, or by pouring small cups of water over the statues.

"You are the old ones now," Chantou joked to Mali and Rotha as they settled in for lunch on their mat in the shade.

"Jah, enjoy being dry!" joked Sokha. "Your turn is coming. It will soon be time to throw water on you!"

But Mali had a surprise. She lifted the large banana leaf

covering from the food tray that sat before her, exposing five 12-inch charred bamboo sticks.

"Kralan!" Sokha shouted. "You made it!"

"It's not as good as usual, and we'll have to share, but I worked with what I had," Mali said. All the children pressed their palms together in thanks. Peeling the bamboo back exposed the sticky rice mixed with beans and grated coconut. She had stuffed the mixture inside a bamboo stick and slowly roasted it on a charcoal fire at a neighbor's house to surprise everyone.

"Where did you get the coconut?" Rotha asked? "I can't find one anywhere."

"I traded one of your cabbages for it, so it's from you, too," Mali said. "And Aunt Ary prepared sticky rice with mango, so we have two treats!"

Ary uncovered her dessert tray with a smile, nodding at all the thank-yous.

"Where has Keo gone?" Mali asked as Ary rationed out her treats.

"He went home to meditate. Sometimes all this excitement is too much for him. He needs his quiet time."

"To meditate or nap?" Rotha asked with a laugh.

Ary smiled and shooed his joke away, "But he'll be back in time to be washed!" she said. Giggles echoed, and sticky smiles snickered in collusion as the heat of the day surrounded them. With full bellies, the families lazed on their mat.

Sokha turned on her back and looked up through the leaves to see the clear blue sky. *I wish it could be like this every day—all the food you can eat. And dessert—and everyone laughing and dancing.* She felt one foot touching Chantou's foot and the other touching Kunthea's foot as they rested beside her in contentment.

"What's this? Everyone sleeping on the first day of the New

Year?" Keo said. Sokha opened her eyes and towering above her stood Uncle Keo.

"Sugar sleep," Mali said. "We've had our fill!"

"You look refreshed," Ary said to Keo.

"I am, and ready," he said with a jovial grin. The children ran with their cups to the cistern by the temple where a line had formed. Sokha carried Vibol.

"Be careful, or you'll spill it all before you have a chance to wash your parents!" she warned. With a mix of reverence and joy, they sprinkled and poured water on the hands and feet of their elders, washing away any misdeeds. Before long, the air shimmered with silver rain as Khmers all around them flicked water droplets on those they loved.

"I think this is your favorite part of the New Year!" Sokha laughed as Vibol stood dripping wet.

"The sun will dry him soon enough," Mali said.

Their shared joy melted into the late afternoon sun as the festivities ended, and the troubled world crept back in.

Once home, Rotha turned on the radio.

Sokha closed her ears. The festivities were over for another year—back to routine. The rainy season would soon begin, but here in the city, they could not grow rice, and no fruit trees lined the path to school. Nostalgia for the farm washed over her.

10

Rotha

Three days later, on April 18th, in the stifling city, Rotha stood beneath his house holding Boran's old radio to listen for news. Buddhist prophecies circulated in the Khmer Republic. One talked of a Bodhi tree with a flat stump, the roots do not grow...a poisonous cobra hides quietly at the same place[1] As he fumbled with the knobs, a neighbor stopped by and handed him a small cup of iced coffee, a rare treat.

"Thank you, Bong!" Rotha said with a bow after placing his radio on the rickety chair that stood near the road by his house. "I'm having trouble with this thing lately—poor reception. But I'm glad we made it through the New Year," he said, holding up his cup in gratitude.

"Haven't you heard?" his neighbor asked. "The Khmer Rouge took over the Capitol yesterday—Phnom Penh is liberated. The Americans have left. The war is over."

Rotha froze. *Phnom Penh is less than two hundred miles southeast of us.* A trickle of sweat dripped down his side. His radio crackled. He fidgeted with the knob to pick up better reception and snorted in frustration. He knew the situation was dismal, but now he felt sick. He'd heard stories of the ruthless Khmer Rouge cadres. "The rebels won? What of Lon Nol?"

"He flew away with the Americans a few days ago. The Khmer Rouge bombed the airport and surrounded the city. They are claiming victory. A few scouts have gotten through here with reports."

Rotha shook his head. "What now? Are we a communist country?"

"I don't know. But who cares who wins? They're all corrupt. Look at it this way, at least the war will be over," his neighbor said, leaning against the wood post of the house. He took a drag on his cigarette, blew the smoke out sideways, and finished his coffee. "Why are you so upset? Someone had to win sooner or later."

Rotha could not pretend to be casual. He gulped all his coffee in one swallow and grabbed his radio. Listening between crackles, he heard reports on Khmer Rouge Radio announcing the victory. His neighbor was right. *Are they coming here? Are they marching to Battambang city right now? What will happen next?* Abruptly, Rotha excused himself to notify Mali of the news. In a corner of their house, Mali and Rotha huddled by the radio, so Sokha and Chantou would not hear them speak.

"Can we put on some music?" Sokha called to them. Mali and Rotha ignored her and spoke in strained whispers. Three-year-old Vibol started fussing, toddling from person to person for attention as if he sensed danger in the room. The radio went dead. Chantou wore a look of worried concentration, but Sokha continued to lament her boredom.

"Rotha and I still need to work, so you stay inside. We won't be long," Mali said to Sokha. "We won't venture very far. Do *not* go outside!"

"You're always worried about nothing," Sokha said, trying not to sound disrespectful. "I'm eleven—almost a teenager!"

"Just do as I say," Mali said with an intensity that made Sokha go quiet.

"Chantou, I want you to come, too. We'll sell these last few cabbages faster if you help. I'll meet you downstairs in a few minutes," Mali said and left the house.

Rotha split up from the girls to sell cabbages, but what he really wanted was information. Mali and Chantou went one way, and he went the other. "I'll meet you back here in twenty minutes. Be right here before dark," he said. "Stay together."

Rotha had chosen his side of the street so he could talk to an old friend of Boran's. He knocked on the door, and an older man, a retired general, appeared. "Rotha, why aren't you home with your family. It's not safe once the sun goes down," he said.

"General Lim…"

"Don't call me that. And do not speak of your father-in-law's title anymore. Government officials are being hunted down. Come in. I don't want anyone to see us talking."

"If they ask, I'm selling cabbages." Rotha held out his wares. "I need information. What is happening? What can you tell me?"

"The Khmer Rouge has won, taken over the Capital, and they are telling people to leave their homes. Battambang province and many others have surrendered, too."

"Leave their homes? Why?" Rotha asked, his heart pounding.

"I really don't know. They claimed the Americans were going to bomb the city, but I only heard that a bank was blown up in Phnom Penh."

"A bank?"

"Yes. There is much confusion right now. You best get home to be with your wife and son. Wait! Hold on." General Lim walked into another room and came back in seconds. He stuffed a pile of riels into Rotha's hand. "I'll take those cabbages," he said. "Now go. And be safe."

Rotha stuffed the money in his pocket and rushed back to the meeting spot. He did not run or draw attention to himself, but all of his senses sharpened. The shadow of moving leaves made him twitch; he kept thinking he saw someone move right next to him. *I must calm down. I must think. Tomorrow I will warn Uncle Keo.*

The girls returned within minutes with one unsold cabbage left. "It's okay, we can eat it," Rotha said. "I got a very good price for all of mine. Let's go."

They returned home to hear Sokha singing a children's song with her younger siblings. The sound of her voice calmed Rotha's nerves. *I need to tell Mali, but I don't want to panic her.* He took a few deep breaths and called her to the back of the house where they could talk alone.

"I've learned that the war *is* over and there's a lot of confusion in the Capital. Someone blew up a bank, but I don't know why."

"Are you sure this is true?" Mali asked.

"I think it is. General Lim is one of Boran's most trusted connections."

"Should the girls continue to go to school? Is it safe? Sokha has no idea what's happening, but I think Chantou knows more than she admits." Mali's voice cracked, and her shoulders slumped.

"Let's keep Kunthea home from temple school. The other two can go. Chantou will look after Sokha, and the school building is more secure than our house. Besides, school is within walking distance, and we should have some kind of advance warning if anything is going to happen. Perhaps with the war over, things will calm down in a day or two."

Mali stepped into her husband's arms. "I hope so. I hope so," she repeated.

Rotha squeezed his eyes shut. *I'm sorry I didn't tell you everything.* Steadying his heart rate, he held his wife close, making a conscious effort to remember the shape, smell, and warmth of her, a memory to sustain him through whatever lay ahead.

11

Sokha

As Sokha strolled down the street with Chantou on her way to school, she overheard people speaking in hushed but animated tones. Overhearing one man say, "Things are moving toward this side of the country," she wondered. *What things?*

The girls stopped at a road crossing and could not hear each other over a group of men arguing nearby. Once clear of them, Sokha asked, "Why do so many people look angry and upset lately? What's going on?"

"I don't know," Chantou said. "It's none of our business anyway. Come. Stop staring at them." Sokha felt uneasy ever since the New Year ended. Mali and Rotha seemed strained, and many of her schoolmates were absent.

Sokha entered the date on the top of her paper as she sat in class: April 24, 1975. She copied her notes from the board along with her classmates. Hearing a commotion, she looked up as a man rushed into the room. He urgently whispered to her teacher, and her teacher turned to face the class. "Everyone, go home. Now!" he ordered.

No one moved. *We just got here*, Sokha thought. *Is this some kind of test?*

The teacher snatched up papers as fifteen students looked at each other with raised eyebrows. The man's stricken face quieted the room as he looked at his students. "You must leave. Go straight home. Do as I say," he said, and he strode out the door leading the way. Sokha grabbed her bag of supplies and filed out with her friends.

Outside, Sokha heard crying and saw people running in the street. Her eyes darted around to find Chantou, but she could not see faces. Action blurred the scene. Little children stumbled alongside fleeing parents. Fathers yelled, "Hurry up!" Mothers clutched their babies—everyone ran as if demons were chasing them.

"Chantou!" she cried, but someone pushed her out of the way from behind, and she took off running, afraid to look behind her, afraid of what was chasing her.

Sokha sprinted. She focused all of her attention on getting to her house, to her sisters, and when at last she stumbled over the threshold, Mali grabbed her shoulders and looked at her with something bordering on madness in her eyes and yelled, "Come! Let's go! We must get out of here. Pack a few of your things. Fast!" Mali spun around and pulled a sack of rice from the shelf.

Sokha turned and saw Chantou frantically stuffing clothing in a bag. "You made it home before me. Why didn't you wait for me?" Sokha asked.

Chantou gripped two shirts in her fists. "I couldn't find you! The soldiers—the ones in black wearing red kramas and caps— they're taking over the country! They have ordered everyone out of the city. Now pack!"

Within minutes, Sokha gathered her things and ran to Mali.

She followed her as her sister took her mother's photo of her father dressed in his military uniform and buried it in the rice storage bin beneath the house. Mali then hid the photo of her mother's face deep in her pouch. "Do not talk to anyone about our parents. Our parents are dead!" Mali called across the room to Sokha and her sisters. "They will kill us if they know that Ba was an officer in the old government! Say he was always a farmer. Do you hear me?" Sokha nodded. Tears welled in her eyes, and her heart thrashed wildly in her chest.

Following Chantou, Sokha rushed out of the house carrying a sack of clothes, her books, her lantern, and a bag of rice that Mali insisted she carry. Chantou brought pots, dishes, a sack of rice, and clothing. Mali clutched Vibol and a bag of clothes with cups and baby supplies padded in her bag, and Rotha carried heavier items. He urged Kunthea to stay close.

"Don't leave my side, no matter what," he said.

Kunthea struggled to keep up with her little sack of clothing, asking questions. "What's wrong? Why are we leaving? Where are we going? Why is Sokha crying?"

"Keep quiet. Just follow," Rotha said. "Come along. Quickly!"

Outside, soldiers were broadcasting from trucks rumbling down the street, "All military and government employees, leave your weapons here in this pile and go this way. Everyone else, you must leave the city now. You do not need to bring anything with you. You'll be back in three days."

The street throbbed with a chaotic blur of bodies running, screaming, crying, and zigzagging across the road. A sharp sound like the pop of a firecracker rang in Sokha's ears. She saw a man a few feet away stop in mid-stride, his body jerked, blood sprayed on the street, and he fell with a thwack! *Who is shooting us? Why?* Two soldiers, their chests wrapped in bullets in the shape of an X, surrounded the fallen man and started dragging him away. Sokha stopped running and gulped for air.

Mali grabbed her upper arm. "Don't stop! Keep going!"

As if jolted awake from a dream, Sokha ran. She trained her eyes on her sisters, terrified that she would be separated from them. She tried not to see anything but Mali's back directly ahead of her, but it was hard to keep up with everyone frantically weaving in and around her.

Stifling heat and cries of panic filled her head, making her temples thump. Rotha strode quickly even though he carried a big sack, and Mali clung to Vibol while Chantou grabbed Kunthea's small hand.

Sokha's nostrils filled with the acrid smell of human sweat and fear in the smoldering heat. The temperature topped 100 degrees, and Sokha and her family were swept into a human river flowing in one direction—away—on the only paved highway out of the city. In the swarm, Sokha saw a grown man carrying his frail mother wrapped in a sheet, his face strained with the effort. She saw teenagers on bicycles with family members packed around them, men on motorcycles that could not get through, and others pulling carts piled high with supplies and children.

Soon, the crowd grew so dense that people could not run, but walked. Young soldiers dressed in black pajama-like uniforms pointed their guns, and yelled, "Keep moving! Go. Go!"

"Everybody! Over here!" Rotha called to his family. "Stay on this side of the crowd, don't go in the middle. Stay where I can see you," he said. They stuck together at the edge of the mob. Panic gave way to exhaustion. Sokha walked without water until her lungs burned. She walked past an injured woman crying for help on the side of the road and paused, but Rotha urged her on. "There's no time to help. Come on."

No time to help. Sokha remembered her parents handing out bags of rice to people on the road by their farm, hiring homeless vagabonds and paying them with food, giving money to the poor. *What is happening to everyone?* She felt a wet stream running from her nose, tasted the saltiness on her lips, and she wiped it away with her wrist.

"Uncle Keo! What about him? What about Aunt Ary and Chhay?" she cried to Mali.

"Uncle Keo is smart. They'll find us," Mali called back.

Soon the pace picked up again. Sokha covered her nose and mouth with her school collar as she passed dead bodies near gullies along the way—men in government uniforms—Lon Nol's soldiers that must have been killed in recent battles. She stumbled, and her sandals fell off. "My shoes!" she called to Mali.

"Keep going!" Mali said without looking back.

Sokha's heart broke. *My feet hurt, and no one cares. I have no shoes!*

Finally, Rotha stopped, and the family gathered near him. "There must be water here, the soldiers are letting people stop. Let's eat and rest a bit," he said. "I'll gather sticks for a fire. We'll need to boil the water." They stepped off the roadway near a pond in mid-afternoon with several other families. Sokha rubbed her feet and picked a splinter from her heel wishing she could cry on someone's shoulder, but there was no sympathy to be found.

Soldiers sat nearby against shady trees in the oppressive heat. Chantou cut up a mango and handed pieces out as Mali attempted to feed her agitated three-year-old a piece of banana. After their snack, the family tried to rest on the ground close to one another while Rotha watched over their possessions, but they did not rest for long. With soldiers urging them on, they packed up to join the multitude of strangers again, responding to marching orders from the rebels who showed up randomly to prod the weary masses along.

Sokha's family trudged through the dank heat.

"Uncle Keo! Here!" called Rotha when he saw him through the mob. "Over here! Come with us." Mali and the girls ran toward their aunt and uncle. Chantou ran to Aunt Ary and helped her along. Sokha noticed that Keo hobbled on sore feet, and hugged him.

"My feet hurt too!" she said. "I lost my sandals!" Keo gave Sokha a sympathetic sigh.

"Ary, do you have any spare shoes?" he asked. Ary dug through her bags. "I think I packed most of mine," she said. Within minutes, she pulled out a pair of sandals. "They may be a little worn, but they should work," she said and handed the sandals to Sokha.

As the paved road gave way to dirt roads in the countryside, the soldiers led everyone into the jungle on a path thinner than the road had been.

Hours later, the weary mob stopped as the sun retreated from its fiery onslaught, and the air cooled down. The dense trees of the jungle made evening darker, and the forest pulsated with wild animal noises. People prepared what little food they had brought along and camped with their families.

Sokha watched as Rotha unrolled the two woven mats he carried, the ones that were used at their joyful picnic only days ago. Keo unrolled his mats a short distance away. The twinkling of campfires spaced apart gave light, and the low hum of families whispering among themselves drifted in the air. Rotha made a fire with twigs collected by the girls, and Mali put on a pot of rice. She cautioned everyone not to eat it all and saved a few rice balls for morning.

Sokha scraped the empty pot with a piece of bark and washed it with leaves and some water as best she could, and when all supplies were stowed away, the family settled down to sleep on their mats on the ground.

Rotha stood guard this first night. Even though Sokha felt stressed, she was exhausted and fell asleep, wedged between her sisters. When it was still dark, she heard Rotha's raspy warning. "Wake up!" Sokha jumped and saw three aggressive-looking monkeys lurking nearby. She huddled with her family.

"Bang on this pot—as loud as you can!" Mali said, handing her a pot and a stick. Sandwiched between Chantou and Mali with Kunthea clinging to her leg, Sokha hit the pot and tried not to look directly at the sharp teeth gleaming before her.

"Don't show your teeth. It will aggravate them." Rotha whispered. "Grab the food bag, Sokha."

Rotha pointed his machete at the screeching animals to distract them as Sokha pulled the bag closer. Chantou and Mali made loud noises and threw rocks to ward off the lunging monkeys. Vibol wailed, adding to the loud chorus. At last, the defeated tribe loped off to steal food from someone else. The family stayed close for the rest of the night with their rice and fruit tightly squeezed between them and tried to doze before dawn.

At sunrise, large hungry rats skulked around family campsites in search of scraps. Eager to press on, Mali doled out sticky rice balls to her sisters. "I don't know how much we'll stop to rest, so make the most of these," she whispered.

Sokha tucked her rice in the sack she carried, and the family began moving with the crowd again. In spite of all the people amassed together, their trek was eerily silent—everyone afraid to speak. Her mind and heart raced. *Where are we going? How far must we go?* The swarm of people and soldiers kept moving, but they traveled more slowly than they had been now that the city was far behind, and because they were exhausted. Strangers begged each other for morsels of food, so Mali talked to the family when they paused to sip some water she had boiled the night before.

"We know this is hard," Mali said, "but we must take care of what little we have. Do not give food away. It's not like life on the farm when we had enough to share." They walked all day with only an hour to rest around noon, but the jungle provided shade, so it was not as hot as walking out of the city.

"Stay close together and try not to speak with anyone," warned Rotha.

On the second night, Uncle Keo, Chhay, and Rotha took turns watching for thieves, now wary of humans and animals after their food. The adult in charge of the lookout held Rotha's machete.

Rotha and Keo cautioned the younger ones, "Don't make noise! You must be quiet." Mali and Ary cooked more rice before they all slept, and once again, reserved extra for the following morning.

Sokha had her notebook and pencil from school, and each night after dinner, she wrote a short note about her day. *Dear school friends. Are you all running too? Are you scared? Do you have enough to eat?* But after three nights, Sokha lost interest in writing and lost all sense of direction for they walked and walked as if they would do nothing but walk forever.

Someone told Mali that they had entered the district of Moung-Ruessei, about thirty miles southeast of Battambang City, but all Sokha knew was that this was a dry, desolate place. A clearing surrounded by more forest.

"Our food is gone," Mali said to Rotha. "I have two cucumbers and a little salt. And what will all these people eat? It's the end of the rice-growing season; crops have been sold. There won't be another rice harvest until November."

Sokha felt relieved to hear Mali's questions and asked a few of her own. "Why are we all crowded here? Will the soldiers feed us?" she asked. Rotha had no answer.

Through a loudspeaker, a male voice blared: "You must build

a shelter for your family. We will settle here until further notice."

Ragged people stared in disbelief. "Build a shelter?" Sokha heard the question over and over, but her family knew immediately that they must gather raw materials and get to work, for the rainy season would soon be upon them.

Rotha, Keo, and Chhay began helping each other construct crude huts raised a foot off the ground using bamboo slats they cut and tied together. The girls collected vines and leaves for roof material and ended the day scavenging for food. The first few nights, they slept under a crude roof with no walls.

Sokha listened as Rotha spoke around their evening campfire. "I don't think we will be returning home as the soldiers promised," he said. She saw Mali's eyes widen in fear as if she had thought the same thing but would never say it. Sokha blocked out his words. He couldn't be right. She turned away from him and banished the thought from her mind.

12

Moung Ruessei District in Battambang Province
May-August 1975

Mali berated herself out loud. "Why didn't I take more food when we left? Why did we sell all those cabbages?" She scooped a few cups of water for boiling from the only nearby water source. "Chantou and Sokha, can you pull some water spinach and water grass from this pond for soup? And don't drink any water until it's been boiled."

"Water spinach soup for dinner?" Sokha mumbled.

"It's all we have," Chantou said. Sokha rolled her eyes.

Rotha busied himself, finding and arranging three large rocks with kindling to create a better cooking fire, and Mali placed her pot on top. The greens and a pinch of salt from Mali's stash simmered into a bland communal soup.

"We'll have to make do with two meals a day," Mali said to the group assembled around her on the ground. After eating her share, Sokha's stomach rumbled with hunger, and she sulked. She couldn't wait for this to be over, whatever *this* was. *Why do we have to live this way?*

Sokha and her family settled into a surreal routine living among displaced families, while the soldiers surrounding them began to hold meetings among themselves. At first, they left the families alone to raise shelters and rest after the long trek. Foot sores were washed and wrapped with whatever cloth or large leaves people could find, and some families bartered—a sliver of soap for a few pinches of salt, or tea for sugar—until supplies ran out completely.

Sokha caught a couple of puny fish in the pond, and Mali boiled them in water with salt. The next day she snagged a small crab for the pot. Every family member scavenged for food, and every scrap went into the communal bowl to share. Sokha remembered her childhood on the farm, her fascination with bugs and animals. She was grateful that she was quick enough to catch a grasshopper and patient enough to find mud crabs in their hiding places.

While out searching one day, Sokha stuck her hand in the pond and grabbed a frog. Although frogs were considered lucky in Cambodia, she saw no signs of good fortune around her. She and her family were thirsty, hungry, and aching, and her frog would go into the cooking pot to nourish them.

One by one, after arriving in this starving camp, her family caught the cramping sickness—diarrhea expelled with mucus and blood. Other families suffered, too. Within days, people grew so ill that no one could hide it. Unable to find a private spot —and beyond the point of caring—people of all ages crouched outside their flimsy huts to relieve themselves. A vile stench permeated the air. Khmer Rouge soldiers kept to the perimeter of camp wearing their red-checked kramas like surgical masks.

An elderly man died first, and then a woman and child, followed by too many to count—their corpses left unattended because relatives were too weak to bury the dead. Death became a familiar presence, and the comforting rituals associated with the passing of life no longer existed. A muted grief shrouded the camp.

Sokha closed her eyes, tied a piece of cloth over her nose, and tried to recall the scent of fresh air. Night after night, she dreamed of the farm where the air did not stink of human waste.

Her mind darted back and forth between her new reality and the teachings repeated by the temple monks: "Do not harm living beings or take a life." *Why does the Khmer Rouge not offer medical help or clean water? Why are they letting their own people die? Where are the monks?* In a flash, she realized she had not seen any saffron robes in weeks. *Where are they? Were they killed? The soldiers do not honor the sampeah; they do not chant or pray.*

With the dry season ending and the rainy monsoon season beginning, picked-over trees bore little fruit, but the rains would bring out more fish and other creatures, and plants would thrive again.

Sokha noticed cycles of suffering. Many who survived the cramping sickness fell sick again from sleeping on the muddy ground with open sores, and some grew ill from eating poison plants.

With so little food available, Uncle Keo taught his family what to eat and not to eat, but when hunger gripped them, people took chances. Sokha was surprised to learn that she liked eating crickets. At first, she and her family ate the whole cricket after cooking it on charcoals, but then they learned to twist the head off and pull the guts out neatly before roasting what remained. This way, they tasted especially good.

Sokha also relished tree ants when she could find them before someone else. She used a hollowed-out half coconut tied to a long sharp stick with a string and then held it up to a nest in the tree. When her stick poked the nest, many eggs and ants fell into her cup. Sometimes she had to climb a few branches up the tree to reach the nest. Whenever she did this, her thoughts returned to her mother. *See, it is good to be a girl who climbs trees. I can find food, Mae.* But then she remembered the pride that Mea took in washing and mending her school uniform, and felt ashamed of her soiled clothes and matted hair.

Standing on the ground, looking up through the foliage, she thought she found a nest. Sokha began climbing the tree to take a look, and as she took a break to anchor herself on a higher branch, she spotted Rotha swaggering in the distance with a dead snake coiled around his neck. "Rotha!" she called.

"Come see what I killed," he said proudly. "Some meat we can all share."

That night, after Mali doled out the meat on small lily pads used as plates, Sokha chewed on a piece of snake and winced. "This tastes awful!" she said.

"It's meat," Mali said, "Eat it." *Why does she have to be so cross?* Sokha wondered.

"It's tough and has too many little bones," Sokha said. Rotha threw her a disgusted look and took the meat from her.

"No!" she cried. "I'm hungry."

"Then stop talking and eat," he said and plopped the snake back on her lily pad.

Sokha tried swallowing small bites whole to get the sinewy flesh down and made faces at Chantou who ignored her and ate the snake as if it were a piece of fish. *Chantou is so perfect. She never makes anyone mad.* Sokha glared at her.

After the meal, Rotha used his machete to finish cutting and splitting bamboo for the construction of the walls of the hut he'd started before getting sick. The family huddled close together for security, but Sokha still felt bugs crawling on her. At first, she tried to swat the insects away each night, but after repeated orders from Mali to "lie still," she surrendered and let them creep on her body. She also gave up trying to swat all the mosquitos that bit her at dusk when they loved to swarm. Soon she was covered in red swollen marks like her sisters and Vibol.

Moods flared as the family huddled around a campfire with nothing to do.

"Stop scratching," Chantou said to Sokha.

"Here," Uncle Keo said to the children gathered on the ground. "If you wet the fire ash and dab some on your bug bites, they won't itch as much." While rubbing ash on her arms, Sokha noticed Mali a short distance away taking out Mea's picture and holding it in her hands. Mali stared at the photo, and then closed her eyes and straightened her back, lifting her head skyward as if she would float upward. When she opened her eyes again, she gazed at the photo once more before folding it and carefully placing it in her pouch. While witnessing this private moment, Sokha offered a prayer thanking Ba and Mea. *Please watch over us, and next time help Rotha catch a big fish instead of a snake.* She drifted off to sleep and dreamt of someone tickling her ear.

A harsh voice broke the silence of an overcast dawn, a morning that still felt like night, and Sokha's eyes flew open. "Everybody rise! All who have not registered must come at once. You must turn in your weapons and unnecessary possessions." She heard the order repeated by a soldier striding through the encampment with a gun slung over his shoulder; a few minutes later, Rotha urged his family to hurry.

Mali, Kunthea, Sokha, and Chantou gathered their sacks. Sokha looked at Rotha, ready to follow him, and saw him press his machete close to his side. She knew this tool was a family heirloom passed down from his father, a family treasure. He used it daily for self-defense, to hunt, split open coconuts, weed his garden, and cut bamboo. With the look of a warrior, he clutched the length of it against his body.

Mali scooped up Vibol, and they started walking to the registration area when a soldier darted out toward Rotha, causing the
whole family to jump.

"What's that?" the soldier asked. He yanked the machete
away from Rotha and ran his fingers along the handle. Rotha's
face reddened with fury. "You won't be needing this," the soldier
said. "You will only need the farm tools we say you will need."
He pointed the gleaming blade skyward as his lips curled into a
snarling smile before he met Rotha's angry eyes.

Sokha shrank back at the soldier's cruelty. His brash display
of superiority showed how much he enjoyed his newfound
power. He looked younger than Rotha, and yet he spat disrespectful words at her brother-in-law. She was sure Rotha would
punch him, but he didn't. Mali stood close to Rotha, clutching
Vibol to her chest.

Sokha saw Mali gently elbow Rotha's side as if to remind
him what was at stake. Rotha's icy stare made Sokha's stomach
roil as she imagined what a fight with this soldier would look
like. She watched her oldest sister fix her eyes on her husband
as if pleading. Slowly, she lowered her eyelids and head as if
signaling a sampeah of respect to Rotha.

Rotha turned away from the soldier. "Come, we must regis-
ter," he said to his wife and her sisters. Sokha's family waited
in a long line as the sun rose overhead, and the day's heat
spread like a thick blanket upon them. Most weapons had
been taken from people when they first arrived. Rotha had
been careful to conceal his machete. Sokha sensed his fury as
he shifted his weight from foot to foot, clenching and
unclenching his fists.

Cocky young soldiers strode alongside endless rows of
people repeating memorized phrases as the procession inched
ahead. "We have conquered the imperialists! We must now work
together to rebuild the country. Those of you from the city must

shed your western ways. They are the ways of the enemy!" They harassed each person who stepped forward for review.

"Oh, look at this!" a soldier laughed as he held up a handful of colorful sampot garments. He threw the fabric at two soldiers who danced in circles waving the clothing as they imitated young women. "Bracelets, rings! All garbage now," he said. "Your long nails will be put to good use digging up weeds!" He waved the weeping girls away.

The next man in line placed his belongings on the table. "Hand over your watch," the soldier said. The man unclasped his watch, dropped it in the soldier's palm, and left the line, his head hung in resignation.

"Anyone with coins, take them out of your pockets now," a soldier called over the crowd. "They are no use to you now, hand them over. Everything belongs to Angkar. Angkar will meet all your needs. And don't try to hide anything. We will find it, and you will pay!"

Sokha's mind swam with questions she dared not ask. *They constantly speak of Angkar as if he or she is a God who can provide everything for everyone. Who is this mysterious person? Where is the great Angkar?*

Sokha's family had little to give away except a few pieces of clothing, a beaded bracelet, Rotha's watch, some clothing and cooking utensils.

"Keep the pot to boil water and keep these cups and bowls," the guard said. Mali nodded. She did not turn over the photo of her mother, and Sokha wondered where she hid it.

When her turn came, Sokha handed over her notebook, and the soldier threw it on a raging bonfire. She gave her pencils and her New Year's dress to him next, relieved that no one made fun of her dress.

"That lantern?" the soldier asked. His lip twitched with impatience.

Sokha hadn't realized she was clutching it to her chest. As she handed it to the guard, she seethed inside. Chantou stepped up next to her, and hands shaking, she dropped all of her belongings at once, eager to leave the area.

Rotha had already lost the most valued possession of the family, and he stood by clearly trying to keep his temper in check. Mali kept making eye contact with him.

After the last person had registered, an announcement blared. "All families will now attend a meeting." Stripped of their belongings, the ragged refugees left their flimsy huts to gather around the leader in a common space. Dozens of families sat nervously on the ground to hear what would happen next.

The leader of the group appeared indistinguishable from the other soldiers except that he held a long stick. He had the darker skin of a peasant and a shiny gold tooth and stood on a small platform dressed in black pajama-like clothes. A red checkered krama circled his neck. "Comrades! I must tell you that there are no homes to return to. This will be your new home." Chatter and sounds of alarm rose from the people seated on the ground.

"Silence! Do not interrupt me when I am speaking! I have good news. We have defeated the American imperialists and the oppressors!" he roared. "Before, you were told you had independence, but many in the country did not see that independence—only those in the capital with their monuments. Those who suffered under Lon Nol are now free. Equal. We will rebuild our country and restore its greatness. We will grow enough rice for all to share. Our work will follow the sun as we labor happily for Angkar!"

What is he talking about? I liked my old life, Sokha thought. She noticed that one soldier looked suspicious and crazy. His eyes darted around the large group assembled as if he expected to be attacked at any moment. He took a few steps forward, reached down, pulled a man up from a sitting position in the front row and lugged him forward by gripping his shirt as the leader thundered, "This man is a traitor! He has betrayed the revolution! He was a policeman in the city and has committed crimes. He's an enemy of the state and must be removed." Sokha wanted to stop looking but stared the way one stares at an animal stalking prey, frozen in fear. The crazy-eyed soldier held a long stick. He let go of the man in one abrupt motion, stepped back, lunged, and cracked the policeman's back with his bamboo stick. The policeman fell hard on his face.

Vibol let out a startled cry when he heard his mother gasp, and Mali hugged him close. Sokha's hands flew to her mouth, and she rocked in place. *How can they do that to a police officer? Why isn't anyone fighting back?*

"This man will be executed. If anyone here knows of anyone among us who has been a soldier in Lon Nol's army or who worked in that corrupt government, you should turn the traitor in as soon as possible or face punishment yourself."

Sokha could not hear what he said next. Her mind turned inward, as if she had suddenly been transported to the dark hole on the farm hearing threatening noises in the distance. The last thing her mind registered was the rallying cry: "Long live the revolution! Long live the revolution! Long live the revolution!"

"We must begin at once to produce rice if we are to eat!" the leader pronounced.

Sokha and her sisters were escorted to a rice paddy and divided into groups to plant rice.

"Where is Rotha going?" Sokha asked Mali.

"He's helping to clean up the camp," she said.

Later, Sokha would hear that he had to help dispose of dead

bodies: bodies of men, women, and children who had died of dysentery and starvation from the long march and harsh conditions.

She heard one cadre say, "Our soldiers don't need to be anywhere near those filthy corpses riddled with disease."

13

Moung Ruessei District in Battambang Province

S okha's family entered their hut and sat together in a tight circle, Mali whispered, "We must be very careful what we do or say. If you are asked a question, give a short answer. Say that we are simple farmers and no more. Do you understand?" Her sisters nodded.

Rotha also nodded. "These soldiers—they seem to want revenge, but why? We are Khmer."

"I don't know," whispered Mali. "They treat us like the enemy. Five months have passed, and nothing gets better."

"They don't trust us," Rotha said. "Most city people followed Lon Nol or had city jobs and possessions—and they think that's evil."

"I want to go home," cried Kunthea.

Mali grabbed her shoulders and shook her. "Shhh! Not so loud. You must not cry in front of the soldiers. Do you hear?" Mali said.

"I'll take her," Sokha said and settled Kunthea in her lap. "I feel the same, bong," she whispered to her little sister as she held her tight. Chantou sat alone and slightly apart from them staring ahead, as if she saw an apparition.

You should get some rest," Rotha said to Mali, his voice full of concern. "We have all seen enough tonight. Try to erase it from your mind."

"Maybe we should try to get away," whispered Mali. "It can't be this bad everywhere. Did you see that crazy soldier?" Sokha's ears perked up like a hopeful puppy.

"You are not making sense. You saw what happened to the policeman tonight," Rotha said. "It has shaken all of us. We must sleep—they will wake us early." He paused, and Sokha's heart stopped for a second at the sight of Mali's icy stare.

Rotha looked away first. "All of you," he said. "No talk of soldiers, no calling them names or talking about them, ever! If anyone heard you, they could report you...."

Mali turned sideways and laid down, and her sisters slid down beside her.

∼

The rain began to fall in short, violent bursts, and the heat and humidity intensified. Mud surrounded every hut—the only benefit being the frogs, snails, and small fish that surfaced.

Everyone had been put to work as the soldiers began to organize work groups by age tasked with digging trenches, planting rice, and tending animals. Some men helped build a collective kitchen, and rice rations were a welcome addition to the dismal routine, but it was never enough.

Days and nights went by before Mali brought up the subject of leaving again. "I can't stay here, Rotha," she said. "They are beginning to split up families, and we must try to get away before it happens to us."

"I want to go, too," said Sokha, crushing her body against Mali's side. Rotha looked resigned. He let out a heavy sigh.

"I will talk to Uncle Keo when I can. You know how hard that is right now, but I will try. We can't go without him," Rotha said.

"Thank you!" Mali said, and lowered her eyelids as if in prayer.

Sokha's heart leapt. *There's a plan! We're getting out!* She directed her expression to Chantou, her eyes glinting with excitement, but Chantou sat in stillness, and Sokha could not understand why this news did not make her happy.

"Do not do or say anything to anyone to make them suspicious. Don't smile or meet the eyes of any soldier, and do everything they tell you to do," Mali instructed her sisters.

After the evening gathering of lectures and the goals of Angkar, Mali asked, "Why didn't you go talk to Uncle Keo?"

"I have not found the right time. I have to find a way not to get caught."

"He was right there," Mali said.

"Yes, but the soldiers were alert tonight. We can't make them suspicious."

Sokha began to lose hope. *Maybe this plan will never happen,* she thought.

The next few nights, Keo was nowhere in sight. "He's probably off treating sick comrades around the camp," Rotha said. "Many people are sick. Some have eaten dirt and made themselves sick." Mali shook her head in disgust.

Finally, one overcast night, Rotha spotted his uncle, and Sokha saw him use his eyes to alert Keo that he had a message. She did as Mali had told her and turned away, careful not to look at the men, but inside, she had a positive feeling.

Keo drifted aimlessly toward Rotha, pretending to look for a place to sit. People were jostling for spaces on the ground competing for areas covered with grass or dry patches of dirt, although it didn't matter. It rained on everyone every day now. Nerves were frayed, and two men got into an altercation that drew the attention of the soldiers, so Rotha spoke quickly to Keo while all eyes were on the argument, and the soldiers were yelling.

"We are going to run," he said. "I'll come to your hut after midnight when most of these soldiers drift off. Be ready." Keo nodded, the creases around his eyes deepening.

When silence fell over the commune, and the girls had slept for several hours, Rotha roused his wife with gentle taps. "Now," he whispered. All the sisters heard him and slowly stood up.

Mali scooped up Vibol, and he woke up babbling. She put her hand over the child's mouth. "We are playing a game. We must be very quiet and walk in the dark," she whispered into his ear. Rotha snuck over to Keo's hut and slid inside.

"Now," he said, and motioned to his own family to wait a few seconds. Rotha held his pointer finger to his mouth to quiet any attempts to talk as the family observed Keo, Ary, and Chhay emerge from their hut and file in behind them.

Sokha stepped as silently as she could, but after fifteen minutes, she found it difficult to walk softly. As planned, she stayed directly behind Mali, gripping a piece of her shirt while Kunthea clung to Rotha's shirt and Chantou ushered her from behind.

Twigs snapped beneath their feet, and Kunthea could not keep her high voice quiet, but they made it to the dirt road leading out of the commune undetected and walked for thirty minutes when a commanding male voice broke the silence.

"Who are you, and where are you going?" No one answered. The soldier continued, "You think you can get away? We told you there are no homes left. The cities are bombed out," the soldier said. "Come with me." Out of the shadows, two more cadres with rifles began to escort them. The family crowded together. The night closed in as black as charcoal, the darkest time before dawn, and the soldiers led them to a narrow trail in the trees where owls screeched. Sokha shuddered with fear as she imagined a hundred glowing yellow eyes trained on her. It took every bit of concentration to put one foot in front of the other.

After an hour or two—she couldn't tell how much time had passed—Sokha wanted to rest but didn't dare say anything.

"This is not the way to camp. Where are they taking us?" Mali whispered to Rotha.

"I don't know," he replied, and stumbled when a soldier poked him in the back with the butt of his rifle and said, "Shut up and walk."

Sokha let out a gasp, and Mali put her free arm around her shoulder to shield her. Mali's other arm held Vibol, and when she looked down at her younger sister, Sokha saw that Mali's eyes had filled with tears, and this frightened her more than anything.

14

Tuol Prum Commune

Rotha and Keo's families trudged after the soldiers through packed dirt trails until they came upon a clearing a couple hours later. "Sit here and wait," instructed the taller soldier. On the damp ground, Sokha leaned against Mali who leaned against Rotha. October was the rainiest month, and it seemed they were seldom dry. She dozed on and off between bouts of shivering heightened by anticipation.

In the light of day, she wiped her gooey eyes and looked around. This new village appeared more orderly than the first village. Scattered open-air structures with thatched rooftops dotted a circular clearing, with a communal cooking area on a platform in the middle that contained two large pots hoisted above cook-fires. Surrounding these structures stood hastily built huts situated in straight lines jutting out from the center. Sokha thought that if she climbed a tree and looked out, the village would look like a spider.

Not far from her family, she saw a few other families huddled nearby. They must have been caught like us, she thought. *The soldiers must be out all night looking for runaways. There must be many trying to escape, or maybe these people didn't follow the soldiers to begin with and have been hiding somewhere.* A well-armed soldier strode over, pointed, and told Rotha and Keo to take their families and stand at the back of a forming line. "You are in Tuol Prum village and must all be registered."

The interrogations started again. "What is your name? Age? Who are your parents? Did you work for the government? What relation are you to each other? What job did you do?" Sokha answered, "I'm eleven years old. My father was a farmer. He died of sickness. My mother died after him. We walked from Battambang city."

"Comrade, report to the food distribution area for a meal, and after you eat, you will attend a meeting with our village chief." Sokha and her family sat together after the interrogation, grateful for the ladle of rice soup with overcooked bits of pumpkin squash.

All afternoon, the village chief stood in front of the amassed group of haggard evacuees to educate them about their new environment. "From now on, because we are all equal, we will dress alike. No one will have more or be better than the rest. We will dress the same, in black – no colors or decorations. Hair will be worn short, no longer than your ears. We are not vain like the imperialists. Cut your hair, or we will cut it for you."

Sokha wished she could ask a question: *How can we cut our hair when the soldiers took everything from us?*

The chief talked on. "If you have secretly kept photos of your old life, you must burn them. Thinking too much about your old life is harmful, and it will be punishable as the crime of memory sickness. Sokha thought of Mali and the picture of Mea. *Will she get caught? Did she already get rid of it?*

The Chief's voice stalked her. She felt his voice like a physical blow. "Angkar is now your mother and father. Angkar will provide you with all you need. Some of you have tried to return to your old homes in the city. Make another attempt, and you risk death for treason!"

Sokha held her breath.

"The past is over," he continued. "We need all of you to reach our goals, to show that we are a united country, united in our goal of mastering independence! We are now equal and will work equally hard for the good of Angkor! Laziness will not be tolerated. Traitors will be harshly punished."

Sokha sat with her family in silence. *Equal? How can you call us equal when you carry guns and threaten us while we have nothing, not even our own food?* The words vibrated in her throat, wanting to jump out.

The chief talked on and on until finally, he called to his cadres. "Issue the clothes." Each person received a neatly folded uniform and a pair of new sandals. At first, Sokha felt a tingle of happiness to have new shoes and clean clothes, but when she dressed, she saw that the sandals were made of old rubber tires that were too large for her feet, and the waist of her pants hung on her hips. Looking around, the last of Sokha's optimism evaporated at the sight of so many people oddly dressed in the same drab costume. She now lived in a sea of identical-looking people, and a sense of doom overtook her brief moment of excitement.

The rest of the day, she watched newcomers report in, and like a voyeur, she glimpsed things not meant for her eyes. A crass young guard calling a soft-spoken middle-aged man a liar, a beautiful young woman humiliated, called a slut for her pink blouse. Some were removed from the line to be "reeducated," even though some people whispered that to be "reeducated" meant to be tortured or killed. *How can dirty young soldiers get away with killing elders?*

At the evening meeting, Sokha gathered with her family

once again. "Sit in a circle around this bonfire. We have a demonstration for you," a soldier directed. Sokha's heart thumped. *Will they burn someone?* She clasped Chantou's hand and squeezed.

Once assembled, the chief appeared with a wooden box of confiscated items taken from people at registration. He pulled a pair of reading glasses from the box and held them up. "See these? Reading glasses," he yelled. He threw them on the ground and crushed them with his foot. "No need for these anymore. Reading is a crime. Time spent reading could be better spent working. We will be too busy working to read here. He pulled a book out of the box and threw it on the fire. Flames shot up, and he continued to feed the fire with books and papers until the fire raged. Smoke filled everyone's lungs, and their eyes watered.

I wish the monks could walk through the smoke and pull out the books without burning their hands. They could frighten these soldiers away with their robes the color of fire, Sokha thought.

"You must forge a revolutionary mindset, a new character, and you will succeed," the chief continued. "Let me share a parable with you. Have you seen an ox, comrades? He eats where we command him to eat. If we let him graze in this field, he eats. If we take him to another field where there is not enough grass, he grazes all the same. When we tell him to pull the plough, he pulls it. He never thinks of his wife and children. Comrade Ox never refuses to work. Comrade Ox is obedient. Comrade Ox does not complain. Comrade Ox does not object when his family is killed.[1] This is the revolutionary character. And now, comrades you will be given a few days to build a home for yourself and your family before you begin work. Have courage, comrades. With hard work, you will soon have more rice than you can eat."

Sokha thought about the chief's words and the story he told, about the revolutionary character he said she must possess. *Could I ever be like the Ox? I must pretend—to stay alive, but I will always be the daughter of a Khmer General, the daughter of Boran and Davi Sang. Angkor is not my mother and father and never will be.*

15

Tuol Prum Commune

After three days, as promised, the leader announced, "Working for Angkar is a great *honor!* Do not shirk your duties. We are all working toward the same goal. Your duties will be assigned according to age." With that, people were corralled into age groups: Rotha would plow the rice fields, Mali and Chantou were placed in a group to plant and weed, and Sokha and Kunthea would tend animals. The elderly would watch children or tend vegetable gardens. Vibol would spend his days with a group of children too young or frail to be trained as soldiers.

As a Kru Khmer, Keo was tasked with visiting the sick. His son, Chhay, was placed in a male teen work crew to dig canals, and Ary was awarded a vegetable garden and herb patch specifically designed to meet her husband's needs—ingredients for the medicine he mixed. Aunt Ary looked at her son and nieces with a guilty expression as if she got off easy. Chhay's face held a look of panic, his eyes boring into his mother's face.

Sokha felt lucky. She knew how to lead animals and missed her friend, Cow.

After each work unit assembled and received orders, the leader spoke again.

"From now on, the workday begins when you hear the loudspeaker at 5:00 a.m. You will report directly to the meal distribution area to obtain your daily assignment and work location for your group. There will be no morning meal until we meet our rice production quotas. At noon, if we are on schedule, you will again hear the loudspeaker and report to the kitchen for lunch and a half-hour break. Work will begin immediately after lunch until the loudspeaker directs you to return home or to a meeting."

Sokha looked at Chantou to see if her sister was thinking what she was thinking. *No morning meal. Twelve hours of work each day. Meetings at night. I'll be apart from my family most of the day.* She looked at the girls in her group, but they were assigned to different grazing areas with their animals which meant she would be alone much of the time, and so would little Kunthea. *Kunthea must be terrified. I'm glad she's only in charge of the chickens!*

"Remember, the food we grow is for the good of all. As we start producing food, you must not eat any. If you eat the food you grow, you are stealing from your comrades. All food belongs to Angkar, who will distribute food fairly and evenly at mealtime."

Sokha knew this was a lie. The soldiers looked stronger and healthier than the workers. Many of the farmworkers had not yet recovered from leaving their homes in the city.

The leader began to explain how to grow rice for the benefit of the *new* people. "The long rice-growing season begins at the start of the rainy season in May, but we will also be growing short-season rice when it's dry, so we will be growing rice all year long," he said. "First, the fields are plowed. We use manure to fertilize. In those fields, workers will plant seeds or seedlings from May to July, then they will weed and maintain the fields. At harvest time, the rice will be hand-cut, tied in sheaves, dried, and threshed. We also have comrades digging canals and irrigation ditches. Our whole country is at work! You will work efficiently and without complaint. Now go, and labor happily for Angkar!"

Is he kidding? Happily? Sokha thought he sounded like a puffed-up rooster crowing to idiots. She already knew how to grow rice. But as she looked around, she saw many faces frowning with worry. *Maybe a lot of people here don't know how to work in a rice field. Maybe they worked in one of the big city buildings and never worked outside.*

"Go now!" The leader ordered. Sokha sprang to attention and looked at her sisters. Kunthea flashed her a frightened look, and Sokha tried to appear brave. "You can do it. Do what you're told, and work hard," she said.

Sokha absorbed the many ways that people were regarded by the regime. She heard soldiers refer to people as old or new. The "new people" were former city dwellers, spoiled by western ways and considered lazy, while the ones they called "old people" came from rural farming backgrounds. "Old people" were uneducated but trusted by the regime because they resented the haughty pride and riches of the city residents—the way the city snobs looked down on them even though they worked hard to provide food for the country. Unfortunately, her family had left the farm four years ago to live in Battambang city. They were considered new people, assigned to the hardest labor.

On the fifth day, after an evening meal of rice porridge— Sokha called it water porridge—the loudspeaker announced that there would be a meeting. "All are required to attend. Do not go back to your sleeping areas. Stay here."

The leader droned on about the achievements of Angkar. Sokha struggled to stay awake, to raise her fist in support of the new regime she detested more each day.

Haggard families trudged back to their shelters in the dark. *Home* was a small hut they built themselves—with straw walls, a roof made of palm leaves, and a bamboo slat floor. As insufficient as it felt, it was better than some of the huts other families had constructed, and Sokha felt sorry for the people who slept outside on the bare ground because they had no idea how to build anything.

"These meetings take up too much time. The sun is almost down," Sokha complained. Mali threw her a harsh, *be quiet* look. Sokha was eager to use any remaining daylight minutes to forage for edible plants, bugs, or animals before resting with her family.

"But I'm still hungry," Kunthea complained. Mali pointed inside the hut.

"You will both stay here, go to sleep, and stop talking. No more complaints. No more words. You will get this whole family in trouble!" Sokha listened to her sister but wanted to be outside looking for something to eat until it was pitch black. She couldn't sleep on an empty stomach. The hours dragged on, and she missed her sleeping mat.

"You must learn to live as we had to live in the jungle," a soldier had said when he took their mats away. As Sokha stretched out on her side, the bamboo slats pressed into her ribs, and she thought of Kunthea's question earlier. "Why do the soldiers break reading glasses?" Mali had answered, "Because it means they had enough money to afford them, that they were rich and spoiled. We must learn to live simply now and not ask questions." Kunthea looked puzzled and offended. The look on

Kunthea's face made Sokha want to cheer her up, but she didn't understand either, and she was always being told to be quiet.

The soldiers once again divided chores. Sokha was directed to feed and care for several buffalos. These prized animals were used to break up the ground in preparation for planting since Angka had shunned modern machinery. Even though she was responsible for a large group of livestock, the work suited her.

One day, as she tended a group of buffalo, one wandered off to eat grass in the water. *He's making my job easy*, she thought. He was a hefty beast with big horns, and Sokha had been ordered to wash the animals. In her black rubber sandals, she stepped into the water beside him and began scooping handfuls of water over his back. The cool water on her feet relieved her from the afternoon heat.

"I know this feels good. It feels good to me," she said. Talking to the animals made her feel less alone. As she bent to scoop up two handfuls of water, a searing pain bolted from foot to calf.

"Off! Get off me!" she screamed. The buffalo's hoof sliced into the top of her foot, pressing her into the mud as the water turned to red ink around her. She stopped breathing, felt light-headed, and gulped for air.

"Help me!" she cried, but no one heard. With a loud grunt and all her might, Sokha pushed the buffalo as hard as she could and pulled her foot free. She hobbled out of the water, nearly fainting at the sight of the huge gash. In agony, she made her way back to camp, her foot gushing blood. Since everyone was working, the area was deserted. As soon as she reached her shelter, she collapsed.

"Sokha, wake up!" Sokha heard a trembling female voice in the distance, felt a hand tapping her cheek.

"What?" she asked in a fog before a wave of pain ran from her foot up her leg. Aunt Ary hovered above her in the hut. *Where am I? Why is my aunt with me?*

Sokha raised her head off the bamboo floor, looked down the length of her body, and saw her foot wrapped in a banana leaf. "Stay still," she heard. Ary pressed her palms on Sokha's chest to lay her down and soothed her. "Shhhh. Try to rest," she cooed. I have wrapped your foot. I must go back to tend the gardens before the guard comes. I will tell him what happened so you won't get in trouble. You rest."

Sokha's foot throbbed every minute of the day and night as if the jaws of a rabid animal chewed it to the bone, and sometimes she cried out. When her sisters heard the guards, they told her to be quiet. "They are already unhappy that you cannot work. Hush, you will be punished for crying," warned Chantou. Sokha didn't care. *How can crying be illegal? The laws of Angkar are stupid!*

Within two days, the gash swelled into a moon-shaped well of putrid pus. With Uncle Keo's help, Mali mixed a poultice to treat the infection, and the treatment cooled her injury for a while, but the infection soon raged back. Sokha cried in pain. "Please take me to a hospital," she begged.

"There are no hospitals in these camps," Mali soothed. "It will heal in time. You must be patient." Mali's eyes flashed with all the anger and disgust she could not speak because she was unable to help her young sister. Finally, when the sore festered, the leader sent a comrade to apply leeches to clean up the bacteria. This treatment did little to cure the infection, but the fact that someone finally helped her eased Sokha's mind.

Her days off work did not last long. Two mornings after the leeching, Sokha was told to report to work. The guard spat his words at her. "You have rested enough. If you are no use to us,

why should we keep you around? Your wound is not life-threat-
ening. Get up and do something, you lazy girl!"

Sokha limped out of her hut with clenched teeth. She kept a
safe distance from the largest animals and tried to avoid
standing in dirty water. Her gash remained covered, but it was
impossible to keep clean. No one stayed clean in Cambodia
anymore. Every night, after sitting through dinner and the
required gathering afterward, Uncle Keo applied salves and
wrapped a clean banana leaf around her foot to treat her visible
wound. But his healing touch and the soothing words he whispered in a voice evocative of her father's, healed her from inside.

September blew in as the rainiest month; blackberry clouds
hung low in the sky and burst into monsoon winds and rain that
drenched the rice paddies now tall and wavering in glorious
shades of green. There were brief periods of rest, and Sokha
began to feel better.

Her gash grew smaller and smaller until it closed up. Sokha
thanked Keo for his skill because the village chief had changed
his plans and decided he needed several young girls in the rice
field. "There is much work to be done. You should be honored
for this chance to please Angkar," the chief declared. Sokha
knew the real reason that younger people were being put to
work in the rice fields: malaria and dysentery had reduced the
number of healthy bodies to do the work, and the soldier's stom-
achs were screaming for rice. With her foot healed, Sokha
enjoyed the feeling of silk mud between her toes. The hard work
made her naturally thick leg muscles stronger, but her sunken
stomach ached for rice and meat.

By November, it was time for the second crop to be planted
in a new field nearby. The first crop would be harvested in
December. While bending in the rice field, Sokha felt the hot
sun burn through her black shirt, but at least she knew what she
was doing. The brigade leader had beaten one poor girl on the

spot for making a simple mistake. Sokha's parents were farmers, so she knew how to plant rice in a neat row. Her sisters knew how to do it, too.

While working, she had time to think. She was a young child during the civil war, and her parents shielded her, but they must have known the danger surrounding them. Sokha remembered her father's dark gray uniform with stripes on the arm—stripes of honor. Out in the field, she realized, *I only knew him as a father and a farmer, never as an officer. But I know he was not like these vicious soldiers.*

Sokha had been told that her family frequently moved when her father served as an officer. But he was only about fifty when he retired to the farm. *Why did he do it? Did he move our family to Battambang to protect us? Perhaps he knew that communism might someday rule, and farming skills would benefit his children.*

Perhaps.

With plenty of silent time to think, Sokha had questions. *Did Ba see what was coming, know he could not protect his family and kill himself, or did he simply die of cancer? Did he train her to live a peasant life in anticipation of a communist takeover?*

Sokha could only guess. Her older sisters did not want to revisit the past—they could not talk openly and risk showing their emotions. Her father's life, his service, his secrets, and intentions had drifted away with the smoke of his cremated remains.

16

Sokha

Each morning, Sokha scooped a handful of sand and rubbed it on her teeth with the bottom hem of her shirt, then rinsed her mouth with water. Hunger and thirst bred sour breath that felt impossible to freshen, but this daily ritual made her feel more human. Next, she drank as much water as her stomach could hold without cramping because it would be a long stretch of time before her next meal of watery rice.

At least I'm here with the family, she thought. *I wonder where the soldiers sent Rotha.* Sokha remembered the stricken look on Mali's face when she heard the news that her husband would be sent away on a special project.

She looked over at her sister's serious face. "Don't worry, he'll be back. He's strong," she said, trying to soothe her sister, but Mali still looked anxious as she dealt with cranky Vibol. Sokha was also concerned, but she didn't want to show it.

"Hurry up, bong," Chantou said. "Time for work."

"They make us be on time for work, but they took all of our watches away! It's so unfair to punish people like that."

"Shhhh," Chantou said. She shook her head, afraid that someone would hear her sister.

Sokha rolled her eyes and closed her mouth. She walked in silence with her sister and sat among a sea of workers to hear their assignments called out. *I'm sitting next to my sister, and I can't even talk to her.* She tried communicating with her eyes, but Chantou stared ahead, uninterested in the faces Sokha made.

The soft thump of rubber sandals drumming the ground made for meditative mind wandering as Sokha followed her group to the worksite. As she walked along, she heard a chorus of birdsong—lyrical chirps calling to each other. Lost in the harmony of sharp and flat notes, she imagined that she had wings lifting her on a cool breeze to a hidden nest where her mother dropped off packets of food. A slight smile crossed her face as she lost herself in fantasy.

"Stop!"

Sokha nearly crashed into the girl in front of her at the sharp call of a female guard. Angry that her daydream ended abruptly, her muscles clenched. The moon-faced leader at the head of the line boomed out work orders as her stubby pointer finger shot toward each worker in turn. Sokha thought, *your dirty nails would never have been acceptable at my old school*, but she stayed silent as the girls peeled off and walked to their appointed spots on the dirt. *I can endure hunger and hard work, but it's just as hard to endure not speaking, or sharing my thoughts. I wish I could scream!*

An hour into the monotony of digging a new canal, a young girl tried to sneak into the worksite from behind some bushes, but a guard saw her, recognized her hunched back and guilty face, and shouted, "Comrade! Over here!" The girl scurried over, her face pinched with dread.

Pointing to the sky, the guard asked, "Where is the sun? Can't you see it's been daylight for a while already?"

The girl looked down, her shoulders collapsing into her sides as if she had folded in half.

"Look at me when I speak to you!" the guard ordered. As the girl raised her chin, the back of a hand hit her face, and the sound snapped nearby workers to attention. "This is a warning," she said. "If it happens again, you'll be more than sorry. Now get to work and make sure you are the last one to leave today." Sokha stared at the guard with contempt as she learned the rules by watching others suffer when they broke them.

Sokha and her sisters made a contest of trying to identify who might be a member of the *Chlop* militia, the young secret agents radicalized by the Khmer Rouge leaders. Most were orphans with no family members, easy to indoctrinate to revolutionary ways, and desensitize to violence. Some were ruthless, trained from birth to swear allegiance only to Angkar.

Sokha thought about these child soldiers, many her own age or younger. *They love Angkar, and Angkar isn't even a real person.* She glanced at one who lingered near the edge of the worksite. *Look at her*, she thought, as she spotted the girl no older than nine, *she's well-fed and healthy and looking for her next victim. Does she really believe that Angkar is her father and mother? What kind of father never protects his young? What kind of mother beats up her children for no reason?*

Because of these spies, Sokha's family rarely spoke to each other when anyone stood nearby. They stopped praying together after seeing people sent to re-education camps for displaying any religious behavior. Sokha began holding conversations in her imagination. She remembered her father saying, "You are a bold one," and it gave her strength.

Rare conversations with her sisters were received as gems, words to be turned over and over again in her mind.

One afternoon, Sokha found a frog in the rice field. She rolled it up in her shirt before anyone noticed, and saved her delicacy to share with Chantou. They placed it on hot coals in the fire pit by their shelter and turned their backs to everyone while they devoured their meager portions.

"Bong, what day is it?" Sokha whispered to Chantou.

"I have no idea. What does it matter?" Chantou said.

"I miss the New Year party."

"I miss Pchum Ben and the festivals at the Pagoda."

"Will we ever have fun again?"

Chantou turned to her sister. "I don't know," she said. "Let's not talk about it. We have a meeting to attend." Sokha wanted to talk about it. She wanted to reminisce with someone who shared her past, a past that was fading from her memory with each harsh day like the old photographs of her parents.

Lies and slogans blared in Sokha's ears as she sat on the damp ground. "Every day is a holiday with Angkar! Thanks to Angkar, we are free masters of the land! It is a great honor to live in this revolutionary country," the village chief bellowed. "But we have rules that cannot be broken." Sokha sat up straight.

In the silence that followed, four soldiers led a teenage boy and girl to the front of the group and tied them to separate poles. Sokha leaned forward. The leader announced, "These comrades are not married, yet she is pregnant with his child. This is a crime. You are all children of Angkar and will only marry the one person that Angkar chooses for you, and no one else. These two have broken the rules. They are enemies of the state, and they will be sent to prison to receive their punishment. Their baby, once born, will not live." Sokha fought to control the expression on her face. The young teenage girl stared down at her feet and wept while the young boy looked miserably at his girlfriend tied up a few steps away.

Tears pricked at Sokha's eyes, and she dared not look at her family members, or she knew she'd bawl. On her walk home, she overheard two women. "They will smash that baby against the Chankiri tree, so it doesn't grow up to take revenge on the soldiers for hurting their parents," one said.

"Is that true? What those women said?" Sokha asked Mali in the hut.

"We should not think about it," she said. "But do not let your guard down around the soldiers, even the young ones. Try not to be alone with a male soldier. Some girls have been hurt in private. Keep your eyes open and your mouth closed." She looked at Sokha. "And *never* talk back to them."

17

Dessert

Nine months had passed since they'd fled the city and a life of three meals a day. "Tong Tong," Vibol said. Tong Tong was his name for Mali. "If I work, I will get more food. Can I work?" He had asked this over and over again, and Sokha saw how it hurt Mali's heart.

"Someday soon," she said and held him close. "But look, I have a gift for you." Mali took a rice ball the size of an almond out of her pocket. She had saved it from her dinner. She tucked the tiny bit of rice in Vibol's mouth, and the boy ate hungrily.

"I want more," he said, opening his mouth, no bigger than a bird's.

"There is no more, and it's time to sleep. Lay down. I'll rub your back."

Sokha watched her sister giving food away like Mea and thought *mothers are the kindest people in the world*. She recalled two boys fighting viciously over a piece of salt the size of a pumpkin seed that one of them had been given by a soldier who wanted to see them fight. She pushed the thought aside and

pictured her mother's face, finally remembering her as young
and vibrant instead of old and sick.

Sokha and her sisters spotted Rotha walking into the camp with
a group of men. Mali ran to him, pulling Vibol along with her.
As they approached the family, they spoke in hushed tones.

"Where were you? Are you all right?" Mali asked.

"Yes. We finished our job ahead of schedule, so we are on a
short break. How are you? Vibol looks thin." He picked up
his son.

"We're all thin," Mali said. "It's good to see you. Come, let's
eat."

"Tonight, all will receive dessert. We have prepared Nom Plai
Ai," Rotha's brigade leader announced as families reunited and
assembled. Sokha's mouth watered just thinking about these
delicacies, glutinous rice balls with palm sugar inside.

Vibol chirped, "Tong Tong! When I get my rice ball, I'm
going to swallow it all, and then I'm going to die of happiness."
Everyone laughed except Mali.

After the usual insufficient portion of rice gruel was doled
out, the sticky rice balls were passed around to a field of eager
faces. Vibol held on to his morsel and watched his mother take
the first nibble of hers. His face beamed at the look of pleasure
on her face, as she tasted the sweetness of the sugary center. He
did not know that she planned to give him the rest of it after he
finished his own.

"Go ahead. Try it," Sokha urged as she looked at Vibol. "It's
delicious!"

"Little bites," Mali said. Vibol had never tasted this treat.

In one swift motion, he popped the rice ball into his mouth,
tried to swallow it, and began choking.

Mali gasped in horror as she watched him struggle for air. "Rotha! Help him!" she cried. Rotha grabbed Vibol's legs and held him upside down. His small body jerked, and finally, the dense white ball fell out of his mouth. As soon as Rotha put him down, Mali scooped him up and cradled him until he caught his breath.

Vibol curled into his mother. After a few minutes, he looked up at her and said, "I still want my treat."

"Small bites," she cooed, and she broke off tiny pieces of her remaining dessert and fed him slowly.

"Mmmm," Vibol said.

In the hut that night, Mali talked to Rotha about Vibol, and they decided he should start working. In the morning, as they walked to work, Mali took Vibol's hand and walked him to the soldier in charge.

"Can he work today?" the soldier asked. Before Mali answered, Vibol's head nodded yes. He was eager to be like the others. The sight of his tiny frame made Sokha feel a flutter in her chest—he'd been frail since the day they left Battambang. When she saw him with his group, he looked smaller than the rest, so small that she ran to help him arrange the rice plants in his bundle in such a way that it would be less clumsy.

For a while, he managed, and he received a few teaspoons more rice than he received in the children's camp, but it soon became evident that he was too weak to keep up.

Sokha's back ached from moving heavy bundles of rice plants and bending all day in the searing sun. The leaders had announced that a new goal had been set—to produce three tons of rice per hectare throughout the country, a superhuman task. If one person in a group turned out to be the cause of the group not finishing, she was called to a "private" meeting for a warning, and if she did not do better the next day, the entire group was penalized.

After a few months, the Khmer Rouge separated Sokha's family as they had many other families. Mali remained at Tuol Prum with Kunthea and Vibol. Rotha was sent to work on another hard labor project with a group of grown men, and Sokha was sent to a new work camp with Chantou.

As she walked for a few hours to the new work camp with a large brigade of young teenage girls, passing tall trees and thickets, thoughts of the *Neak Ta* kept entering her mind. She had always trusted the tree spirit that connected her to the land of her family. *The spirits must be very angry to allow this much pain and suffering. I must be careful and stay out of their way.*

18

Moung
May 1976

S okha and Chantou stood clustered in a nest of young people. "If you used to live in the city of Battambang or Phnom Penh, come over here," announced a soldier who stood by the village chief. He tapped the ground next to him with a long stick. Most of the group walked over to where the soldier stood. Chantou and Sokha joined them. "You are in group one—new people," he said. "You must learn to work hard and be independent. You have been used to enjoying the work of others. Now you will see what it takes to grow your own share of food," he said. The village chief nodded in agreement.

Another soldier stood several feet away. "If you are age ten, eleven or twelve, come here," the soldier instructed. Sokha threw a panicked glance at Chantou.

"Go on. Go," Chantou grunted. Sokha walked over to join the younger girls.

"You are group two, the preteen workgroup," he said when the last girl stepped over.

"May I speak?" Sokha asked the soldier.

"Yes, comrade." Chantou sent her sister a warning glance from a few feet away.

"I'm twelve," Sokha said, in a self-assured voice. "I am strong. I want to work hard for Angkar to rebuild our country. I'm sure I can keep up with group one if you let me."

The soldier's mouth twisted into a sadistic grin. "You are a good comrade!" he shouted. He threw an amused look at the other soldier. "We will make sure you do keep up. Group one works longer hours, and you must do as much as the others or be shamed. Permission granted." Sokha held back her smile and nodded. "Report to group one."

Chantou exhaled, her worried eyes searching Sokha's face for sanity. Later, as they sat under a palm tree surrounded by a cluster of high grass after their evening rice ration, she chastised her sister. "Are you crazy? My group is going to be worked hard. You could have gotten off easier. I cannot protect you out there!"

"I want to work with you," Sokha said. "I'll do it. I'm strong." *What does Chantou mean she can't protect me? I thought we would protect each other.* Sadness welled up inside her. "Are you upset with me?"

Chantou looked at the sky. "See how it changes minute to minute from royal blue to purple to pink. In a short time, it will go from all this color to darkness," she whispered.

Sokha sighed. "But are you mad?"

"You want too much. You worry me. You always think you can do anything, and because of that, you'll get yourself hurt one day."

"I won't. I'll be careful. I'm twelve now, anyway. I wish you wouldn't be angry with me," Sokha said, her voice defensive.

"It's not me you need to think about, it's the soldiers. Don't talk to them. Just do what you're told."

"I'll try," Sokha said and elbowed her sister who remained

silent. Sokha perked up. "Admit it, you're glad we'll be together, right?" Chantou gave her sister a worn-out look.

"As long as you don't scare me to death before I starve to death!" the girls started laughing and immediately checked their surroundings.

"Hush," Chantou said. "We'll get in trouble." Sokha basked in the sound of her sister's laughter all the way back to their sleeping quarters.

After sunset, the girls slept back to back in long rectangular palm-thatched huts with packed down grass for a mattress. In the morning, they rubbed cold morning dew from their faces and arms. They rinsed their mouths with water and spit into the grass, scratched the goo from their teeth, and rinsed again.

Group one assembled.

Each girl assigned to digging was issued a tool called an azada that resembled a sharp hoe made to dig through hard clay. "Take care of your azada," the brigade leader barked. "If you break it or lose it, you will be severely punished. Follow me." The girls passed a large pond, the size of a lake, topped with lily pads. Sokha longed to eat the lily stems with Mea's homemade dip. Across from the pond stood an impressive temple.

The temple at Moung sat atop a dozen aqua-colored tiled steps with rose-colored tiles running down the center as if a king's carpet had been unfolded from above. The heavy dark wooden double doors of its entrance were framed in tiles etched with a rose and leaf pattern. Layers of red roof tiles with spires representing enlightenment made the roof stand out from the pale peach exterior. At the foot of the temple stood several ornate stupas containing the remains of devout Buddhist monks, and painted statues graced its courtyard: roaring lions and tigers and elevated statues of the Buddha. The sight gave Sokha peace.

.   .   .

At first, squeezing the handle of the azada and striking the earth made Sokha feel powerful, but her shoulders soon tired. In the hot sun, she excavated parched or soaked dirt depending on the day, and all the dirt she shoveled, Chantou carried away in buckets on a bamboo pole across her back. Most days it rained for about an hour, making the heavy wet mud feel like cement, causing the thin pole to cut into Chantou's boney shoulders. But after a hot, sunny morning, fresh rainwater licked off parched lips tasted like nectar sent from above.

Sokha struggled through the first week, determined to prove to everyone that she could keep up. She noticed that even though she was thin, her arms grew strong. She used every mental tool at her disposal to get through the day and keep up with the other diggers. She counted, she sang to herself, and she chose mantras to repeat to keep her mind off the burning in her forearms, shoulders, and elbows, and she felt the pain she observed on Chantou's face every time she lifted the pole across her back.

On one particular evening after dinner, in the food distribution area, the leader pointed to a betrayer for everyone to see as an example. "This man has stolen from you. He has taken what is yours!" This had become ritualistic, but something about this man particularly struck Sokha. He had resistance etched across his face—a look of courage—an expression not often seen anymore. He stood tall and defiant as soldiers shoved him back and forth, making the crowd jeer at him. "He will die for his crimes," the village chief said before ordering that the man be taken away.

The following day, Sokha felt weak with hunger while digging in the heat; the hot sun hit the right side of her body with its full intensity. She tried turning to distribute the burning sensation, but could not find a comfortable position, so she asked permission to use the outhouse to take a short break. The latrine consisted of four stalls separated by half walls, with nothing but a deep hole covered with a board over the top to create a makeshift toilet. The walls were so low that people could see each other's faces—men and women together. Flies buzzed, and guards were supposed to spread ash over the feces to kill the stink in these pits, but it didn't help. Her trip was quick, and on the way back to the worksite, she wondered: *What would happen if I asked respectfully for something to eat because I'm working so hard in the older group? The soldier granted my wish once already to join that group. Maybe if I'm honest, and don't steal, they will give me a little something.*

With this in mind, she drifted toward the cooking platform instead of the worksite. Halfway there, she heard angry voices and instinctively crouched behind a nearby empty hut.

Peeking between bamboo slats, she saw two soldiers by the hut of the man who was killed the night before. His wife had recently given birth, and she was allowed a few days to feed her newborn before returning to work. Sokha heard cries inside the house that quickly turned into hysterical wailing, and then she saw a soldier come outside with the woman's infant. He threw the baby up in the air, and for a second Sokha saw his tiny figure suspended against the blue sky. Shots rang out. The soldier fired at the infant in mid-air, and the baby fell to the ground with a sickening thump. Sokha held her mouth to keep from making noise while her whole body convulsed, but she could have cried out loud. For nothing could have been heard above the piercing screams of the infant's mother.

Sokha hurried back to her worksite, the words of her sister repeating in her head.

"Bong, you are twelve, and although you can hold a sharp tool and work with older comrades, you still think like a twelve-year-old. I'm sixteen, but I can't take care of you here! You must look out for yourself."

19

January 1977

"How long have we been in Moung?" Chantou asked.

"I don't know. I can't keep track. And look at you, Bong, you're so skinny, you look like a boy," Sokha said, teasing.

Chantou made a face to say she did not like that comment one bit. In a mocking voice, she replied, "You're still built like an ox." She paused and added, "A tall, skinny ox."

"A beautiful ox," Sokha said with a sly smile. Looking around at the other comrades, her mood sobered. All of the workers looked like willow limbs, thin and droopy, and Sokha knew Chantou no longer bled each month as young women were supposed to do; and she never started bleeding, but she was glad.

The meal plan differed at this camp. Workers received a morning ration and an evening ration. "We are behind schedule," the village chief complained as wilted workers congregated beneath the shade at noon. During the hottest part of the day, they received clean water and a short rest, but no food.

"Some of you will have to return to work instead of resting for an hour." He randomly pointed to several people, including Chantou and Sokha. "You'll have to get back to work. We must all try a little harder if we want to be self-sufficient."

Sokha and Chantou took a long drink, picked up their tools, and walked.

"The guards are not coming," Sokha said as they followed five other workers.

"They're not stupid. They're in the shade," Chantou said. She slowed her pace and let the other workers walk ahead. "Let's look for food, just for a moment. We'll never get another chance like this."

Sokha grinned. Not far from the worksite, the girls entered a rice field, pushing through a thick section of rice to scavenge for any edible scrap of food in a puddle of water that might be home to small fish or snails.

Concentrating intently on their foraging, each girl scanned the ground when a man appeared. The girls crouched low. He wore no cap or gun, only his checkered krama, but he carried a long stick. He was not tall or broad-shouldered, but he looked menacing. "What are you doing?" he asked.

Chantou's head jerked up. "Oh! We were sent to work," she blurted.

"Well, you are in the wrong place and have damaged the rice crop stomping around in here. I want you to carry that bundle and place it away from the water," he said, pointing to a pile of rice.

"We did not damage the rice," Chantou replied. Sokha looked from her sister to the man.

"Yes, you did!" he said, stabbing his stick into the ground for emphasis.

Sokha froze. *My sister is always careful. Why is she talking back? She'll get us killed!*

Chantou tried to signal Sokha with her eyes not to follow the man, but Sokha was afraid to disobey. "Come over here. Come see where you caused the damage where I'm standing," he said, staring directly at Sokha.

"No! She did nothing," Chantou insisted, pulling her sister backward.

"Come. That's an order!" Sokha took two steps forward.

"Bong! Don't go!"

"But he is ordering us..."

"Both of you! Over here! Now!" the soldier yelled at them. Sokha once again tried to move toward the soldier, but her sister grabbed her hand and said, "We didn't do any damage!" Spinning toward Sokha, Chantou screamed, "Run!"

Sokha's mind went blank for a second before she wheeled around and ran behind Chantou in the direction of their worksite, hearing the soldier behind them. She tripped in a panic, and her sister pulled her up. "Don't look back. Just run!" she cried.

Sokha's rubber sandals were clumsy. One fell off, and the few little fish she had found floundered out of her pocket while the soldier chased them. After rounding some bushes, they no longer heard his steps, but they did not turn to see if he was there. It was just a quarter-mile more to join their work crew.

Panting behind the bushes, the girls stopped. They scanned the area for the soldier but could not see him. It was almost as if the soldier stopped chasing them. After a minute of quiet, Chantou looked over at Sokha and hissed, "Why are you so stupid? He was luring you to the tallest bushes so no one could see what he would do to us. He was going to rape us or kill us with that stick! He had a killing stick!"

"I was afraid," Sokha said. "Why didn't he catch us?"

"He was probably from the men's shelter, not a soldier at all," said Chantou. "I don't know. I've never seen him before, and if he was a guard, I think I'd know him."

The two sisters did not see the strange man again. Sokha figured Chantou was right. He wore the scarf, but she didn't know if he was a soldier or an imposter from the men's camp. At night, Sokha had nightmares that the man trapped her like a cornered animal in her hut, his menacing eyes gleaming in the dark. She woke up, sweating and shaking. *Why does hunger make us so stupid?*

It was here in Moung that Sokha and Chantou first heard the moans and cries of people being tortured in the temple, and when the cries began to upset workers in the field, a loud-speaker blared to cover up the noise—as if the sound of revolutionary music could still the imaginations of those who might be punished next.

The evening meetings that took place about three times a week now reminded everyone that "Angkor has eyes like a pineapple," and the higher organization could see everything at all times. Sokha didn't believe it anymore. At first, she feared the Angkar could read her thoughts, guess her exact location, see everything she did, but it slowly dawned on her that Angkar was nothing more than a bunch of mangy soldiers being told what to do, not some kind of God. She still secretly prayed to Preah Buddha.

Still, she struggled with all the speeches she had heard. They filled her head with thoughts of the collective, of being a good comrade, of feeling like a bad person for wanting anything— more food, a nice house, fine clothing. The monks had also said, "Let go of worldly things." *Who was right? They seemed so different, and yet the same in some ways.*

When she was around her family, she felt one way—secure. When she was out working among others, she felt on her guard all the time. She had been told time and time again by her family not to trust anyone, and she didn't. Not trusting was almost as exhausting as working because she had to watch and listen all the time.

The guards were not as attentive as they had been the year before. Often they were preoccupied with picking dirt from their fingernails or squatting in the shade talking to each other when the leader was not around.

Sokha had slipped snails in her pocket on her way to work, and she was eager to cook them on any hot coals she could find after the evening speech. Chantou had begun to do the same, letting go of her careful tendencies.

The sun threw colors on the sky that quickly faded to black, as the girls exchanged knowing looks on their way back to the hut. They quickened their stride, and Chantou stumbled. Sokha caught her before she fell.

"Bong, I can't see the ground," Chantou said. "I can't see the trees."

Sokha held her elbow. "It's only because of the dark. No stars tonight. I'll guide you. We're almost home." *Home. Did I just call it that?*

Once inside, Chantou said, "I still can't see. I need vegetables."

Sokha knew her sister needed certain foods to help her eyes, but she didn't know which ones or if any such vegetables or fruits were left in Cambodia. *Uncle Keo knows. I wish I could talk to him right now.*

The following morning, Sokha woke up before her sister. When Chantou opened her eyes, Sokha watched her. "Are you able to see?" she asked.

"Jah. I can see again."

"Your eyes have returned with the sun," Sokha said. "There's something for night blindness. I have heard Uncle Keo mention it, but now I can't remember.

"Being blind may not be the worst thing that could happen to a person," Chantou said, and the venom in her voice made Sokha wonder what Chantou meant. *I've been thinking only of myself, but my sisters have seen things, too. Did someone hurt her? What happened to her to make her wish for something so awful?*

20

Sokha

A new national anthem had been adopted in 1976 to commemorate Independence Day, which fell on the day the Khmer Rouge rode into Phnom Penh to liberate the country. It was decreed that this would be an annual holiday going forward, and all workers were granted a day off, but before people could leave, they sang their new patriotic song in unison.

Had two years already passed? Sokha was in no mood to celebrate one of the most traumatic days of her life. She winced at the lines she had to sing under penalty of death:

Hurrah for the 17th of April!
That wonderful victory had greater significance
Than the Angkor period!
We are uniting to construct a Kampuchea with a
New and better society, democratic, egalitarian
And just.

Fists punched the air in unison as the song leader pumped the crowd for enthusiasm, and afterward, everyone celebrated by sharing a meal of rice with bits of fermented fish and greens as a holiday treat.

"This tastes so good. I wish it could last forever," Sokha said.

"Me too. But we better enjoy it now. Don't eat so fast," Chantou whispered.

Leaving the gathering, Sokha asked, "Bong, do you feel well enough to visit the family?"

"I feel better. Jah, let's go. But can we return here before dark? I feel unsteady in the night with my poor eyes." Sokha agreed.

The girls set out for Tuol Prum, a few miles away, and as soon as they arrived, they collapsed on the bamboo floor. All they could do was gaze at their family members who shared few words. Sokha had the dismal thought that their lives were like the record player used years ago in the city school. The record skipped and skipped as it played the same notes over again and again. Still, Sokha needed to see her sisters, to know they were still living, and to keep their family bond intact, no matter what kind of junk the soldiers preached.

The only update spoken was that Rotha was still not back, and Mali had not heard anything from him. Once that news was shared aloud, it was not brought up again.

In the afternoon, Sokha and Chantou picked some leaves, boiled them, and shared a humble soup. As they sat crossed legged drinking the dingy broth that lacked sweet or bitter, tang, or zest, that smelled faintly of muddy water, Sokha's imagination lit up. She held her cup and inhaled as if taking in a fragrant broth and smiled.

"Ah, I smell fish, coconut milk, curry," she whispered.

Kunthea was the first to catch on. She looked in her cup and said; "I see juicy bits of pork and spring onions on piles of rice."

"Sour soup," whispered Mali, and she drank her soup down in one gulp.

Chantou closed her eyes. Holding her cup high like a chalice, she whispered chicken, carrots, rice, sweet peppers, and Mea's fish sauce."

"I wish," said Kunthea, suddenly looking sad. The mention of Mea made everyone quiet.

Sokha searched for Keo before the end of their visit, but Ary said, "He's been sent to another place for a few days." It was only then that Sokha noticed the look of loneliness etched on her Aunt's face.

There was little time to talk, so Sokha looked left and right to check for guards and got right to the point: "I came to ask him what vegetable will help Chantou's eyes. Do you know? Do you have any to offer?"

"Carrots, sweet potato, and mango would be best, but I have not seen a mango on a tree in years, and all vegetables are collected by Angkar," Ary whispered.

Sokha stood quietly for a moment. Several paces away, she saw a guard. "I see," she said. "We must return to our camp before the light goes. May comrade Keo return safely," she said.

As the girls walked back, the sun began to set, and Chantou urged Sokha, "Walk quickly."

Once they entered the grounds, Sokha led her sister to their hut. "Five steps more, now turn right. We are here."

Concerned about Chantou's night blindness that grew worse with each passing week, Sokha talked to her unit guard. "My sister cannot see at night. Is there a vegetable you could give her that might help?" she asked.

"Comrade, it's easy to cure," he said. "At nighttime, pick up a lily pad and fill it with water, and when you go to her, she will not see you. Look close at her, and aim the lily pad at her face, then throw it in her face. Wham! That will cure it. When she is scared, the blindness will be over. If it does not work, you need to do this again and again." The guard chuckled and kicked the dirt with his feet.

Sokha stared at him and said nothing. *What a stupid cure,* she thought. She wished she could say the words out loud. Instead, she took the soldier in with her eyes and summed him up in her mind. *You are a nasty fool. The monks would have whipped you and made you kneel on jackfruit, and I would have loved to see them do it to you. I hate you and everyone like you.* Sokha immediately checked herself, understanding that the hate she felt right now was no better than this soldier's hate. *I wonder if karma is real. I don't know what's real anymore.*

When they finished building the dam weeks later, Chantou and Sokha were permitted to visit family until informed of their next assignment by Angkar. Once again they walked to Tuol Prum. As they approached the village, Sokha noticed that the simple huts that had dotted the landscape now had bamboo walls, and some had doors that offered a bit of privacy. This place had become more of a permanent housing area than the worksite camps.

"Do you think we'll grow old and die living like this?" Sokha asked.

"If we keep living like this, we won't grow old," Chantou said.

Kunthea had turned ten, and she still worked with the animals, but she cared for the larger animals now, and Vibol was nearly six, but he looked like a four-year-old. Ary had been given permission to check on him when he was too sick to go to the children's camp. The girls found him asleep on the floor and jostled him. He managed a weak smile, but it was not long before the two aunts snoozed beside their nephew in the stifling afternoon heat.

When Mali returned to the hut after work, Sokha and Chantou greeted her, but Sokha felt awkward as if she had invaded Mali's space. "Our job is done. We are here awaiting orders," she told her sister. "Is it okay to stay with you here?"

"We'll manage," Mali said.

Mali squatted to rub Vibol's back, looked at Sokha, and said, "We have nothing" as though each word scraped her dry throat. She greeted Chantou and added, "But you can join us to get a rice ration." Mali picked up her boy, and they all left the hut, spotting Kunthea along the way. Although bonded by history and parents, Sokha felt herself drifting apart from the family she seldom saw.

Sokha noticed changes in the communal space, too. New tables lined the perimeter, but the rules remained. Only kitchen workers could dish food out of the pot. As they waited in line for a portion of rice, Sokha reflected on her changing relationship with her sisters. While she still loved them, they no longer knew each other intimately. Mali, the surrogate mother and mentor of all the sisters, now had no resources to help them and no power to protect them. Maybe it was hunger, or Mali missed her husband, but Sokha sensed surrender in her oldest sister. For the first time in her life, Sokha was glad she was not the oldest sibling bearing the burden of family stability.

I hardly know Kunthea at all, she thought, *and yet I was so excited when she was born.* Kunthea's chubby infant legs once kicked with delight when Sokha made faces at her; and now her legs were as swollen as logs, mined with infected bug bites. Mali told her that Uncle Keo said he wished he had some Moringa seed oil to treat her edema, but he had none.

At dawn, Sokha did not hear a wake up call and a guard did not check the hut. Mali said it was because this camp was well established and ran smoothly. The workers who survived generally followed the rules, knowing that punishment could be severe.

"Would you like to go outside?" Sokha asked her youngest sister. Kunthea nodded. "Climb on. I'll carry you."

Kunthea weighed less than a bundle of rice as Sokha carried her on her back down a short path to the water where they could try to find amaranth to make a morning soup for the family. They woke up extra early and could boil the water before work. Sokha wondered what Kunthea's leader was like, but didn't pry. They had to be quiet while foraging. With a few handfuls of greens stuffed in their pockets, and Kunthea carrying a bladder of water, they made their way back to the hut.

"Arkoun," Kunthea whispered in Sokha's ear before she slid off her back. *What a beautiful phrase,* Sokha thought. *Thank you. We have so little to be thankful for.*

By the following morning, Sokha and Chantou were reassigned to a new project a distance away, and the sisters parted. The word, arkoun, sang in Sokha's head like a song as she followed her sister and comrades to work.

21

November 1977

I t hadn't rained for days and days. Chantou and Sokha hiked uphill with their workgroup on a thin mountain trail.

Sokha's rubber tire sandals scoured her feet with dirt and pebbles along the way. When at last she and her comrades reached their destination, there was nothing to see but forest surrounding large patches of dry land. From a distance, they could see two work sites. One was just starting, and the other was teeming with male workers.

The girls were tasked with building a dam to prepare a rice field. Part of Sokha's group cut down trees, and in those clearings, others dug the hard, rocky soil. Sokha was assigned as a digger with her sister.

Half-dead trees wilted in the cracked earth. It was one thing to be hungry, but not thirsty, too. The two sisters slept on the ground, but this time they each had a plastic sheet to use as a ground cover or rain shield—if only it would rain.

On the rare occasions when it showered, Sokha scooped up

water from the ground knowing it was dirty, but she could not help herself. She spat out twigs and swallowed grains of sand. Food rations remained small, but they satisfied Sokha even less because of the intense heat and lack of water. It took all day for workers to carry water in a huge barrel on a cart to the workgroup.

Sokha could not believe she could be hungrier than she had already been, but she was. There seemed to be no end to how miserable a person could feel and still possess a beating heart.

One evening, after she and her sister had ingested their meager ration of food, Sokha spotted what she thought might be a Sdav tree. She knew the leaves to be healthy, but they tasted bitter.

Picking a few, she offered some to Chantou. "Try this. I think Uncle Keo told me we could eat these leaves," she whispered. The girls chewed the leaves just enough to get them down their throats. Sokha put a few more in her pocket with the two snails and one water chestnut she had found while digging in the dam.

It took only days for her comrades to start fainting from dehydration. Thirty people shared one bucket of water. A portion of one scoop per person had to last hours. Sokha's lips cracked, and her skin started to flake off.

While digging in the direct sunlight on an afternoon like any other, she heard a loud pop. The comrade on her left, a girl whispered, "Did you hear that? It sounds like a gun." She heard another pop and looked around. "What are they shooting?"

"Go back to work," yelled the unit guard in their direction.

In the distance, a man could be seen running away as soldiers chased him. He was a worker, and Sokha recognized him as a comrade's father. Another man had accused him of eating a bite of his rice when he wasn't looking the night before, and he must have decided to run before he was punished. The running man had pale Chinese skin, and the Khmer Rouge often killed the Chinese for no reason in their quest to build a "pure" Khmer society. Gunshots rang out again, and Sokha saw the fleeing man fall face down. A few steps away, she saw her comrade, a girl her own age, shaking and crying.

"Don't cry!" Sokha whispered. "If they see you cry, you will be punished because you are his child!" As they continued to feign digging, they saw soldiers tie the man's hands together and drag him behind a horse. It wasn't clear if he was dead or alive. Sokha felt sick inside and thought she might vomit in the canal, but her stomach was empty. Her eyes darted from the girl to the guard. *What if this was my own father—how could I watch this and do nothing?*

"Back to work!" the leader shouted again. "Stop staring and dig. You will stay here until your work is done!"

The girls stood still a few seconds longer. Sokha watched her comrade out of the corner of her eye and wished she could comfort her. She saw her runny nose, her anguished face, but she kept quiet. "Everybody! This is your final warning! Return to work!" boomed the voice of the brigade leader.

Sokha lifted her azada and struck the ground. Her jaw clenched. *I hate these guards! I hate the Khmer Rouge. I hate this place and my life!* She looked around every time she raised her azada and felt the vibrations of rage in her fellow comrades. She heard the screaming of their silent tongues every time their metal struck the dirt. They exchanged glances, and their glances burned through her, sliced her into two people—the frightened girl who worked—and the defiant one, who would never pledge her loyalty to the Khmer Rouge.

During the evening meal, Sokha searched out the daughter of the killed man. When she saw her, she gazed into her eyes, speaking without saying, offering without anything to give, loving without words.

Conditions in this work camp soon grew so dire that the

favored guards began to suffer. The land was too dry to make progress without water. Shortly after the killing incident that Sokha witnessed, she and her sister were marched back to the Moung work encampment, the job left undone. Both girls feared retribution for failing to achieve Angkar's goal, but no one said a word about it.

Sokha's first long drink of clear cold water felt like an infusion of life. She could feel the cells in her body plumping like berries, and her tongue unsticking from the roof of her mouth. Their meager evening meal tasted like a feast.

While sitting with Chantou in their hut, she thought about the horror she had witnessed but no tears came. In a flash, she saw herself as if from above, slowly becoming someone who had grown numb to torture and death.

A few days later, when Chantou walked alone with Sokha, she leaned in and asked, "Remember our comrade who lost her father?" Sokha nodded. "Her mother was taken last night by the soldiers. Now she's all alone."

"Oh no," Sokha whispered, but she wasn't surprised.

"Ba used to say that if you bend one stick by itself, it will snap, but many tied together will not break," Chantou said and brushed her sister's hand with her own as they made their way to the rice field.

22

Keo

Keo surveyed the hut he built years ago at Tuol Prum. He and Ary had been allowed to stay in one place as long as he traveled to treat the sick or wounded. He had improved the walls by adding thin strips of wood and recently added more palm leaf to the roof. He wondered about the passage of time, how it expanded for stress and sorrow, covering everything, never seeming to end, but contracted in joy. He struggled to keep track of time. *Almost three years since the Khmer Rouge takeover. Year 1978. Seven years since I watched Chhay chase ducks on the farm or saw Ary laughing at sunset as she wiped the mango juice dripping down her chin.* He looked over at his wife now, thin and brittle with pain.

"Ary, we must go to our meeting," he said. Every time he looked at his wife, he heard her unspoken question: *where is my son?*

I suffer, too. I want my boy back, his expression replied. Ary picked up her pile of weeds and walked them to the compost pile. She brushed off her hands and joined him.

The crazy-eyed soldier had recently been charged as a traitor, and Keo worried about the paranoia spreading among the ranks of the Khmer Rouge. After leaving the unusually harsh gathering, his stomach sent acid rising into his mouth.

Over the last year, these programs had turned into a crazed kind of spectacle involving criticism and self-criticism. Keo hated to see Ary frozen in fear as soldiers encouraged comrades to point out anyone who lacked the revolutionary spirit.

"Tell Angkar everything! Pour boiling water over fermented fish, and you will see the worms come out," the leader yelled.

"That man over there tried to eat some of my rice!" a young man called out.

"Comrade. Come here," the leader called to the accused. "On your knees and confess."

"I didn't do it," he said.

The soldier struck him in the head. "Only the truth will do! You will tell the truth one way or another!" Two guards took the man away for reeducation.

How many times have I heard a soldier say: if you are honest, if you confess, you will not be harmed? They are liars. Sadistic killers. Keo had seen the bodies of those who confessed.

On the way back to the hut, Ary offered a slight look of relief. No one she knew was sent away for re-education.

Keo felt the need to be alone. "Ary, I'll be along shortly. I must go collect some root scrapings before it gets too dark," he said.

Ary's downturned eyes told him to be careful, but Keo knew his traditional medical skills were highly valued by the leaders, and he was safer than most. Although Keo already had enough sugar palm root to treat malaria, he walked toward a stately tree on the commune, his every move considered, his face void of emotion. A tired-looking soldier stood watch nearby, his checkered krama hung limp around his neck, and his Mao cap half covered his eyes. He can't be twenty years old, Keo thought.

"Where are you going?" the soldier called.

"I am Kru Khmer. I need to collect some medicine," Keo said.

"I am watching you. Do not go beyond my sight." He waved Keo on with the automatic weapon strapped across his chest.

Back on his Battambang farm, the spirits of the land guarded his family through the life-giving force of his oldest sugar palm. Its extensive root system and unique properties offered unmatched benefits and beauty. He remembered it as a tall green umbrella, a shelter from the blazing sun. He missed that tree as if it were a dear friend.

The single towering stem of a palm could rise twenty-five meters high, dripping succulent palm juice from both male and female flowers in its green canopy. A single tree could produce palm fruit, thatching for houses, mats, baskets, and wood for furniture or dugout canoes. Its roots and male flowers made medicine for malaria.

But its spiky fronds, sharp and serrated like the French bread knife or the teeth of a chainsaw now made Keo cringe. He had never seen one used as a weapon before today.

His mind struggled to forget the image of the blood-soaked bandage around the young boy's ragged neck—a boy only slightly younger than Chhay. There was no chance to save him, and they considered him an enemy anyway. Were they testing Keo's loyalty, gauging his reaction? Keo suffered exhaustion from trying to keep his emotions in check and not show his disdain.

What kind of person cuts the throat of another with a life-giving palm frond? It seems like every blade of remaining grass in this country has been paid for with a human life cut short. Khmers fighting Khmers. Who will I be told to treat next? How many young people beaten, shot, or carved up with infected wounds all for nothing?

He bent to slip off his sandals and knelt before the tree as if collecting samples from its roots—an act for the guard since he would never invade a tree unless absolutely necessary. He would pray, and no one could stop him. His bare toes clutched the earth, his knees pressed into the ground, binding his legs and organs to the collective energy of his ancestors. Under a sugar palm, he first heard his father tell him: "Keo, perform most of your cures during the earliest part of the day when the spirit wakes fresh—when the mind is clear—that's when the bark, roots, and herbs you have mixed will most easily enter the body to work their magic." Keo listened and conjured his father's face, his wide flat nose, the mole on his left cheek, his squinting eyes.

I never wake fresh in the morning anymore. I fear my spirit could break if this goes on too long.

He imagined his palms together in prayer as he dug his nails in the dirt beneath the tree and filled his heart with forgiveness. *It is not the tree that is to blame for the violence of men.* In silence and shame for his squeamishness, he forced himself to remember who he was.

Thank you father, grandfather, and ancient healers of my family. Thank you for sharing the well of your knowledge and the wisdom to calm and cure instead of hurt and kill. I shall clear my mind and bind myself with the sick to chase the illness from their bodies. I shall do this to honor you. Help me clear the hate from my mind. Keep my hands steady, my heart open. Protect Ary and her family. Chhay, wherever you are, I am with you.

With a deep breath, he grabbed a handful of useless twigs, stood on shaky legs, and returned to his hut for the few hours of sleep he desperately needed.

23

Sokha
June 1978

The brigade leader announced, "You have two days leave. We are waiting for more supplies. You may go, but return on time, ready to work."

Sokha and Chantou decided to visit their family at Tuol Prum. They walked at a leisurely pace on the dirt road that led to the home village. Few words passed between them until Sokha noticed a field of corn ready to be harvested.

Sokha stared. "I want..."

"Don't look," Chantou said. "It's not there. Keep walking."

"But look!"

"It's Angkar's corn, not ours!"

Sokha could not remember the last time she tasted fresh corn.

"Stop staring," Chantou said. Sokha could not drag her eyes away. Her mouth watered. She knew she would be in grave danger if anyone caught her stealing, but she felt like she would die if she didn't eat the corn. For the rest of the day and into the night, she imagined the plump golden kernels; she could taste its sweetness bursting in her mouth, sliding down her throat, reaching her eager stomach. She didn't want to endanger Chantou again, so she decided to get some by herself.

After a somber reunion with her emaciated sisters and nephew, an hour after everyone fell asleep, she crept away in the dark to the private property. The moon and stars her only light, she kept thinking *I can do this. No one will see me in my black clothes. I can get this corn.*

When she found the cornfield, she ducked and scurried in, breaking a few stalks as she tried to conceal herself. Focused on the corn, she ignored the sounds she made in the noiseless night. She broke off a few ears of corn, her eyes bright with excitement at the touch of the corn's silky ends in her hands. Crouching between the stalks, her ears perked up. *Did I hear something? The rustling of trees? Steps. Feet stomping toward me!*

"Who's there?" a man shouted. Sokha crouched as close to the ground as she could. "Who is it?" he yelled again. Sokha held her breath, and before she realized what had happened, her hand flew to her eyes as a beam of light sliced through the darkness onto her face. She jumped up and tried to run.

The stocky farmer strode over and grabbed her before she could escape. He gripped her bicep like a vice and yanked it as he flashed his light at the picked ears of corn a few steps from her feet.

"Thief!" he cried. "I got you. You will not get me in trouble!"

As he squeezed Sokha's arm, she pleaded with him. "I'm sorry. I'm hungry!" She looked at the angry farmer and cried, "Take it back. I will go. I won't come here ever again!"

"I must report you. Come!" He yanked her arm and dragged her to the meeting place where the village chief slept nearby. Sokha sobbed and could barely stay on her feet to keep up with

him. The meeting hut had four thick poles holding up a roof
that covered the cooking space.

The farmer secured Sokha's wrists behind her back with
rope and tied her to one of the poles. She sank to the ground
crying with her head hung low in submission, her chest exposed
in a vulnerable way. She wanted to hug herself, fold into a ball,
but she could not. "Please don't wake him. Let me go. I will do
anything you ask," she pleaded, but the farmer stomped away in
disgust.

A few moments later, the chief stood before Sokha. "Show
your face to me!" he commanded, but Sokha kept her eyes cast
down as her shoulders shook in terror. Suddenly, she felt
someone grab her hair and snap her head back. The farmer, the
chief, and a soldier looked into her face. The chief's voice
growled, "You are a thief, a betrayer, and an enemy of the
people!"

"I won't do it again!" Sokha cried. "I deserve to be punished. I
will not steal again."

"Shut up! I'll deal with you tomorrow." He turned to the
farmer. "You have done well. You will be rewarded for catching
her. You may go now." The farmer nodded in agreement, and the
chief and his cadre stomped back to their beds to sleep.

Sokha sat outside tied to the post, listening to every sound in
the darkness and wondered if anyone in her family stirred in
their sleep and noticed her missing. She heard a rustling noise
beyond the trees. A vicious monkey or a cat could spring on her
with jagged teeth. The cool breeze felt like a wet snake slithering
across her mid-section. Nervously, she rubbed one foot against
the side of the other for comfort.

*I was stupid—stupid to steal—stupid to get caught. Chantou was
right. I should have listened to her and ignored the corn. I am selfish,
no good.* Images of others killed for their crimes flashed before
her eyes—the young lovers, the starving father—the baby shot

because her father broke the law! *What will they do to my family?* She tugged at the ropes binding her wrists and felt blood trickle slowly into the palm of her hand.

Then she thought of the corn and her hunger, and she salivated in spite of her fear. *What does it matter? I am going to die slowly of starvation or quickly today. Let me die bravely. Please don't let it hurt. Sisters, forgive me for stealing.*

The hours stretched from seconds to minutes and slowly swelled into excruciating hours as Sokha's stomach burned, her nose ran, and her eyes stung. She licked her salty lips as stars slipped away into the watery black of night, and dawn rose up in a foggy mist bringing with it clouds of gnats that darted into her face. She rolled her head from side to side to avoid them, spitting a few from her dry mouth.

A young soldier suddenly appeared and squatted to face her. "Sleep well?" he asked with a snide laugh. He pulled out a cigarette and lit up. After the first puff, he blew smoke in her face. "We're calling everyone to meet you," he said before standing and pacing back and forth between the poles as he waited for work crews to gather. "The chief will soon be here, and he did not sleep well last night. Someone woke him up!" He laughed again and crushed his cigarette out so close to her legs that a spark flared on her calf.

Within minutes, the village chief arrived. "Show them your face," he ordered Sokha as comrades started to arrive at the food kitchen.

"Come see the thief! She tried to steal food from you, comrades! Come tell us her name and the name of her family," he shouted. He smiled, exposing his gums. Sokha watched the line of workers through her swollen eyes. People filed by her as the soldier persisted, "Who is she? Does she belong to you?" It was common knowledge that if anyone claimed her, they would be guilty by association. A line of blank faces blurred before her.

When her oldest sister approached, Sokha felt her heart sink. Her face flushed with shame. Mali kept her expression steady, her lips pressed tight, and walked by. Chantou ignored her and tugged Kunthea along. Next, Uncle Keo approached. He had treated many soldiers and helped their families when they had fallen sick, so he was well known among the leaders. Keo walked up to Sokha, looked closely at her face, and said, "This is my niece."

The chief stared at Keo and nodded, but he did not pull him aside.

What will they do to my uncle? Sokha wondered. Nausea roiled her insides. *Uncle Keo! Can you save me? Will they hurt you if you do?*

Sokha was not untied until everyone in the village looked into her face and acknowledged that she was a thief. When the guard untied her hands, he demanded that she stand to face her comrades. Sokha could barely make her legs straight after being tied to the pole through the night, and she stumbled.

"Tell everyone what you have done," the chief bellowed as the soldier shoved her.

"I tried to steal some corn," she said, trembling and weak with hunger. "I am a bad comrade. I deserve to be punished." Sokha could not say more. Her body swayed with dizziness as she rubbed her sore wrists.

"You!" shouted the village chief, fanning his pointed finger across the entire group. "Look at her face. Her life will end today. If you steal like her, you will get the same." Sokha's body shivered. She was despised—worth nothing. Hunching her sore shoulders further forward, she waited for a gunshot to go off, and tried to brace herself. Nothing happened.

The chief jabbed his finger into her cheek and bellowed again, "Remember this face, the face of a traitor! He stared at the faces before him and finished. "You are dismissed. Go! Report to work."

The meeting area emptied quickly as every comrade hurried away except Sokha's uncle. Keo stood humbly before the chief. "May I speak?" he asked.

"Yes," the leader said.

"My niece, she has worked hard for Angkar. She has confessed her mistake. She knows the rules, but she was not thinking—she was selfish for one moment. Please have mercy on her."

The leader, knowing that Keo had saved a member of his family, paused for a minute.

"Comrade Keo, I will spare her, but she must still be punished. I will send her away to work harder," he decreed. He looked over at Sokha, cut his eyes, and said, "She will work all day long, and then work an extra shift until midnight. Stealing is a serious crime."

"Thank you. I give you my word that she will not disobey again," Keo said. With a nod of the chief's head, a soldier yanked Sokha away. Keo did not meet Sokha's eyes, and she longed to tell him she was sorry, but the word seemed useless anyway. It changed nothing.

The guard grabbed Sokha by her scrawny arm and pulled her along. She gave one last mournful look at her uncle before she was dragged down the dirt path and tied to a tree with two other offenders.

Now a part of the criminal group, shame and humiliation consumed her. She was no longer considered a good comrade, and she had lost the comfort of working with her sister. She had endangered her uncle. Sokha would have to face her punishment alone.

24

June – August 1978

Sokha felt as if she had lost a limb without Chantou. She marched beside fellow criminals along dirt roads, through the smoldering heat, into the shade, and over rugged uphill paths until a voice yelled, "Stop!" A feeling of isolation tempted her to collapse and give up—no family, not a familiar face anywhere. Her head hung like the defeated crown of a flower pummeled by torrential rain, too weak to stand up. But her conscience spoke: *Why did I put my family in danger like that? Did I renounce them as Angkar says? I have betrayed them. The look on their faces hurt more than the ropes cutting into my wrists. They could have killed Uncle Keo for claiming me. I must stay alive and be there when he needs me someday. I must pay him back. Why didn't I listen to Chantou?*

"Everyone sit, and don't move," yelled the brigade leader. He looked distressed, disoriented or lost, and he convened with his other cadres. They had climbed some mountain and stopped in a place that looked like it had been chopped up, barely cleared.

Walk, wait, and work. The words repeated in Sokha's brain.

There's never anything worth waiting for. She looked around at the other prisoners. None looked threatening. They could have been her neighbors or school friends from the city.

As Sokha sat, she could not stop thinking of Chantou and how much she missed her. Chantou, who walked her to temple and school. Chantou who loved to tell her stories, like the one about a rich man and his strong bull. She could imagine Chantou's singsong voice telling her, "The bull's name was Delightful, and he was the strongest one in the land. He was treated well by the rich man who gave him plenty of food and affection. Although the rich man loved the bull, he once tried to look strong in front of others by betting that his bull could pull more weight than any other. He whipped the bull and called him demeaning names. Sokha had cringed at that part, thinking of Cow. The rich man looked foolish when his bull did not budge to pull his cart, and he lost a fortune.

Afterward, the bull told the man that he deserved honorable treatment, for he had always served the rich man well, and the man understood. He made another bet, but this time, he fed and watered his bull and asked the bull to *please* pull his heavy cart. He gave the bull an affectionate pat on the shoulder, and the bull pulled hard to help his master win his fortune back."

Sokha remembered how Chantou burst into laughter when Sokha looked at her quizzically and said, "I didn't know bulls could talk."

"You're missing the point, Bong! Bulls only talk in made-up stories—not in real life!" she said when she stopped laughing. "The monks will teach you that what you give to others, you will receive in return. Give kindness, and you will get kindness. If you're mean, others will be mean to you." Chantou loved playing the teacher. "This is Karma, doing the right thing because you know you will suffer if you don't."

Chantou always understood this—from the time she was a little

*girl. She found hundreds of ways to tell me to be careful, to follow
rules, but I did not listen; and still, she protected me.* Sokha hung her
head in shame. *I'm so stupid! I'm sorry.*

"Don't *feel* sorry. Work hard to be better," her mother used to
say. Sokha straightened her back.

Uncle Keo had always been kind. *I will be careful like Chantou
and kind like Keo. I'll try to survive for them.*

Despite her mental resolve, Sokha barely kept up with the
heavy digging in the canal. She squared her shoulders and dug
through the pain that shot from her hands through her arms
and backbone with every strike of her spade. At night, her neck
and shoulders ached no matter how she tried to position herself
to sleep. The ground made a hard bed, and she found no
comfort. She swept the thorns and stones away and piled a few
leaves under her neck, and she ached for a velvety moss crib and
to feel the warmth of Chantou next to her.

Slowly, she recognized a pattern of events that made her
shrink into herself and compelled her not to think about
breaking any rules. First, the guards continually recited a direc-
tive that they said came from the top leader of Angkar who
would soon be revealed: *There will be no complaining. You are to do
what you are told to do as instructed without question, in rain or heat,
in the dark of night—without fail.* Secondly, she noticed over the
course of weeks that a Chlop would lurk nearby as comrades
arrived or left for their work detail. She observed how the ones
who talked to each other were targeted. A day or two would pass
before one or the other would be escorted away at night and
never be seen again.

In the shadows of nightfall, Sokha heard, sensed, and
smelled terror surrounding her. Was it the voices of the dead she
heard as she tried to sleep, or was it an animal crying? Taking a
deep breath to calm herself, she drew in the scent of decay and
tried breathing through her mouth.

This work project was doomed to fail...the earth would not open up to the sharp metal that tried to pierce it. Sokha imagined Neak Ta spirits drifting over the soil and telling it *No more!* She knew when to dig, and as soon as the guard turned away, she stopped to rest. In the evening, she noticed fewer prisoners than usual in line for rations, but she gave it little thought. She slurped down her sickening portion of maggoty rice and returned to work three hours more.

Then, one night, a guard said there would be no work after dinner. "Go to your shelter and return to work in the morning," he ordered. No one asked why.

As she walked in silence to the common sleeping area with two other girls, she heard a shriek. Turning her head toward the sound, she stared through a stand of trees and saw the outline of a structure and some figures in the distance. She and her comrades froze. "What was that?" one of them asked.

"Over there," Sokha mouthed. She pointed and touched a finger to her lips to signal "be quiet." She looked around for guards, and when she saw none, she walked across the path to a patch of bushes and hid in them. A moment later, her two curious comrades joined her. Because they were all reed-thin and dressed in black, the bushes concealed them entirely.

The outline of an abandoned temple appeared in the distance, and the guards stood in the foreground near a large circular shadow—a ditch. The sun was slowly slipping into the horizon, so she squinted her eyes to see. Positioned around the wide hole stood ragged men and women, their wrists tied one to the other like the string of paper dolls she once made in school to represent her family.

She spotted a soldier with a rifle strapped to his chest. When he approached the ditch, he walked behind a criminal, but he didn't touch his gun. Another soldier strode over and untied the prisoner. And then she saw the long stick. The soldier with the gun picked it up off the ground and struck the criminal on the back of his neck. The criminal teetered for a split second before the soldier pushed him into the pit. A female prisoner let out a scream, and she fell next.

Sokha's mind raced back to a different man holding a stick; the one who tried to lure her in the rice paddy when her sister yelled at her to run. Chantou had saved her. Unable to keep from watching, she put her fingers in her ears to block out the sound of crying and begging. When all of the bodies fell into the pit, a bulldozer came around the temple wall and scooped a layer of dirt on top of them. Even after two loads of soil had been poured, the hole remained deep, and Sokha could hear the muffled moans of the men and women wafting upward through the dust. People she knew at this camp—some who might have worked alongside her—were being buried alive, groaning like ghosts calling from the grave.

Sokha wondered what these people did to deserve this torture or if they had simply been accused of eating something forbidden by the Chlop militia. She saw these child spies as blood-sucking ticks clinging to the Khmer Rouge for nothing more than an extra ration of food. *How could they send people to this pit?* She had always been taught to honor her family, and nothing else could feel natural to her, and yet she was here, a betrayer. Sokha worried that her sisters hated her for stealing. She ached to see her mother's face and knew that her father would never stand for this. She yearned for Ba's protection. She wanted to hear him stop these soldiers with his General's voice and the full force of a father's revenge. Confusion wracked her brain. *Who am I? What have I become? Will this ever end, or is this the way it will always be?*

The temple stood in the background like a powerless deity. Hollowed out by the Khmer Rouge, the temple was a cicada shell, casting shadows of death that released unearthly cries.

Standing there, with a chorus of death flooding her ears, Sokha folded forward, slipped off her rubber sandals, and padded back to her hut on bare feet, watching intently for any form, movement or shadow. Behind her, she barely perceived the sound of her two accomplices following. She practiced taking as few breaths as possible, breathing in slowly through her nose.

I will disappear.

I will dissolve into nothing.

I will not be killed here.

As she settled herself to sleep, she recalled her first night at the camp when the leader said to her group, "You have no rights here. You are no better than animals, and if you can't work, you will be treated like a useless animal."

Sokha heard the restless spirits of the dead roaming the camp that night. She hugged her knees to her chest as she tried to visualize the faces of her family, but all she kept seeing was a rice pot, full to the brim with steaming jasmine rice, a strange image conjured by an all-consuming hunger, more powerful than fear.

Days later, Sokha and all of her comrades were summoned to a meeting to listen to an official radio address—a speech by a man claiming to be Cambodia's official leader, and for the first time, he was announcing to the world that Cambodia was a communist country. The head of Angkar now had a name: Pol Pot.

She closed her ears to most of what this leader said because her mind was consumed by thoughts of the Buddhist monks. They must have all been killed. How else could a temple become a place of doom? After the long speech, she returned to work until ordered to return to her hut.

I will not love Angkar. I will never honor Pol Pot, no matter how much time passes, and no matter what they do to me. I love my family

*and believe what the monks have taught me. I will pretend to be a
good comrade. I will endure like the lotus seed. Nothing is permanent
—not even this pain.* She slept on the ground, soaked in tears.
*Mea. Ba. I did not mean to get everyone in trouble. Please protect
Uncle Keo.*

She woke up choking on dry leaves, her teeth gnashing
particles in the back of her mouth. She must have tried to eat
them in her sleep.

For days on end, Sokha started work while the sun still hid
beyond the edge of the world and labored until it grew too dark
to see. Living on one meal a day at noon, the ranks of her
comrades grew thinner and thinner. At night, if her fear didn't
keep her awake, the loud snorts and honking snores of her
exhausted fellow workers startled her awake.

Still, she worked.

Her body moved, but her mind drifted in and out of reality
—in and out of inescapable guilt and self-loathing.

In brief lucid moments, she had flashbacks of life before the
revolution.

The further away her beloved Cambodia receded from her,
the more she remembered it as a poem—waking each morning
to the sound of birds in the rustling trees, the clean, fresh air, the
rippling pond. In her glorified past, the sun did not burn her
skin, the farm animals nuzzled her hands, and her parents stood
near enough to hear her call. Cambodia rose in her imagination
like a perfect oasis of tranquility as she dug the earth beneath a
merciless sun, as she lay half-dead on the barren ground, as she
felt the sharp blade of hunger slash through her restless sleep.

On a foggy morning, weeks later, the brigade leader called out
three names. One was "Comrade Sokha."

"Come here!" he boomed. "Do not report to work. Wait here," the leader ordered. Sokha caved into herself and looked anxiously at the other two ragged workers standing beside her.

Sokha watched the remaining workers march away with their tools. *This is the end. They are going to kill us.* Her nails dug into her wrist, and she could barely stand upright.

"Follow me," the soldier ordered. Sokha trailed behind— every step a conscious effort. After a mile, she realized her small group had left the work camp. *Where are we going—to a ditch?* Her heart pounded. The trek continued until she recognized the landscape. Tuol Prum. *They kept their promise to Keo. They are returning me alive, but barely. My family must hate me. Will they recognize me? Will they ever forgive me?*

Once released, she fell into Mali's hut, ragged and exhausted, and slept. When Mali returned from work, she knelt beside Sokha.

"I'm here. Water?" Mali fed her sister small sips. "Come, you can have some rice. You must eat." Mali helped Sokha to her feet, supporting her as she hobbled to the food distribution area for the evening meal. There, Chantou rushed to sit with them, and Keo walked by passively. He whispered something to Mali but barely looked at Sokha. The sight of his face made Sokha want to kneel and beg forgiveness.

As she ate, she learned that Rotha had not yet returned and that Keo's teenage son had been sent away. Ary's face was taut and lined with age. Sokha listened in a haze.

As she walked back to Mali's hut with her sisters, the village comrades scorned her.

"Hey thief!" a boy hissed as they passed.

"Stay away from her. She is the selfish one who took the corn!" a woman warned her children.

Their words could not pierce Sokha, for she was so hungry and sick that she swayed and saw sparkles. After a comatose sleep, Sokha woke up, disoriented. Hearing shallow breathing nearby, she turned her head and saw a hollowed-out coconut shell cup next to her. Beyond the cup, her nephew lay gravely sick on the floor. *Mali must have left this water for us. This may be the year we all die.* The thought came without any feeling attached.

As an unexpected arrival, Sokha was not immediately assigned to a work camp, so she collected her rations and "slept like the dead," as the guards had often told her to do.

25

Tuol Prum Village
October 1978

Sokha had recovered enough to work, but Vibol did not. Mali stood vigil beside her son anytime she was not in the field.

"I can't understand why they don't feed us more," Mali whispered. "It's been years. We should have enough food by now." Sokha's eyes darted around. She did not want to go back to a punishment camp ever again.

Mali continued, "There have not been as many soldiers around here lately. We don't know why." She stroked Vibol's thin arms. The morning gong sounded, calling everyone to work.

"The huts look different now. Yours looks better," Sokha said, standing.

"Uncle Keo helped me. He worked on his, and then since Rotha has not come back, he helped me. We had rain coming in, so he thatched the roof, and now we have solid bamboo walls.

He said we should make peace with this place. It's going to be our home." Sokha knew from Mali's face that she had not accepted these words as fact. For although Mali was a proper Khmer woman who possessed endless patience, a woman who could endure change and deprivation, no one would tell her what she should or shouldn't wish for. She cut her eyes at Sokha and said the word with conviction. "Home." She said the word as a goal, not a lost dream.

Sokha nodded her agreement. "Home," she mouthed. The word held a thousand pictures in her mind, and Mali's determination germinated a seed of hope.

Mali squeezed her son's hand before standing to leave. Six-year-old Vibol looked like a stick figure engraving on the temple wall—all arms and legs, all bone, no flesh. "You go along. I'll be there soon. I need to find Uncle Keo and see if he has any more medicine."

Watching her oldest sister grieve without tears made Sokha yearn to run into her arms, but if she did, she was sure someone would have to pry them apart.

At the end of the workday, Mali rushed to her son to take him for his daily meal, but Vibol's weak legs could not carry him, and his cries were the cries of a mewling kitten. She met Sokha and her sisters at the communal kitchen where she took three bites of her thin rice porridge and began to walk back, hiding her bowl under her shirt. All three of her sisters ate quickly and followed one by one. Although Mali offered food to her son, he would not eat.

Sokha watched Mali peel off a long piece of tree bark that contained a soft pulp inside. She scraped off the pulp and dipped the stick of bark in a drop of honey that her uncle had given her. She rolled the bark into other shavings, and it dried into homemade incense. Using a sliver of bamboo as a candle that did little more than smolder, she made her offering to Vibol.

Vibol was fading into death. Sokha breathed in the humid air of the hut to calm her mind. *The monks told us after Ba died that each moment is precious because death is certain, even though the time of death is uncertain. But here, there are no monks to chant the sutras, no comforts to ease Vibol's transition, and no customs to ease our grief. If Vibol dies, Mali will go with him.*

Sokha shook the thought away. *I must never think such a thing again. I must be present and offer prayers, as the monks would do if they were here.* In her mind, she tried to remember the sound of the smot chanting she had heard long ago. Chantou and Kunthea sat on the opposite side of the room with pained expressions on their faces.

Like everyone else, Vibol wore a black outfit. He lay on the bamboo floor before his wilted mother. Mali drank in the image of his small body for several moments before she removed his clothing. Sokha watched her oldest sister hold the red-hot point of the incense to the cloth and burn several holes in his shirt and pants so no other spirits would take these from her child. With her finger, she put a smudge of black ash from the pot on Vibol's bottom to mark him in his next life. Together, Sokha and her sisters offered silent devotions for the boy. Then Mali gently dressed him again.

Quietly, Keo stepped into Mali's hut with his medicine bag, and Sokha saw he was limping. She tilted her head and knit her eyebrows as if asking, "What's wrong?"

"A bad sprain," he said. "Later, will you come to my hut, Sokha? Perhaps you can help me." Sokha said yes with a nod.

Turning toward Mali and Vibol, Keo met Mali's eyes with love and knelt on the bamboo floor.

"Uncle is here," he whispered in Vibol's ear. He lifted a clay bowl and polished rock out of his bag and used them as a mortar and pestle to grind hand-picked pieces of bark into a fine powder. Sokha watched him choose a dry root from the Mrom tree. Keo had once told her that traditional healers use every part of this tree—the bark, leaves, and roots—because it contains protein, vitamins, and minerals. He placed the root in his bowl and began scrubbing and scraping it into the water, and then used another chip of bark she did not recognize until he was satisfied with his mixture. Sokha observed him carefully, concentrating on identifying which bark he used by the color and texture of it, and paying attention to how he prepared the mixture, so she could learn. Once he finished adding each ingredient, he poured this liquid into a dosing cup. It was known that no one could drink from the medicine-mixing bowl, although Sokha wasn't sure why.

Holding the cup in one hand, Keo lifted Vibol's head with his other hand and patiently helped the boy sip. After Vibol consumed every drop, Keo's lips moved in prayer, but he did not pray aloud in case a guard walked by. When he opened his eyes, Sokha knew he had finished, and she helped him stack his medicine bowls and followed him to his hut.

Keo sat on a small wooden bench and showed Sokha how to unlock the muscle that plagued him. "Learning to live means learning to release," he whispered. He then instructed her to apply a greasy yellow salve and wrap his calf with a cloth. When Sokha had tucked in the last piece of material, Keo chanted healing prayers to himself, so she silently made up her own prayer on which to meditate. *Preah Buddha, breathe life into Vibol. Cure Uncle Keo's pain and protect my sisters. Please protect me, too.*

On the floor of the hut, Sokha contemplated her Uncle's words over and over. "Learning to release." Does he mean releasing only muscles or hope? Does he mean releasing thoughts of returning home? Is that what he's trying to do with Mali—help her forget her happiness, so she stops missing home? Before falling asleep, Sokha decided she needed hope. She needed to remember happiness, even if it slipped away a little more each day like a fish from her fingers. She could still watch it through the water, gliding free.

Keo administered his herbal drink to Vibol every day, and he made a small amulet for Vibol to wear hidden beneath his clothes for protection. Each evening, after returning from work, Sokha witnessed Mali pressing her hand to her child's chest to feel the birdlike beating of his heart.

Sokha's grief multiplied when she dwelled on the irony that her family spent every waking hour digging canals, moving dirt, planting, weeding the fields, and harvesting massive bundles of rice only to starve to death. Her family sat vigil beside the sick child every moment they could, sharing any food they found, and after several days, Vibol stirred. Within weeks, his eyes began to shine with life again. He would not run, jump, or work, but he might live. A kindle of hope lit in Sokha's heart.

"He will see his father again," Mali said. "Rotha will come back, and he will see his son."

"Have you seen the trucks driving our rice crop away?" Chantou whispered to Sokha after work.

"Jah, the rice we grow for Angkar! Where is it going?" Sokha asked.

"I heard a soldier say it's going to China because they gave us guns."

"What? I don't..."

"Shhh! Not so loud." The girls looked around. The area was clear. Chantou continued, "Uncle Keo told Mali that the Khmer Rouge soldiers were fighting the Vietnamese, and Pol Pot was torturing some of his own soldiers."

"Why?"

"He suspects everyone now, even soldiers."

"This must be why we have been fed less food. It goes to the Chinese."

"Jah, because they help us. That's why less soldiers are here...off fighting."

"I don't know which side I want to win."

"I don't either. I don't care. I just want rice."

Sokha was stunned that her sister would talk to her about this out loud. Chantou had grown bolder while Sokha had grown more careful.

Sokha tasted rice in her dreams until they morphed into nightmares of Khmer Rouge soldiers punching her in the stomach. She awoke in the fetal position, sweating and gasping and recalled her father's voice telling her that the monks came for alms because they owned nothing, not even a grain of rice.

"Why?" she had asked in her childish voice.

"Because they practice letting go of all craving and attachment, and this leads to 'vossagga' a kind of happiness and peace."

"What is craving?"

"Wanting."

"They never want *anything*?"

"No, because wanting and craving creates suffering."

Sitting in her hut, Sokha tried to renounce her desire for food. *Yes, wanting is suffering, and I want rice! How did the monks do this?* The word thrummed in her temples.

Vossagga. Vossagga. Vossagga.

26

Sokha

In the dry month of January, Sokha and Chantou were assigned to work in the rice fields at Tuol Prum. Compared to Moung, it felt easy. There were fewer guards, and they were close to family again.

While walking back from the outhouse, Sokha overheard one soldier tell another soldier, "The cook will prepare Num Pachak for the whole village tomorrow!" He spoke intentionally loud as if wanting everyone around to hear. Later, rumors buzzed through camp that the leader had a plan to poison the soup to kill everyone. Comrades whispered to each other when the guards looked away, and the air hummed with excitement and dread.

Let them worry about death, Sokha thought. *I'll look forward to soup!* Sokha dreamt of sumptuous bowls of Num Pachak all day. Images of steaming bowls of broth with chicken and lemongrass, potatoes, cabbage, onions, and thick, tasty noodles flooded her mind. Once she heard the name of the soup, she could not stop salivating for it. She remembered Vibol choking on his dessert. *At least I would die happy!*

"Will you eat the soup tomorrow?" Sokha asked Chantou as they sat with the family slurping their thin ration at supper. The girls sat on the ground with Mali, Kunthea, and Vibol.

"I'd like to," Chantou said. She lowered her voice. "But what about these rumors? Why would they poison it? Then they'd have no one to work the fields."

"Nothing they do makes sense, so why try to figure out why?" Mali said. "I doubt there's any Num Pachak, anyway—just another mean trick."

On their way back to the hut, Sokha watched Vibol walking, a sight she thought she'd never see again. At first, Mali had held his hand, and he walked unsteadily, but within a few weeks, he had mastered his legs. He continually begged for more food in his childish voice, and it tugged at her heart. Sokha considered his recovery. On the one hand, his life was the answer to all their prayers, but on the other, he would soon be called to a children's brigade. Mali kept telling the guards he was still weak, that he needed more time, but he was scheduled to start work training in February. With Rotha gone, Sokha could not imagine Mali getting along without her son. Vibol was clearly Mali's reason for living. In the midst of all these thoughts, Sokha heard a loud pop.

Mali's head swiveled around looking for the source. She grabbed up Vibol in one swift motion.

"My stick. I dropped it," he cried.

Sokha reached back and pulled Kunthea's hand. Gunshots rang out again, and the sound of stomping feet grew louder and louder.

"Hurry! Run!" Mali said. One by one they ducked in. "Get inside. Quick. Yuons! Vietnamese uniforms. They are attacking!"

Once inside, Mali took charge. "They are fighting the Khmer

Rouge. Stay away from the door and window." Sounds of grunt-
ing, shouting, and gunfire kept everyone's ears on alert. Outside,
the fighting continued for hours, until it gradually faded into the
low hum of distant moaning.

Mali rose, bent over, and scuttled to the window opening to
peek outside. A male voice hissed at her, "Stay where you are!"
She crouched low and ran back to cower in the center of the
shelter.

"Why did you look out the window? You could be shot! Stay
away from there," said Chantou.

"Where is Rotha?" Mali worried aloud. "We can't go
anywhere without Rotha." He'd been away for nearly two years
now with no word. "How will he find us if they take us away?"
Panic singed the edge of her words.

"Nothing's happened yet," Sokha said. "Besides, Rotha
would look for you. He would never stop looking." Mali closed
her eyes as she nodded in agreement. Speaking the words aloud
padded Sokha's hope.

The hours dragged on until Chantou asked the question on
everyone's mind: "Will they take us prisoner? I couldn't bear it,"
tears streamed down her face, and Sokha shook with fear.
Chantou grabbed her in a hug. It was the first hug Sokha had
had in years, and the feel of warmth, of closeness, seeped into
her. Within seconds, Kunthea joined them, squeezing between
them in a three-way hug.

Vibol squirmed and grunted and tried to untangle himself
from his mother's lap, all four of her twig-like limbs caging him
in, and for some reason, this made everyone laugh.

Kunthea wiped her face. "I'm hot and thirsty," she cried, and
Chantou handed her a cup of water.

"Don't drink it all. It's all we have left until we can get out of
here," Mali said.

Listening without seeing. Hearing without knowing, they

waited hour by hour through the pitch-black night in the airless hut. Intermittent flashes of light lit their faces. Loud shouts made them jump. They heard the thump of punches landing, bodies falling. They smelled smoke in the distance. And then... eerie silence. No one slept.

As daylight approached, a low chatter could be heard, so Mali peeked outside again. "It looks like the Vietnamese have won," she reported in a hushed voice.

She stared out a corner of the window opening, her eyes squinting in the sunlight.

"What do you see?" Chantou asked.

"Gray uniforms. Vietnamese soldiers all over camp," she said. "Over by the food shelter, Khmer Rouge soldiers sitting on the ground with their hands tied behind their backs. Vietnamese soldiers guarding them." Dirt and gravel crunched followed by a reverberating squeal and thud.

"I think I hear trucks," Sokha said.

"Jah. There are three big trucks arriving. Now they are loading Khmer Rouge soldiers in the trucks. Some don't look alive. We can't go outside."

"What's going to happen to us?" Sokha asked. Chantou wept and tried to turn her face away from the younger children, but Kunthea saw her and began crying, too. Sokha struggled to hold her emotions in check.

"I don't know. But if they wanted us, they would have taken us by now." Mali said. Chantou wiped the tears from her face and hugged Kunthea. Sokha held Vibol while Mali kept watching as another hour passed when all of a sudden, she peeked out and saw Vietnamese soldiers running from hut to hut shouting, "Santran!" (You are free!) "The war is over! You may return to your home villages."

"Look. Come look!" Mali called, and all of her sisters crammed their faces through the small opening to see.

People flowed out of their shelters in a state of disbelief, many crying tears of relief.

"They aren't going to kill us?" Sokha asked.

"They saved us?" Chantou said. "They are letting us go?" She wiped her face. Squinting people emerged from their huts and hobbled to the latrine. The soldiers held their guns down and nodded at the workers.

"We will not leave without Rotha," Mali said. "We will all wait together."

"I'm hungry," Kunthea wailed.

"Me too!" Vibol cried.

Sokha saw people rushing to the food area. "Chantou, let's get some rice!" she said, her face eager with excitement.

"How can we carry it? Pockets?" Chantou asked.

Mali handed her two coconut shells. "We can bundle some in our extra shirts, too," Sokha said.

"Be careful!" Mali called after them.

The girls carried what they had and sidestepped the blood-soaked ground. The food supply area looked like a New Years party gone wrong. Food flew everywhere. People pushed, shoved, and ate rice from the communal cook pot with their hands. Bags of rice were slit open, and people took as much as they could carry. Sokha grabbed a nice-size rice pot from the shelf to keep for the family and filled it. Chantou stuffed raw rice in her pockets, filled the coconut shells, and balled up cooked rice to carry back.

"Look at all that rice!" Mali said, the worried look on her face dissolving. Sokha gave Vibol and Kunthea each a ball of cooked rice.

"I'll make a fire and cook some more. Vibol, stay close. Don't wander. Kunthea, please watch your brother."

"Keo! Ary!" Sokha called as she saw Uncle Keo and his wife move toward them carrying a pot and a bulky sack. Chhay was not with them. He still worked on a mobile brigade and had not yet returned. All around, a sea of people in black pajamas called to family members.

"Let's eat together," Keo said. "Can you believe this happened? I'm so glad you are all unharmed. Some people were injured in the fighting. I may have to help some of them. I'm going to check around. Here, I found a block of salt and grabbed some rice, and Ary picked her garden clean! She has sweet potatoes! Chantou, you get a little extra for your eyes!"

"In a mischievous voice, Sokha said, "I can't see either," and Uncle Keo swatted her away with a grin.

"I'll be back in a little while. Ary—girls, stay here."

Ary sat next to Mali and began scraping dirt from potatoes. "We're eating our own food. It's like a dream," she said. "And soon, maybe Rotha and Chhay will come back."

Sitting on the ground near the fire, the family ate outside in the open until their bellies were full. Wedged between her sisters, Sokha took her food last. For so long, she felt selfish. She had stolen food and put her family in danger. *If we can be free, I will take very little for myself. I'll give back to my family for not abandoning me after my crime.*

Ary handed her a small boiled sweet potato, and she let the soft center of it melt on her tongue. She did not want to drink water for fear of washing the taste away. The hot rice tasted dense, like her mother's rice, and a small amount filled her up. She wanted to feel happy, but all around them were soldiers, Vietnamese carrying off the dead and watching for any violent eruptions. *Should we feel safe? Are we really free?* The original elation of hearing "Santran" dissolved as she looked around. Guns piled up, bodies in trucks. New soldiers in charge...their declared enemies now their saviors.

A cacophony of voices rose in the camp as people spoke in normal voices, the sound overpowering to Sokha's ears after years of silence and whispers. *How many words have I held inside? So many times, I wanted to say something and could not. I can't even remember what I wanted to tell everyone.*

Uncle Keo returned and ate, and then he helped Aunt Ary and Mali hide the remaining food in their hut. It was time to wait. They leaned on each other, and everyone slept, exhausted from the night before. A few hours later, as they sat outside talking, Rotha showed up with an ox and cart that he had taken from the commune where he'd been working. Dark circles ringed his eyes, and his hollow cheeks made him look worn, but Mali cried out, "You're alive!" She threw her arms around him and held him close as they cried into each other's shoulders. "You're alive," she repeated as if she hardly believed it.

When they split apart, Rotha gathered up Vibol who cried out for his mother as if in the arms of a stranger, and Rotha put him down. Mali gave her son a stern look, but Rotha said, "He's frightened. Give him time."

Chantou handed Rotha a bowl of warm rice with sweet potato to eat. "Much better than watery soup! This is so good!" he said between bites.

"Have you seen Chhay?" Ary asked, her eyes hopeful.

"No, I'm afraid not," Rotha said. "Is he on a work brigade?"

Ary nodded.

"What happened at your camp? How did you get that cart?" Mali asked, and everyone gathered around to hear his story.

"The Vietnamese entered our commune last night and killed the Khmer Rouge soldiers so swiftly that it took us all by surprise. We all hid in our huts thinking we'd be killed, too. We heard the yuons yell that we were free! But I did not believe it, because look what happened when the Khmer Rouge said we were free—and these were *youns*, our enemy," Rotha said. The girls all nodded in agreement.

"Everyone stayed inside their shelters, but I poked my head

out and talked to a soldier. He said, 'You are free to go. Go back
to your village. The Khmer Rouge have lost,' so I took a chance. I
ran and grabbed the ox-cart before anyone else did and came
directly here, and no one stopped me. But there is still fighting,
and they are burning some of the leader's huts and villages."

Keo listened intently and said, "I hope Chhay arrives soon
with the same story. It hardly makes sense, our enemies letting
us go. It seems like a good thing, but the youns don't ever do
anything without expecting something in return."

"You are right," Rotha continued. "We must still be careful.
I'm not sure who's in charge of our government anymore. After
the soldiers left, many workers fled with tools. But I knew we'd
need this cart, and I was lucky to grab it first. I also wanted a
knife or a gun but could not find one. Oh, I should not waste
time talking," he said, wiping his mouth with his sleeve. We will
need as much food as possible for our journey home! Let's see
what's left."

Pandemonium still raged in the kitchen. The large soup pot
stood empty. But emaciated men and women leaned into the
one huge cook pot that held only rice, no doubt to feed the
soldiers, and scraped the last of the sticky rice from the pot with
their fingernails. A few large open sacks of rice remained half
full. People shoved each other aside to grab what they could
carry in their pockets without containers. Rotha, Chantou, and
Sokha each brought their one spare black shirt to use as sacks,
filled the pockets and center with rice, and tied the arms into a
knot on top. By the time they left, people were collecting rice
grains off the ground.

"Where's Uncle Keo?"

"Way over there, he's on the wrong side of the kitchen,"
Rotha said. "All the rice is here," he yelled. Keo heard, but he
ignored him.

"Look how much food they held back," Rotha said. "Bags and bags. They could have fed you so much more!"

Sokha loaded the cart. She placed bundles of rice on the bottom and nested a few cups and bowls in the pot. Now they had two pots, one with cooked rice, and one empty one. "I saw some men carrying bags of rice away that were too heavy for one man to lift. It was here all along," Sokha said.

"I don't care anymore," Mali said. "We're going home. It's over."

"If we can find our home," Rotha said. "If it still looks the same."

Sokha lifted her sleeping nephew from the ground and padded him into the cart. "Look! Vibol sleeps on a bed of rice! He smiles in his sleep. This is what a full belly can do," she said.

"I forgot what it felt like to be full," Mali said. She stroked her son's black hair. "Vibol," she whispered like a prayer.

"Come," Rotha said as he took Mali's hand. "Are we all here?"

Sokha watched Keo look at Ary as they stood next to the cart. Ary turned her face into Keo's shoulder and cried. Rotha stood near them.

"Chhay will find us. He knows where the house in the city and the farmhouse stood...he will go to one of those places," Rotha said. "We can't stay here. The youns are starting fires all around, and everyone's leaving. If we stay, we'll be alone."

Sokha reached for Kunthea's left hand, and Chantou held her right. Rotha gave the ox a tug, and the family left Tuol Prum.

And once again, they walked.

27

On the Road

C areful to follow those who knew the way to Battambang, Sokha's family retraced the steps they had taken almost four years ago with thousands of others.

"Lon Nol tried to save Phnom Penh," Rotha said to Keo. "I learned that he had helicopters drop holy sand blessed by the monks around the entire perimeter of the Capital when the Khmer Rouge closed in. By then, he was outnumbered. To this day, I can't believe the rebels won the war." Sokha listened with interest. As a child, she knew nothing about such things.

"What happened to the monks?" Mali asked. "I never saw any."

"The ones who refused to stop praying were killed. Others were forced to work in the fields in black uniforms like us," Keo said. "They were shown no mercy. Many died of disease and starvation. I was sent to treat some of the sick, but I think they stopped eating because they could not stand being called parasites."

Ary walked beside Keo. "I don't want to talk about this," she said. "Can we walk in peace?" Chantou nodded in agreement.

"Of course," Keo said.

"Are we going to the farm?" Sokha asked.

"Jah," Mali said. "But the city is on the way. We'll need a place to rest up." Along the road, they nodded at other families and saw smoke plumes rising in the air. They passed an overgrown lot of rusty abandoned cars without tires and saw Vietnamese soldiers patrolling everywhere.

Days later, when they reached the city, a good portion of their rice was gone because they had many people to feed.

Stepping around deep ruts in a road lined with stained and crumbling sidewalks, the family stared at what was left of Battambang city. Heavy strands of utility pole wires sagged across the street, their gnarly ends dangling in the breeze on tilted stands. The yellow façade of a stately French colonial building wore a dark coat of dust. Mold discolored the shutters that hung half off, and a dirty curtain blew through a broken window. Garbage collected around the foundation, and empty snack bags and papers were caught in the wires above. Vacant shops looked haunted with turned over chairs and cracked vegetable crates, as if left unattended after a storm blew through.

"We should have expected this," Mali said aloud, "but it's hard to see." The White Elephant temple still stood, but it was vacant. Without any monks, it looked hollow. The house they used to live in had broken down and sagged with mold.

Rotha knocked on the doors of several houses and asked where his family might stay. Finally, an older man noticed them and offered the ground level of his stilted home in the open air. The matted floor kept out the rain and sun. After the adrenaline rush of the Vietnamese liberation, and several days on the road, their minds and bodies shut down, and they slept for a full afternoon and night—the kind of sleep too heavy for dreams.

A cat's caterwaul woke them with a start before dawn, and the family huddled around a side-yard fire as Keo brewed ginger tea.

"While everyone hoarded rice, I raided the other side of the kitchen and grabbed herbs and tea!" he said, clearly proud of his cleverness. "I knew where they hid them because the cook doled out small amounts when I treated the soldier's families."

Rotha nodded his appreciation. "I wondered what you were doing over there." He finished his tea. "I'm going to explore a little. I'll be back around noon," he said and stepped into the street. He disappeared down the road toward the market.

"Let's look for something to eat," Mali said to her sisters. "Aunt Ary, would you keep an eye on Vibol for me?" Ary nodded.

Mali, Sokha, Chantou, and Kunthea searched a wide area in pairs to find food. In the city, there were only a few gardens, and other families had already claimed what viable patches remained.

During the Khmer Rouge years, money was banned, and the soldiers burned piles of it, but there might still be packaged food in the markets. They headed there first but found the place completely bare. Other people were searching for goods, too. Mali remarked to Chantou and Sokha, "Can you believe we sold the last of our cabbages for useless money right before the Khmer Rouge took over? We sold at least eight beautiful cabbages. I thought about that every day wishing I had those vegetables back!" she said.

"A cabbage would taste good right now," Sokha said.

"No sense thinking about it. What's done is done," Chantou said.

"Are you sure you're not a monk in disguise?" Sokha asked with a grin. Chantou smirked.

For two more days, they searched sections of the city, and although they found hardly anything, they were free to roam or rest or speak the truth of their minds without fear. Ary and Keo still had a store of roots and vegetables to simmer a soup that was better than the rations served in the communes, and their evenings were spent discussing what to do next.

Little by little, Sokha saw signs of the past returning. People greeted each other with a sampeah, and she heard chanting as she passed one house with many people inside. The sound made her stop and close her eyes to listen. Her mind saw vivid images of the monks she had known.

One old farmer offered Sokha and Chantou several lime green oranges from a tree in his backyard on the far edge of the city when he saw them scavenging. "I was fortunate to be able to stay in my home to keep up this orchard for the Khmer Rouge soldiers," he told them. "I'm glad to see others returning," he said. "It's been lonely here. Take these for your family."

Sokha and Chantou rushed back with the fruit, "Look! Look what we have!" Sokha called. As she peeled and sectioned an orange to share, the citrus aroma made them all inhale. Mali took three bites from one section to make it last. A sound of pleasure rose up from her throat.

Vibol gulped his portion in chunks. He looked like a striped squirrel with bulging cheeks. "More!" he begged with his mouth still full.

"You have got to learn to eat small bites," Mali said. "We'll save these and divide the other three up for everyone tonight." When he whined, Mali pushed him away and scowled, an act that made Sokha take notice. *That's something she would have done before the war. Vibol must be all healed now, and he better behave!*

Other than the oranges, Sokha and her sisters could not find much food in the abandoned gardens they checked. A while later, Rotha returned with a pile of cloth. There's no food, but I found some t-shirts. The girls gathered around. "There were a few shops open, and I rummaged. They were hiding beneath a bottom rack pressed against the back wall."

"New shirts! I can't wait to get out of this black top!" Sokha said. She chose a green one. Chantou grabbed a blue one, and Kunthea's looked like a pink dress on her.

"A little dusty, but new," Mali said, shaking out a tan shirt. "Thank you!"

"I know these are not like the blouses you used to wear, but at least it's something different," Rotha said.

"Let's keep our black shirts for extra," Mali said. "We can wash them and use them as pillows. I think we've seen what there is to see—there's nothing much here for us, and I'm anxious to get to the farm. "Have we rested enough?"

"I have," Ary said, although she looked worn. "Chhay could be waiting at the farm. I want to go."

Rotha nodded his agreement, and Sokha's heart leapt.

Keo sat nearby with Ary. "I feel the same. I want to check our farms," he said. "Let's rest tonight, and go tomorrow. We should be able to find more greens to pick along the way once we get out of the city."

In the morning, Keo brewed a pot of root tea while Ary prepared a vegetable soup before everyone began the trek home. They had to stop twice to rest during the hottest part of the day, so the trip took longer than usual. The landscape hadn't changed much, but many landmarks were missing or altered to the point of appearing unfamiliar.

"Have you not seen any greens to pick?" Sokha asked her uncle.

"Not much, the path is trampled, and we should not veer off

too far. There are landmines, and Khmer Rouge soldiers may be hiding out. Look, every fruit tree we pass is stripped clean."

When they finally recognized a few tall palms at a bend in the road, Mali sensed they had arrived at the right spot. "Stop," she said. "We're here."

Sokha looked around and hardly recognized anything. She longed to see her house the way it used to be, but all she saw was abandoned land, overgrown bushes, and tangled weeds.

Rotha led Vibol and Kunthea to a patch of grass under a palm tree, glad for a break, and Keo split off to continue down the road with Ary.

"We'll check back with you later this afternoon," he called behind him. He had a hint of eagerness in his voice, as if he might find Chhay on his property waiting for him.

"Are you sure this is the farm?" Sokha asked.

"Jah, there's the temple." Off in the distance, she could see the top of the temple school she attended as a child.

"Where is our house?" She followed Mali and Chantou through the tall grass.

"There's the pond. It's drying up. And over there...look," Mali said, pointing. "That is where the house once stood."

Sokha saw an elevated dirt foundation surrounded by overgrown gardens. "It looks like someone made the house disappear," Chantou said. "How could that happen?" The girls walked closer for a better look.

Sokha said nothing. She gazed around the land as if seeing a battlefield strewn with dead bodies. *It's all gone.*

"At least there's not rubble everywhere," Mali offered. "I wonder what happened to the young couple that took care of the house for Mea...if they made it..." she said, her voice trailing off when she realized where the thought might lead.

"I hate to admit this, but I was afraid we'd find our old house full of Khmer Rouge soldiers," Chantou said.

"I wonder what happened to Cow," Sokha said in a mournful voice. "This doesn't feel like home. Doesn't feel right without the red roof, or Mea and Ba and the animals."

Chantou grabbed Sokha's arm and pulled. "Let's check Mea's garden for something!" Sokha blinked and snapped out of her trance. The girls ran and fell to their knees to dig through vines and weeds until Sokha pulled out a thin carrot.

"This is for you, Chantou. Remember? Uncle Keo said you need to eat carrots for your eyes." She dusted off the small orange root and handed it to her sister. Chantou took a bite and crunched. Sokha dug in the tangled weeds again, her mouth salivating, but could not find anything more. She slapped her hands together to clean off the dirt.

Mali circled the footprint where the house once stood, and her sisters joined her.

"It's creepy here," Chantou said. "This place is full of ghosts."

"I feel it too," Mali said. "And the gardens and rice fields. Almost all weeds. Mea's hard work, all wrecked. Remember how she grew such beautiful vegetables? She grew so many she could give them away to strangers." Her voice broke, "Mea cared for everyone."

Tears slid down Sokha's face. Chantou started weeping, too.

"Enough. Come, sisters. Let's go rest in the shade." Mali put her arms around their shoulders, and they joined Rotha.

"Should we stay and try to build a new home?" Mali asked.

"I would like to do what you want, Mali, but there are few villagers and many soldiers nearby," Rotha said.

"I'm not sure we could manage alone out here anymore," Chantou said, a worried look crossing her face. "The rice field needs to be started over, and we only have one azada to work with."

"Maybe we could get Mea's garden going again," Sokha offered, sniffing.

"We have no seeds, and it would take weeks or months," Rotha said. "Before she died, Davi put Mali in charge of it, so I want the decision to be yours, Mali. This all belongs to you and your sisters. Perhaps we could come back in a few months?"

"Do you think it's safe here now?" Mali asked.

"I have no idea. Are we part of Vietnam now that they beat the Khmer Rouge? Will we be treated well? We will probably be safer living near others since we don't know how many Khmer Rouge may have escaped to the jungle. I think we should leave," Rotha said. "Maybe we could check housing around the Psar Nath market area of the city," he suggested. "One man on the road said there are houses still standing there. We could look for a deserted one to live in. Let's talk to Uncle Keo in the morning and make a decision."

Mali nodded her agreement. Sokha's shoulders sagged as she looked out across the desolate farm.

"Let's rest under this tree and wait for Uncle Keo and Aunt Ary. I hope they found Chhay," Rotha said.

On the quiet farm, Sokha could retrace all the paths she used to run along, through the packed dirt under the trees, through the vegetable gardens, to her climbing tree. She remembered playing with Chhay when Uncle Keo's family visited—how she was the only girl in the family who could keep up with him. Chhay would help Ba by chopping coconuts or pulling yucca. She would rather have hiked the farm with him and climb trees than learn to be a proper Khmer girl. Lost in vivid memories of her childhood, she dozed off.

An hour later, she sat up, brushed off her body, and saw Uncle Keo and Aunt Ary walking toward them. As they grew closer, Sokha saw her uncle shaking his head *no* with a sad look on his face, and she knew Chhay was still missing. *We will have to give up the farm again. My home. My only home.*

"Will you stay and wait for him?" Rotha asked.

"We've gone over and over it," Uncle Keo said. "Ary now thinks he will return to Battambang city to find us—in the house we lived in right before the takeover. I think we will go wait for him there. If he comes here and sees the farm destroyed, that's where he will go. He could be there now."

Sokha wondered where her cousin was and what happened to him. *Is he dead or alive... and if he's alive, what shape is he in?*

28

Sokha

"I still don't know why we can't stay on the farm and build a house," Sokha said to Chantou and Mali as they tromped along the road back to Battambang city.

"The decision is made," Rotha called out, startling her. "It's the right decision. No more talk!" Sokha fumed inside. *Everyone makes my decisions for me. When I didn't want to leave the farm, we left. When I liked my life in the city, we were kicked out. Now we have a chance to rebuild the farm, and no one will do it! When I'm grown, I will live the life I want to live. I'll go back to the farm and make it work, and no one will tell me what to do.* As she walked along, her temple throbbed, and she realized she had been clenching her jaw.

Upon arriving in the area of the Psar Nath market, where Sokha's mother once sold her wares, Rotha and Mali found an abandoned wood house with a red clay roof, and Keo and his family found another empty house a block away.

Sokha liked that the house was raised off the ground like their old home in the country, but it felt wrong to take someone else's place. *What if someone else took over the farm? What then? Would they lose it?* She wondered who had lived here and had trouble sleeping because she imagined the family's owners returning in the dark to reclaim the house. *Are they dead? Alive? Will they be angry if they find us here?*

She relaxed when no one showed up for days. Then, she looked out the window on a sweltering morning and saw a weary couple walking toward the house, their eyes squinting at the door and windows, and she knew it was their house. Rotha had left thirty minutes ago to seek more information. "Mali, Chantou! Someone's coming here," she said. "A man and a woman."

"Let me talk to them," Mali said. "Kunthea, take Vibol outside for a little while, but stay close to the house and don't talk to anyone."

Mali stood in the doorway with Chantou and Sokha close behind her.

"Hello. Come in," she said and greeted the couple with a sampeah.

"This was our home before the Khmer Rouge took over," the man said without any hint of malice.

"We did not know. Many people are trying to find shelter. My family tried to return to our home in the country, but it has been ruined, maybe burned down. We don't know what happened, but it's gone, and so we came here," Mali explained. "Please rest," she said and showed them to the threadbare rug on the floor."

Once seated, she added, "Forgive me. My name is Mali, and these are my sisters, Sokha and Chantou." The girls both offered a sampeah. We have clean water. You must be thirsty." Sokha hurried to fill two cups for them.

"I am Chakra, and this is my wife, Boupa. Thank you for your kindness." He held his cup with both hands and took a long drink, then wiped his chin with his sleeve. "We lived here for ten years with our three boys. In the beginning, we loved it, but you know...."

"Your sons?"

Chakra cleared his throat. "The soldiers separated us from our boys, and we have lost contact with them. We have not seen them in three years, but we hope they will return. We thought they might be here." His face contorted in pain, and his wife looked as if she might lose her composure.

Mali closed her eyes and lowered her head in deference. "This war has taken too much from all of us," she said.

For a few moments, they sat in silence. Then, Boupa let out a sigh and looked at the doorway. "It is good to hear children's voices again," she said. Vibol and Kunthea could be heard arguing over a lizard they were trying to catch below the house. "Are all you women managing alone?" Boupa asked.

"No, my husband, Rotha, is with us, but he is not here right now," Mali said.

"Well, Chakra, I think we can all fit nicely in this house," Boupa said.

"Yes, you may stay for now," he said, his words directed at Mali.

"Thank you! You have a very nice home," Sokha blurted out as she collected the empty cups.

"It was nice...before," Boupa said as she looked around. "We used to have rugs, mats, baskets, and many nice kitchen items and tools, but they are gone. Everything has been taken except this rug, which was underneath the nice one! How has life been here since you returned?"

"We've only been here a week," Sokha said.

Mali joined in. "People are just beginning to come back to their old houses. Many have taken a long time because they are looking for family members like you. Others returned to find the city an empty, quiet place."

"And food?" Boupa asked.

"We have not had any luck finding food. The markets are empty. Mali is trying to grow potatoes in a patch alongside the house, but it has not rained all week. My uncle and his wife have some root vegetables leftover. I'm sure we will share what we find with you."

"We have a few cans of rice and will share it with you, too," Boupa said.

Mali nodded. "Sokha, would you get a pail of water so they can clean up?" Mali turned to Chakra and Boupa and said, "We will leave you to rest after your journey and meet you back here for dinner. I must tend to my quarreling children," she added with a wry smile. "Perhaps we'll have a lizard to roast tonight if they didn't let it get away."

Chakra and Boupa were like sweet grandparents. The rice soup was thicker with a few morsels thrown in, and Rotha had returned with a cabbage that was not very fresh but still tasted good in the soup. Sokha slept soundly that night.

Each day after, the family had to widen the circumference in their search for food until they were exploring the outer reaches of the city. While roaming, Sokha stumbled on a field of sugarcane growing behind a tall rotting fence. She checked around for a home nearby to see who might own it and found no one around. "Let's get Rotha's cart," she suggested, "and cut it down." She and Chantou found Rotha, and he joined them with the azada. By evening, they hauled a heaping cart back to the house, and along the way, Rotha traded a small bunch of sugarcane for a long sharp knife.

With her mouth watering, Sokha picked through the tall stalks of sugarcane to find a healthy one to share with her family. She ripped off the leafy top, and held the long cane in two hands, using her teeth to remove the outer sheath, peeling downward. She cut the last remnants of the sheath off with Rotha's knife and sectioned the segmented stalk into six-inch pieces that she cut in half again.

After rice and soup, Sokha passed around the bowl of sugar-cane sections. Ooohs and Ahhhs filled the room, and sweet sugarcane juice dripped down their chins.

"What an unexpected treat!" Mali said. "Thank you for fixing it, Sokha."

"I'll cut some into sticks to dip in Keo's tea!" Sokha offered.

"Good thought!" Chantou said. "Maybe our luck is changing."

"I don't think so," Rotha said. Chantou frowned. "We've searched all over, and most of the land is dead, the gardens unworkable. If we stay where we are, we will starve as we did in the Pol Pot years." Sokha's shoulders sank. "Uncle Keo said he heard there is food at the Thai border."

"How far away is that?" Sokha asked.

"About 115 km, I've been told, but we will have to go through forest. It will be hard, and we'll need to prepare."

Chantou exchanged looks with Sokha. Sokha wondered if she'd be walking back and forth between the city and country all her life. She felt sick thinking about it.

"You think we can make it?" Mali asked.

"Do we have a choice? The Vietnamese are in power here. At least we are fairly strong right now and have enough food to travel part of the way," he said. "Thailand would be more friendly, and they are not at war."

Mali looked at Chakra and Boupa. "What will you do? Will you come with us?" she asked. Boupa sipped her tea.

Chakra shook his head. "No. If our boys come home, we will be here," he said. "But I think your husband is right. You have many people to feed and must find a better place."

"It will take a day to prepare to leave," Mali said. "I think we should all get some rest."

"So we are walking to another country?" Sokha asked. In her mind, the trip would take years.

"Jah. I agree with Rotha," Mali said. "We don't want to be caught in another trap here."

Shortly after dawn, Rotha left for the market to sell his ox and cart for gold to trade for rice along the way.

"What took so long? Why don't you have rice?" Mali asked when he returned hours later. Sokha and Kunthea quickly stepped aside as Rotha strode toward Mali, his face contorted in anger.

"I've been cheated. I was given fake gold, but I didn't know it. Two men bought the cart—they gave me melted bullet shells, not gold. Rotha pulled the pile of gleaming nuggets from his pockets and dropped them on the ground. They clinked and rolled.

Sokha held her breath. Mali's face remained expressionless. "We couldn't travel with that cart anyway," she said. "You said it yourself, we may have to hide or run, and we don't need a big cart and animal to slow us down."

"But we have no rice!" Rotha fumed.

"No one does. I was wondering where you thought you'd find some," she said.

"Now we'll have to scavenge for food again," he huffed, but some of the steam had drifted off the furnace of his rage. "I should have known better," he muttered. "Filthy thieves! Bastards are everywhere!"

"Rotha," Mali said. "You can stand here and be angry or spend your time looking for food. We leave in the morning." With that, she entered the house.

Rotha stamped his foot, and his face turned purple, but as he looked at Mali's back through the doorway, his face drooped in defeat.

Sokha had never heard Rotha swear like that. *Did the Pol Pot years change us all?* "We still have sugarcane to trade," she said to interrupt his mood.

Rotha kept his eyes on the ground. "I'll take some of that and see what I can get for it," he said and turned away.

29

April 1979

S okha's family followed the footsteps of those before them. As they passed each village, they saw pagodas and old schools full of Youns camping out—young men smoking with guns strapped across their chests or swaggering down the streets, making their presence known. It was rumored that they had defeated the Khmer Rouge in two short weeks in a lightning war.

Once out of the city, they walked long hours for three days past rice fields and stilted homes spaced far apart in the country. Heading north, Rotha asked people along the road, "Can you point the way to the Thai border?"

"You must head toward Banteay Meanchey province. Follow this road to Sisophon and go west." Many other stragglers followed the same route.

They were heading toward the far northwest region of Cambodia through the Cardamom mountains, a Khmer Rouge stronghold where Pol Pot's leaders were said to congregate. It was a forbidding forest throbbing with wildlife: elephants, tigers, and clouded leopards; and during the rainy season, leeches that latched on to any warm body passing by.

"Keep going. Getting closer," Keo urged. The blazing sun forced them to rest frequently and make side trips to seek out food in the markets or woods. Sokha faded into her thoughts. *Nearly four years spent avoiding the chlop militia, fearing that Pol Pot's eyes might bore into me one day; fearing the penetrating stare that would surely challenge me to pledge allegiance to Angkar, and knowing he would detect my disloyalty. Four years spent hiding all my emotions, burying sadness. How many more years must my family sweat under the scrutiny of soldiers holding all the power?*

In every village along the way, Sokha noticed Aunt Ary checking each young male face in hopes she would find her son. A few times, her aunt let out a short gasp of recognition only to hear Uncle Keo say, "It's not Chhay." Sokha wished she could be the one to find her cousin first and present him as a gift to his parents.

Once again, Rotha asked for directions. "You must go west to Poipet. There is the crossing into Aranyaprathet," he was told.

The closer they moved to the border, the more Uncle Keo warned of buried landmines. Years ago, Boran had told him some of the war tricks used to thwart the enemy. "Keep to a packed dirt trail if you can," he repeated, but it was not always possible when fighting broke out. It was not only soldiers they feared but also starving strangers and bandits. And if they had to penetrate the forest, Keo warned them of punji stick traps that might be planted in the ground—bamboo sticks sharpened to a point and coated in human feces buried by Youns to catch Khmer Rouge guerillas. "Look for a light coating of twigs and leaves that seems to cover a hole," he said. A punji stick injury would cause a slow, agonizing death by infection.

Several nights were spent hiding in the woods or shrubs beside the trodden path, hoping they would be passed over.

Sounds of gunfire popped in the distance. There were soldiers in plain sight. Unpredictable soldiers. And Rotha warned, "There are others hiding out. Stay alert."

As the days passed and the forest swelled around them, the trees hummed with life. Cicadas chattered, and birds soared from branch to branch overhead. Soldiers, like fast-moving clouds, flashed between tall overgrown ferns.

Mali suggested they wear their black shirts over their colored t-shirts all the time, so they wouldn't be spotted, but still, Sokha jumped at every sound. At dusk, her eyes played tricks as mist hovered over the treetops, and animal calls echoed. She clung to Kunthea's hand as if protecting her, but her sister's warm hand made her feel safe.

As daylight slipped through dense trees and vines, they tread carefully. When Rotha held up his hand to silence the family, every ear perked up. Pointing down meant *hide in the bushes*. Down they went, squatting thigh to thigh, squished together. All of their senses peaked at once. Eyes saw movement; ears heard crackles, heartbeats thumped, and their noses sniffed for signs of human or animal threat.

Vietnamese troopers clomped along the path hunting for stray Khmer Rouge soldiers. When the woods fell silent again, Rotha checked to see if the way looked clear before he made a hissing sound, his safety call to the family, and one by one, Sokha and her sisters emerged from the brush, feeling each step with their feet for noisy twigs, slowly pushing away branches so they would not snap. Nights in the eerie forest kept Sokha awake long after she tried to will her aching body to sleep. *Who will get us first, the animals or the soldiers?*

The border hung before her like a mirage, a sacred place of sustenance and rest, a shimmering line of hope. *How will it feel to step over this border, to enter a country that's not at war? To stop being afraid?*

After many days, and losing track of time, they began to see more and more Khmer refugees ahead. A few more days and the road clogged with people as well as bands of Vietnamese troopers and Khmer Rouge soldiers, depending on what part of the border people were trying to cross.

"Who can we trust? Who can tell us where to go?" Sokha asked.

"No one," Rotha answered. "You trust no one. I will do the talking."

As Uncle Keo and Rotha whispered, thinking they were out of sight, a soldier in black appeared and asked, "Where are you going?" It was hard to determine which side this soldier was on. Usually, the Vietnamese wore green.

"We are in search of food. We are a family with children," Rotha answered. Keo stepped beside Rotha to shield the girls.

"There's no food here," the soldier said, holding his rifle down. A few other cadres gathered nearby. "You know when you pass this line, you will be across the Thai Border, and you are not welcome. They do not want more people coming across."

With that, another soldier who looked Cambodian called the cadre over. He whispered a few words to the soldier who had spoken to Rotha, and the soldier changed his story.

"Come here. You can cross," he said, and he let the family pass. Rotha hesitated. He looked confused because he didn't know what precipitated this change of attitude. Sokha wondered if the Khmer soldier recognized her uncle. Had he treated someone they knew? As quickly as the soldiers had appeared, they faded into the forest.

Rotha and Keo led their families on the thin, worn jungle path for another half-day with Mali urging everyone on. "Walk faster! Let's get somewhere safe by nightfall." The road began to change again, opening up on both sides with wider and wider clearings.

Sokha's nose caught the scent of rancid humans before she saw them—refugees everywhere. The border area looked like an emerging Khmer Rouge commune. Refugees were lying on the ground, building little huts with branches for roofs, squatting in the shade.

Sokha noticed that a few people were eating food, but most looked hungry and lethargic like her family. *Why have we walked all this way to grow weaker, to feel threatened by soldiers, and find no food?*

Rotha went investigating and learned that the first people who had arrived at the border were given food, but since then, supplies had run out. Mali had one can of rice left in her stash. Sokha sat rubbing Vibol's back in the shade with her sisters while Rotha explored further. When he returned, he had a few cans of rice and a handful of wilted greens. He did not say where he got the food or if he traded something for it, and no one asked.

While eating, Mali and Rotha talked. "We should try to keep walking until we reach a city," Rotha suggested.

"But we don't know where to go," Mali said. "What city?"

"It's too crowded here, and there's nothing to eat. People are fighting. I nearly got pulled into a brawl. We have to get away." Hearing this, Sokha could not help wondering, where is *away*? How far must we go to get *away*?

Rotha picked a path, and the family followed. Sokha felt a little revived from the meal, but she wanted to sleep. Rotha and Keo urged the family on, and as they pushed forward, the unmistakable stench of death permeated the air. Sokha saw a fuzzy figure up ahead. As she drew close, she saw a dead woman sitting by a bush as if sleeping with her baby still in her lap. Flies hovered over their bodies. She noticed a ragged father and child squatting by the roadside, the father looking as lost as the toddler next to him. After seeing a mother with three children sitting in their own waste begging for food, she steeled herself. Dead bodies littered the side of the path, more than she could count, and just as many looked nearly dead. Sokha covered her nose and followed Chantou.

Her family kept all their words and feelings inside.

They stared ahead. They moved on.

30

The Thai Border
Chumrum Thmei (New Camp)
October 1979

Dust motes from hundreds of pairs of trampling feet on the dry earth clouded the air like smoke before the skies opened up and rain turned the red dirt to mud. The road snaked with refugees carrying sopped bundles of possessions. The line of people doubled and tripled in width until refugees funneled into a vast field of bedraggled humans sitting in groups close together. There were no shelters, huts, or structures, only people dotting the landscape and blurring into the mountains far beyond. Sokha squeezed through wet bodies, sticking close to her family members until Mali finally staked out a space of their own.

As they set their plastic sheeting on the ground, Sokha berated herself for imagining some kind of salvation beyond the border. *The life we knew before Pol Pot is gone. We will never live that well again.* The thought felt like the bamboo lid her father used to seal off the world, shutting out the light in the foxhole that smelled of doom.

Rotha read a sign. "We are in Chumrum Thmei," he said. "We're over the border in Thailand. I was told a warlord who hoards food donated by aid agencies runs this camp. Be careful." Rough looking men and women haggled over black market items as men patrolled with guns, although no order existed, and defectors of the Khmer Rouge army picked fights all around the camp.

Sokha felt a flash of fear when she realized that a garden hoe and a knife served as her family's only weapons in this place that looked as if a free-for-all could break out any moment.

The spot that Mali claimed lay on the outskirts of the ever-expanding camp near a tree. Close by, six monks chanted, a comforting sound that Sokha tried to hear above the noise of children crying and men arguing.

Rotha cut a few branches to build a crude shelter for the family and used his other plastic sheet to keep out the rain. "I have heard there's one well for clean water, and workers are digging two more," he said. "I'll go collect some, but we need to see if we can find any food. Pick a partner and forage in pairs. Do not stay away long or travel too far," he warned.

"There's nothing but mud here," Sokha moaned.

Rotha looked around, his face grim. "You're right," he said.

"I may be able to trade a cure for rice," Keo said. "I will ask around the market stalls." He turned his gaze to the youngest girls. "Don't you or any of your sisters venture over there."

"Why not?" Sokha asked.

"There are soldiers from all sides here—hard to tell who's who. Khmer Rouge, Thai, Vietnamese. It's dangerous."

"I'm going to try to find a map of the area at the black market, so let's go together, Keo," Rotha suggested. "I'm sure we'll be able to find something to eat. Mali, stay here with the girls and listen for any useful news."

Sokha leaned against the tree, glad to have nothing to do. *I could sleep for days,* she thought. Kunthea put her head in Sokha's lap and fell asleep. Mali, Chantou, and Vibol slept next to them under the flimsy shelter. Their rest didn't last long. When the sun came back out, the heat woke them up. They listened to the people surrounding them.

A while later, Keo brought back two cans of rice, and Rotha reported what he had discovered. "There are white-skinned people taking refugees away on a bus to a place with shelters and food," he said. "I need to find out where, so I will go back to the market tomorrow. There are no maps, and no one seems to be able to give me directions."

"I heard some of those buses can't be trusted," Mali said. "I have heard some people talking about them. One man said they drove people back to Cambodia!"

"Jah, Sokha said, "I heard a girl say that a Thai man here had asked her if she wanted to volunteer to go back to Cambodia with her family! Why would they ask that? The girl told the man she'd rather die!"

"I'll find out more," Rotha said. "We don't want to do anything stupid now that we made it over the border."

In an animated voice, Rotha relayed a story that sounded like a folk tale to Sokha. "I have heard of a white-haired woman—maybe American or Australian—who is in charge of the bus, and no one, not even the Thai soldiers ever harm her. She holds a position of power." Sokha pictured what this white-haired woman might look like—a wiry woman with skin the color of the palest pink eggshell, robed in a thin flowing dress with see-through colors like a moth's wings.

"No one knows exactly who she is or what gives her such authority, but everyone reveres her," Rotha said. In a rare imaginative burst, Sokha could see her as an apparition flying and swooping down to rescue young children in danger.

Within days, Rotha learned more about this legendary woman. "She is a leader in the American Red Cross. People told me she is both kind and strong. She runs a refugee camp nearby where she cares for many people. No one challenges her because they all trust her. She is the only one in charge of the bus, and she always comes at the same time and place, so people who are fleeing can find her. If there's trouble, she changes the time or place and tries to get word out through scouts."

Rotha kept seeking answers, and after several attempts, he was able to find a scout and make his way to the bus. "It parks by the roadside a few hour's hike from here, usually in the same spot. I think we should try to hike there," he said. "It's a long way, and there are soldiers, but I think we can make it. We must be sure we are all able to get on the bus together, or we will be split up."

The thought of being alone without her family made Sokha shiver. Holding her only possessions, an extra black uniform, a piece of rolled-up plastic sheeting, and a mat she had woven, she set out with her desperate family to walk through the jungle again. They had to arrive at the right time. As it grew later in the day, Rotha stepped up the pace until he and his family were running through the last of the forest path where the red clay turned to hot sand, and he knew that's where the bus would be parked.

"I think we're here," Rotha whispered.

"But where's the bus?" Sokha asked.

"Let's wait. It should come," Rotha said. He wiped the sweat from his forehead. They gathered behind a stand of trees and stared at the road for ten minutes before they heard the crunch of tires on gravel. Sokha saw the bus creak to a stop, the doors folded open, and she saw a shadow move inside before a woman's hands gripped the railing and her head appeared from the doorway looking left and right, her waist-long white hair swaying as she moved—a mythical figure come alive. The woman stepped off the bus looking willowy yet exuding strength. The pale skin of her face appeared luminous as she craned her neck to search among the trees, and she straightened when she noticed Sokha and her family. Waving her arms, she yelled to them in Thai, "Come! Run! Quickly!"

Rotha cried, "Now!" and Sokha's whole family burst from the brush and ran toward the woman. She helped them onto the steps as they climbed in and slid into vinyl-covered benches. From her seat on the bus, Sokha saw the strange woman up close, her translucent skin, her blue eyes, glassy like the blue Ratanakkiri gems she once saw sparkling at the market with Mea. She heard the woman's confident voice commanding a Thai soldier and a driver as if she wore stripes on her shoulders. Sokha held on to the seat in front of her as the bus lurched forward and bounced along the dirt road, tree branches slapping the windows. Vibol cried when his skinny bottom smacked the seat, and Mali scooped him up to secure him on her lap. Chantou put her arm around Kunthea to hold her steady, and the bus bumped along.

Sokha smiled at the white-haired woman to thank her, this ghostly figure who alone held the power to rescue desperate people and whisk them away. She noticed Chantou also smiling at her as if enchanted. *How many lives has she saved?* Sokha wondered. *How many has she rescued? How wonderful to be the white-haired woman. Surely, she will reach nirvana.*

Warm dusty air blew through half-open windows as they made their way to safety. Several minutes later, the bus stopped on a stretch of land carpeted with refugees. Once again, Sokha had arrived at a place she knew nothing about, at the mercy of whoever would receive her and her family.

31

Khao-I-Dang Khmer Refugee Camp

"Look at all these people," Sokha said. Her family kept hearing of places offering rice, but it seemed that there would always be more hungry people than food to feed them.

Keo calmed her fears. "I have a few dried Chres leaves. Help me grind them for our dinner soup," he said.

"Where is there water for soup?" Sokha asked in a morose voice. She sat next to her uncle, who set down his basket and pulled out a small spice sack. "The woman on the bus told me we would receive clean water. We just have to wait a little. Here's the last of my powdered mango leaves. I had hoped to use them for treatments, but this will help us all feel better."

Chantou and Mali arranged what few pots and cups they had on the ground and settled the children nearby. "Thank you, Uncle," Mali said. "We'd better make a sleeping area for tonight." Rotha pushed the long sticks they collected into the dirt and attached what cloth they had to provide shade, but there was nothing left to do, and so they sat.

At dusk, a truck pulled into camp holding twin drums of clean water and refugees scrambled for a place in line. Sokha's family collected their allotment for the next 24 hours: a half bucket of water for each person to drink and cook with, but it was not enough to use for bathing, and Sokha yearned to pour a shower of cool water over her body. The meal that Mali and Keo simmered for supper slid down more like tea than soup. It lent a fragrant aroma but did little to quell the gurgling in Sokha's empty stomach.

Sokha waited for the moon to rise, counting the stars one by one as they appeared until she drifted into a fitful sleep. The sound of distant small arms fire woke her in the morning. *Who has any fight left in them? How many will be left when the killing is over?*

Sitting up, combing the dust from her hair with her fingers, she saw Keo boiling a pot of water, and after his drink, he said, "I'm going to see what I can find to restock my medicine basket."

"May I come with you?" Sokha asked.

"Yes. But check with your sister first." Keo stood up, his back cracking as he rose. He turned his head left to right and tilted ear to shoulder to work the kinks out of his neck.

"May I go?" Sokha asked Mali, who had just rubbed the sleep from her eyes.

"Jah. Go help your uncle," she said. "There's nothing to do here."

Sokha stepped carefully behind Keo, through a maze of tents and bodies, until they came to the edge of the refugee camp where trees and foliage grew. "You are always watching me," Keo said when they were finally able to walk alongside each other. "Remember when you helped me with my sprained foot? You have a gift for healing. Would you like to learn more?" The realization that it was no longer a crime to be educated lifted Sokha's spirits like an unexpected gift.

"Jah," she said, and for the first time in nearly four years, Sokha performed the sampeah for Keo, holding her prayer hands higher, and bowing to show respect for him. As she raised her head, she saw the loving eyes of a father returning her gaze.

"Then, I will show you. Let's go." They entered a trail into the edge of the forest, and after a few minutes, Keo stopped. "We won't venture too far in because we don't want to run into any fighting, but observe carefully. There is medicine all around us."

Bending to inspect the grass and plants on the ground, Keo picked a small bunch of wood sorrel. Tracing the outline of the leaves with his finger, he said, "Deep green. Three rounded leaves on each stem with a taste similar to lemon." He handed Sokha a few bites to try. "It contains many nutrients. You can eat every part of it, stems, seeds, and all. We can make tea with this for Aunt Ary and your sisters."

Sokha scanned the ground for more. "I found some!" She picked a bouquet and stuffed the greenery in her sack.

"Healing is about restoring balance in the body with the help of nature, but in our situation, we must eat anything we find that is edible." He let out a short laugh. "Look here. The tops of these Paco ferns can be eaten raw." He broke one off and handed it to Sokha. The taste pleased her, and she collected more.

A little further on, he said, "It rained last night, so look for mushrooms. The het hu nu grows on dead tree trunks and looks like mouse ears." Keo and Sokha found a few random mushrooms, some Keo kept, others he threw back. Before they returned home, he mentioned a climbing plant called bauhinia and told Sokha, "The young shoots and leaves of the plant cure dysentery, but I don't see any here." Sokha felt a surge of satisfaction as Keo passed along his knowledge of tree bark and plants.

On their way back, Keo discussed how small doses of poison

could sometimes heal as well as any medicine. "It's the dose that makes a poison," he said. "But be careful when eating plants, some can be deadly in very small amounts. I once saw a woman die because she ate too much raw cassava root."

Once they returned to their campsite, they sipped water and sat beneath a nearby tree, sorting all the specimens they found. Keo set out the objects of his profession and used a rock to scrape at a piece of bark until a small hill of fine particles formed. "*A hundred pieces of medicine*," he said as he shaped a small mound. "Every particle counts, each helps the body in its own way."

Sokha thought of her family. They gave her strength in a horrible world, each member of the family helping the others survive in their own unique way like the hundred pieces of medicine he talked about. With that thought came a flash of shame that struck her with its force. *I nearly cost them their lives when I robbed that corn. I was selfish, and I must repay Uncle Keo for claiming me that day. How could I have failed the one man I love almost as much as I loved Ba?*

Keo's low voice shook her loose from her feelings of disgrace. "Traditional healing isn't only about the medicine," he said. "Special chants and prayers go with certain cures, and sometimes a healing touch must be applied for an injury to heal properly. A healer not only mixes a poultice but also uses massage to transport the medicine to relieve pain. Do you understand?"

"Yes—like we did with your ankle," Sokha said.

Keo nodded. "There is so much to know."

"How do you remember it all?"

"It has taken years and years of study and practice," he said. Sokha let his knowledge sink in and realized that she had forgotten her hunger all morning. Her mind began to think about the complexity of the human body and the hidden magic in the world that could alter it. *I might want to be a healer someday*, she thought.

From first light until evening, Sokha watched an endless flow of refugees pour into Khao-I-Dang as aid workers struggled to house and feed them. Her family collected their half-bucket of water a day, and the Red Cross began distributing rice in rations, along with small amounts of other foods like vegetables or dried fish, when available. As a bonus, every ten families shared one chicken a week that they boiled in a communal pot of soup.

Sokha noticed dramatic changes in the camp every day. First, a large bamboo and thatch hospital and clinic replaced the sick tent. Rotha and Keo helped volunteers build long rows of bamboo and palm leaf huts for housing, a series of connecting rooms measuring about 64 square feet each, that kept out the blazing sun and monsoon rains—one room to each family.

Relief workers from dozens of agencies poured in and enlisted the help of healthy refugees to dig trench latrines in the alleyways between houses and along the perimeter of the camp. To meet the burgeoning need for water, a group began excavating wells. The few former professionals who were multilingual and had survived the Khmer Rouge helped translate Khmer into English, French, and Thai for foreign aid workers, and they recruited and trained workers of all types to get the camp up and running.

Sokha organized a game of tag with a few young children as she babysat them one afternoon, and soon several other children joined in. A young Khmer man stood watching. "You are patient with children and babies. How old are you?" he asked.

"I'm sixteen," she said, as a toddler came crashing into her legs to avoid being tagged. She lifted the boy into her arms.

"Can you read and write?"

"Jah. Khmer. I think I remember...."

"Well, Sokha, how would you like a job?"

"What kind of job?" she asked.

"A job where we train you in the clinic. You will be rewarded."

"A clinic like a hospital?" she asked.

"Yes, exactly. You will help people here."

"Jah! I want a real job. But how will I know what to do? What will my job be?" Sokha asked. She had never been given anything for her labor, so she wasn't sure she understood the arrangement. Would she receive gold? Food? She knew that Rotha used to be paid money at the hospital, but money had been wiped out.

"There's an opening at the Mother Child Healthcare Center. You would help pregnant women stay healthy. In return, you will receive a little extra food."

Sokha nodded excitedly. "Like a healer? My uncle is Kru Khmer."

"A doctor's helper."

I'd rather be a healer, she thought, *but a helper would be a good start.* "I need to check with my brother-in-law and sister for permission. I'll talk to you tomorrow," she said.

"If you can do it, please show up at the Health Clinic early tomorrow morning. They really need people like you. You can start right away." Sokha agreed.

On her first day of work, Sokha approached the gated healthcare grounds and told the guard at the gate, "I have a job. Doctor helper." The guard took her name and walked her inside. Sokha squinted as she went from the bright sunshine into the shaded room, and she heard a cheerful voice.

"Good morning! You must be Sokha!" A petite white woman with a white coat spoke in Khmer, but Sokha could tell it wasn't her native language. Sokha noticed her hair, swirled and wound in a graceful design and pinned to her head. *She must be the doctor. Wow. She is a happy woman to be so nice to me.*

"Hello," Sokha said as she looked around the room. In the center sat a table with a bamboo mat on top, and along one wall was a cabinet of supplies and a tall metal contraption that Sokha had not seen before.

"Before you work with the mothers and babies here, I will show you what you need to know. Our patients are lining up already. I'll show you how to check-in the first few patients," the doctor said. "We need to keep track of who is who. Are you ready?"

Sokha nodded as the doctor lifted a clipboard off a peg hanging on the wall.

"First, you write each person's name on this pad. Let's pretend you are a patient." She handed Sokha a pencil. "Write your name on this line." Sokha hadn't touched a pencil in years, and it felt foreign in her hands, but after the first few strokes, she felt relieved that she remembered how to write.

Next, you will weigh each woman," the doctor instructed. "Step up here," she said. "This is a scale. It tells us how much a person weighs, how heavy that person is. You weigh 98 pounds." All you need to do is write the number next to your name."

When Sokha stepped off, the doctor showed her how to measure a woman's height. "You are five feet and four inches. A tall girl," she said.

Sokha proceeded to weigh several women and record their weights on a tablet with the doctor present. "Your job is to keep records of the weights of these pregnant women so they can deliver a healthy baby."

"My sister Mali is pregnant," Sokha said. "Can I help her, too?"

"Jah. And you can tell her that her ability to hold a child

inside shows that she is recovering from the starvation she suffered under the Khmer Rouge. It's a good sign."

Sokha dove into her work with a new sense of purpose. Each day, she learned a little more about nutrition during pregnancy. "I have met many women through my work," she told Chantou. "Now they see me and say hello. I have new friends, and soon, I'll see their babies."

After the first two weeks, Sokha noticed something mysterious and asked one of the translators who worked in the clinic, "Why does the doctor never stay around the camp at night. Where does she go?"

"Some of the relief workers think the camp is too dangerous at night," he said. "They are taken to a more secure location. I think they go to a hotel several miles away."

Sokha nodded in mock understanding because she could not relate to what he said. *They don't feel safe? This refugee camp has been the most secure I've felt in years. After being marched out of the city at gunpoint, starved and worked half to death, punished and released, but then trekking through the jungle, I feel pretty safe here with a room, a job, clean water, and rice!* She shrugged.

The following morning, the doctor returned. "Sokha," she said. "I'd like to teach you to use a stethoscope." The doctor invited Sokha into an examining room where a woman in her seventh month rested on a table. Using the Khmer words she knew, mixed with English and sign language, the doctor began her lesson.

"To locate the heartbeat, feel around the woman's abdomen for the baby's back." The doctor pointed to her own back, and Sokha nodded. That's where you'll hear the heartbeat best." The doctor then palpated the woman's belly, searching for the right spot. When she found it, she placed the round silver end of her stethoscope on the spot, listened, and placed the ear buds in

Sokha's ears. Sokha's face lit up at the sound of galloping and swishing inside the mother's womb.

"It's easiest to hear after the fifth month of pregnancy," the doctor said, stretching out her arms as if she were holding a large belly. "The mother's heartbeat is much slower than the baby's heartbeat. Here, listen. Mother...." She tapped the table with a slow rhythm. "Baby," she tapped the table quickly making swishing sounds with her lips. "That's how you tell them apart." Sokha slowly learned the nuances of each sound and how to distinguish between a healthy and unhealthy heart rhythm.

She also used the stethoscope to hear lung sounds, listening for wheezes and crackles. She practiced taking pulse readings and began asking expectant mothers questions about their eating habits, stressing the importance of taking the vitamin supplement she gave them. *Uncle Keo was right: food is medicine! The small capsule the doctors told her to dole out to young mothers also held many particles of medicine.*

But better than these vitamin pills were the eggs she was given to dispense to expectant women who required extra nutrition. The first time she handed an egg to Mali, her sister held the fragile orb and gazed at it as if it were a nugget of gold.

"Where did you get this?" she asked. It had been five years since she had eaten an egg.

"There are only a few dozen for pregnant women like you. The clinic gets a small shipment each week. Eggs keep your baby healthy," Sokha said. "Inside the egg is protein to make you feel better."

Mali sat on a bamboo chair holding the egg, entranced.

"You're not going to stare at it all day, are you? And don't share it. This egg is only for you!" Mali stood up and hugged her sister with one arm; her other arm carefully lifted away so she wouldn't damage the egg.

"Let's put the egg over here for a moment," Sokha said,

placing it in a wooden bowl on a corner shelf. She had another surprise for Mali. "Please lie down on the table," she said in a mock professional voice. Mali did as her sister instructed wearing an amused look on her face.

Sokha stepped over to the wall where the stethoscope hung on a peg. She carefully took the instrument and draped it around her neck. She lifted Mali's shirt and began feeling her abdomen. Mali flinched, but Sokha gave her a reassuring look.

Sokha then carefully placed the drum on Mali's swollen abdomen. She listened and moved the silver drum a few times before finding the right spot. Once satisfied, she held the drum in place with her left hand and took the earpiece out of her ears with her right hand. She handed them to Mali. "Listen," she whispered.

Mali placed the ear buds in her ears and heard her baby's beating heart. Sokha could tell the exact moment she heard the sound. Her mouth opened in amazement.

"That's your little baby," Sokha said. She squeezed her sister's hand.

After the exam, Sokha told Mali that her baby's heart sounded healthy, and she handed her the egg. "You are to eat this at once. Don't show anyone or it will disappear fast. Okay?" Mali nodded with a smile and tucked the egg in her pocket.

Two months later, in the early spring of 1981, Mali delivered a healthy baby boy, and it was Sokha who helped her breathe through contractions and Sokha who handed the newborn to her sister. At only seventeen years of age, Sokha had proven herself at the clinic.

"You have grown so valuable as an assistant that we can now afford to pay you a small amount for the work you do here in addition to receiving extra food," the doctor said. "Congratulations!"

By now, Sokha regularly administered routine checks,

collected blood and urine samples for the doctor, and measured the diameter of each mother's pelvis.

She also detected depression in some young mothers who had not planned on becoming pregnant. They looked sad and distant and rarely washed up, even though there was now clean water available. "More and more babies are being born healthy," Sokha said to one such woman, "because we have rice every day and good care."

"I'm still hungry," the woman said. "And now another baby to feed."

"But don't you want a healthy baby? If so, you should keep your hands and body clean to avoid germs." Sokha held the woman's hand in her own. "See all this dirt under your fingernails?"

"What are these germs?" the woman asked. "I can't see them." The woman pulled her hand away in protest.

"No one can see them. They are too tiny to see, but sometimes when people are sick, their breath and body can smell bad, and that's from germs. That's how you know you have them." The woman turned her head away and made a clucking sound. Sokha continued anyway, "Germs can get into your mouth, nose, and eyes and make you sick, so you must wash your hands to protect yourself and your baby, especially after using the latrine." The young mother looked at her suspiciously as if she were making up lies. "We no longer have to feel dirty like we did in the Pol Pot time," Sokha insisted. "Won't you feel better to be clean? To smell fresh?"

The woman looked away and stared into space.

"Look at me. I am around sick people all day, and yet I'm healthy. Why? Because I wash my hands," Sokha reasoned. The woman shook her head from side to side and smirked.

"Here, take this." Sokha handed her a sliver of soap. "Please use it. I am telling you to stay clean because I care about you and your baby." The woman caught a whiff of the soap, and her eyebrows lifted as her face softened at the scent of jasmine.

Next time, Sokha thought, *I'll hand over the soap before the speech and save myself some work!*

A few days later, after dinner, a young boy ran to Sokha's house. "You must come quick! My mother. She's having her baby!"

"Get the midwife. The doctor has gone," Sokha said.

"I already tried. She's sick—can't come. Throwing up!" he said.

Sokha ran with the boy, checked his mother, and asked the woman's husband to carry his wife to the clinic. She stayed all night with the woman, who could have been no more than twenty-five years old and struggled with her stethoscope to find a fetal heartbeat. The sound was so weak, she was not sure if she could hear it, and the woman was not progressing with her contractions as she had seen before. Sokha placed cool rags on the woman's head and made her as comfortable as possible.

Sokha heard the door creak as the doctor entered in the morning. "Sokha! What happened? Where is the midwife?" the doctor asked.

"She is sick. She could not help, so I stayed here by myself." Sokha looked down at the young girl on the bed. "She is four fingers, and she has been for a long time."

The doctor took one look at the young woman and reached beneath her skirt for an internal exam. Then she listened to the woman's belly for a heartbeat and walked Sokha to a corner of the room.

"First, you did all the right things, and she'll be okay, but not her baby." The doctor put her hand on Sokha's shoulder. "The baby is dead. I'll need to deliver it or operate. You can go home and get some rest. Thank you. You did everything you could. I hope you know that."

"I'm staying," Sokha said. "She's frightened, and she trusts me." Sokha walked back to the bedside, turned the woman's face to her own, and spoke soothing Khmer words to ease her sorrow as the doctor went about her work. After the baby was taken, the doctor washed and swaddled her, and she handed the female infant over to the mother, but the mother turned away.

Sokha spoke to her for a short time, but the mother wanted to be left alone.

"It's time to go get some rest," the doctor said to Sokha. "You should go. I can handle this." Sokha turned to leave. "But wait. I want to thank you. You are caring and competent. I think you could stand in as a midwife if we are short-staffed. Would you be willing to do that with a little more training?"

Sokha nodded and left, too tired to realize she'd been given a promotion.

~

"Is Rotha still digging pit latrines?" Sokha asked Mali.

"Jah, and he's miserable. What a nasty job. The monsoons make them fill up too fast."

"Poor Rotha. I'm glad I work indoors now," she said. Mali cooked and watched the children, enjoying the extra food rations Chantou and Sokha provided through their work.

Chantou walked through the door, excited. "I heard a Cambodian teacher has opened a small class to teach English to students," she said. "We have a little money saved. Want to go?"

"I was told it would cost 15 baht a month, and there's nothing else to buy here, so I think it might be worth it," Sokha said.

"Girls, check out the clothing I stacked in the corner over there," Mali said. "I was given a bunch of donated skirts and blouses to try on. Want any?" The girls ran over and started looking through the clothes. Their sizes were different. Chantou was slim, straight up and down. Sokha was curvier. They threw garments back and forth, trying them on over their t-shirts and talked.

"Oh, I like this tiger print! Remember all the outfits the girls wore in public school? I miss that school." Chantou smiled, but her smile quickly turned to a look of longing.

"Let's try the classes here," Sokha said. "I can already say a few words. Hel-Oh! How are you?" the girls laughed. "And I get this white lacy blouse," she said, posing with her hand on her hip. Chantou picked up a black button down blouse. "No black stuff. Throw that one out!"

The next evening, the two sisters walked over to the hut designated for school. The room was so jammed that a line formed outside, so they sat along the outside bamboo wall on the ground where they could still hear. The following week, they came earlier and sat in the classroom. Packed with bodies, the heat was enough to make everyone sleepy after a long day of work. Sokha felt sick.

"I don't think I want to do this anymore," she said to Chantou on the way home.

"Me either. Besides, we're running out of money, and we know enough to get by," Chantou said.

"Jah. Let's save our money for when we get out of here."

"Rotha says we may never get out. He keeps signing papers, but nothing's happening."

"We can't stay here forever," Sokha said. "How do you like your job, Chantou?"

"It's okay. Nothing special. I mostly check on people in the waiting room and then clean the clinic. It's boring, but I like being paid. Why do you ask?"

"I don't know. Just wondering."

Sokha felt anxious working at the clinic, but she didn't know why. Sometimes, she grew lightheaded and sweaty watching women in labor. After a string of births with multiple problems, Sokha could not bear to hear another woman scream in pain. She found their cries distressing as if an emotional switch had turned on inside her, and she vividly recalled seeing the baby that was shot in the air by the soldier, a memory she thought she had blocked from her mind. *Working with mothers and babies didn't bother me before, why now?*

"Another miscarriage," the doctor said. "I'll need to do a D&C."

"I'm so sorry. I have to go," Sokha said and stumbled from the room. Outside, she knelt in the dirt and struggled to breathe, her heart pounded, and she saw spots. *I can't do this anymore. Mali is pregnant again. I could never watch her go through this. What if something goes wrong?* As soon as she was able to stand, she waited in the doctor's office to speak to her.

"Sokha, what happened in there?" the doctor asked. "I needed your help."

"I don't know, but I can't work here. I'm sorry! It's all too sad. I don't know why it feels so hard all of a sudden," she said and began to cry. The doctor's shoulders slumped.

"I hate to lose you, but I understand, Sokha. "There are healthy babies, but there are a lot of sad cases, too. You are young. Take good care of yourself. If you ever need a job again, I'll be happy to help you."

Sokha walked home and told Mali what had happened. Tears came again.

"You'll find another job. The Red Cross and IRC are always asking for people who can write," she said. Sokha had a cup of tea with Mali and then went to the camp office to apply for a new job. Within hours, she was hired.

"I've taken a job at the IRC," she told Chantou in the evening.

"Why? Has something gone wrong? Were you fired?"

"No. Too much suffering every day, that's all. I need something different."

"What's your new job?"

I'll be counting all the refugees in the camp, gathering information from group leaders, and sending their names to the IRC, and the names I collect will help people find lost relatives."

"It sounds boring compared to what you've been doing. I thought you wanted to be a doctor."

"I did, for a while, but not anymore. I think this new job will help me feel better. I'll be helping people find each other, something positive." She thought for a moment. "Remember how unsettled we felt not knowing where Rotha was sent in the Pol Pot time? Remember when we were all separated? What if they had kept us apart? These records will help people find their families. It's important work, too."

Chantou nodded in agreement. "Maybe you'll find Chhay!"

"I'll try. I'd love to see him again!"

Sokha earned 300 baht a month. Instead of saving money, she filled out a form to exchange her baht for goods like food, clothing, and supplies. As the family grew, Sokha found there was no money left over at the end of the month. Everyone chipped in to support the best life they could achieve as refugees.

"What are days, weeks, or months anymore?" Sokha asked Chantou. "The Khmer Rouge erased our way of life. Are you ever angry about it?"

"I don't think about it," she said.

"We used to live from rice planting season to rice harvesting season, and now we live day to day, from sunrise to sunset, and what do we have to show for it? No home, no farm, no school... like we had before..."

"Don't think about it too much because you can't change what's done. It's the way it is."

"I know, but I want to have fun again. Don't you?" Chantou yanked Sokha's sleeve and ran away laughing in a playful taunt.

"Hey, you can't do that. You can't pull on me!" Sokha said and chased her.

Sokha loved that her hair was growing. It grew longer and glossier and felt like freedom. Under the Khmer Rouge, everyone had the same blunt cut as if they were all copies of one another, but now, women began to look like individuals again.

As Khao-I-Dang improved, aid workers helped parents build a larger school with bamboo walls, a sturdy roof, and a dirt floor. Many refugees had missed four years of education and were anxious to catch up. This would be a more traditional Cambodian curriculum, not language classes, and it did not cost anything. Sokha signed up.

On her first day, she sat next to a shy girl named Na, who was about sixteen years old but small for her age. A bunch of boys made fun of her, and at first, so did Sokha, but then she felt sad for Na because she had no friends.

On her second week of classes, Sokha arrived at the school and heard three teenage boys taunting and tossing balled up paper at Na.

"What's the matter? You think you're too good for us? You're just a stupid girl," the leader of the bunch scoffed.

Sokha strode up to them and said to the biggest one, "Stop doing that!" The other two boys laughed at her, but Sokha didn't back down. She stepped closer to the tallest boy, her pupils dark with anger, and used the tone she remembered from her father, "If she was your sister, would you do that to her?" She put her hands on her hips, "No? Now look who's not talking! Ha!"

The boy's face flamed red before he recovered himself. "Shut up. I'll kick you even if you *are* a girl," he said.

Sokha balled her right hand into a fist. Equal to the boy's height, she emanated strength and confidence. "Try it! Try it," she dared. Pushing one fist to his nose, she said, "Don't push me. I'll give it right back to you!"

The boy froze at her fist, shocked that a girl would dare act that way. His friends backed off and snickered at him, and the teacher walked in.

Sokha sat on the bench next to Na, who gave her an adoring look. "Thank you," she whispered.

From that day on, Sokha and Na became close friends and looked out for each other. Whenever they had a break, Na followed Sokha around like a duckling.

Sokha inherited her father's height. When she left the clinic, she stood at 5'5" and weighed 108 pounds. She had grown another inch and gained ten pounds since arriving in the camps. Na was short and small-boned and looked to Sokha for protection.

One evening, Na's parents invited Sokha on a trip to the theater. An outdoor stage had been built in a wide-open field near the Buddhist temple at the far edge of camp to provide entertainment for refugees free of charge. Sokha lost herself in the charming story of a prince who fell in love with the King's daughter. "Look at that beautiful dress! It sparkles!" she said to Na who sat next to her. "My little sister, Kunthea, would love that dress! She's not like me. I like to be comfortable and be outdoors," she said.

"And the prince is handsome," Na giggled. Walking back home, the girls kept a few paces behind Na's parents.

"Can I tell you something? Will you swear you won't tell anyone? Ever?" Na asked.

"Jah! What is it?" Sokha said.

"I have a boyfriend," Na said, and her cheeks blushed.

Sokha guessed who it was. She had seen the two staring at each other. "Does he hold your hand?" she asked.

"No. My father would *kill* him." Na paused, then leaned close to Sokha's ear. "But once, in private, he kissed me. It was so fast, I hardly remember it," Na said, giggling. "I pretended to be offended," she added, looking up at Sokha with a devious smile.

"Oh, you are a bad one!" Sokha said and laughed her hearty laugh. "I won't tell. But have your parents ever talked to you about who they want you to marry?"

"No. I hope they allow me to choose," she said.

"Mali and Rotha will plan my marriage. I'm sure of that," Sokha said. "She's told me a million times not to find a boy until we leave this place." Na scowled in sympathy. Sokha remembered the conversation not long ago when Mali had told her. "No boys!" and Sokha responded, "That's easy for you to say. You have always had Rotha, and now you have two children and a third baby on the way to keep *you* company."

Mali smiled back at her. "Jah." She held her hands to her swollen belly. "Babies are sweet, Sokha, and marriage is good, but it's a big responsibility, too. We will find you a nice match when we leave this country."

"I know that. Don't worry about me," she said. "I have not seen anyone worth marrying here."

Sokha loved washing her thick black hair with lavender or jasmine soaps that were more precious to her than money. She now had daily rice along with a little protein and some fruits and vegetables, which made her skin glow. A small seed of personal satisfaction sprouted inside her, and she loved talking to Chantou about boys. One had caught her sister's eye. Reflecting on what Mali said she thought, *maybe I'll wait my turn, and maybe I won't.*

32

Kab Cherng Border Camp, NE Thailand

"Pong. Have you met Pong?" Sokha heard girls asking this question all day long. He was the handsome twenty-one-year-old they all wanted to meet. His clear skin and pleasant disposition set him apart from most of the angry, injured young men in the camps. Sokha spotted him on the first day of her new assignment at the health center where he worked as a nurse practitioner.

Her new job didn't involve delivering any babies, only check-ups. She didn't want to help deliver Mali's third child. A fear had grown in her after seeing many pregnancies go wrong.

"You're not afraid of this tiny needle, are you?" Pong asked a wriggling child. "Not a strong-looking boy like you. Look at those muscles!" Pong said as he squeezed a little boy's biceps.

"No! No. I don't want it," the boy cried and tried to squirm away.

"Okay then, here's a deal. You can pinch my arm on this side as hard as you can while I give you this shot, but you have to stop when I stop, okay?" The boy smiled. In a blink, it was over, and Pong made a dramatic show of how much his pinch hurt.

"The shot didn't hurt me one bit," the boy bragged through misty eyes.

"I told you that you're tough!" Pong sent him on his way and caught Sokha's grin. He smiled back.

Sokha had turned eighteen in the weeks following her family's relocation to Kab Cherng Refugee Camp for another step in the immigration process, and the clinic had practically begged her to work for them because of her experience. *I may like this job, after all*, she thought.

Each morning, Sokha saw Pong on her way to work. The first morning, he only nodded at her and said hello, but on the second day he stopped. "How are you? He asked. She blushed and smiled. Looking in his eyes felt like staring at the sun. "What's your name?"

"Sokha."

"I'm Pong," he said and held the door for her as they entered the health center. The next day, he greeted her and walked by her side. "Good morning, Sokha. How long have you been at this camp?"

"Not long at all," she said. An awkward moment of silence followed. "I have to get to work," she said and hurried inside the gate to the clinic door. *Why did I run from him when I like him? Is it written all over my face? Does he think I'm not friendly? I hope not!*

Each morning after, she searched for Pong. Most days he showed up, but sometimes she never saw him.

"I didn't see you yesterday," she said.

"I missed seeing you, too," he said, his unexpected response making her look at the ground and smile. "I work a second job at the food processing center, and it's in the other direction. I had meant to tell you, but you always seem to be in a hurry."

"You work hard," Sokha said, trying to cover her embarrassment.

"You, too. You have a good reputation with the doctors," he said. "How do you know so much about medicine? Did you go to school?"

"My uncle is Kru Khmer. He has taught me a lot. I also assisted a doctor at Khao-I-Dang." Sokha felt her unease slipping away. *He's so easy to talk to.* They parted ways when they reported to work. *Does Pong like me, or is he this friendly to everyone? I wish I could talk to Na, she would know.*

After work, Pong sought her out, leaned in close to say, "For you," and passed her a note before he hurried away, flashing her one beautiful smile over his shoulder. Flustered, she held the paper for a second before shoving it in her pocket. She felt Pong's breath on her cheek and touched it. Sokha's mind raced. She walked until he was nowhere in sight, leaned against a tree and read the note.

Dear Sokha,
Your name is beautiful, and so are you. I'd like to spend more time with you.
Pong.

Sokha's hand shook. She imagined him writing the note at work. She read the brief note again and again and then tucked the letter back in her pocket.

The following morning, as he strode toward her, her mouth dried up—she felt as if she stood alone on a stage in the theater not knowing what to say, and she knew he anticipated her response to his note. All she could do was smile at him. Every little move she made felt awkward, the way she walked, spoke, looked at him, and looked away.

Day after day, she and Pong met, and he passed her short love notes. His face, his voice, the way it seemed as if he could see inside her—everything about him filled a place in her that had never been reached before. Standing close to his body on the hot clay road made her shiver.

She hid his letters in a thin booklet she had saved from her English class inside the dormitory-style bamboo house she and her family stayed in, and her fingers itched to hold and read his letters all day.

According to custom, Pong never held her hand or embraced her, yet the sight of him made her skin flush, and her body drifted toward him as if being pulled by some invisible force. She had to check herself to maintain her composure. *Why must we live by these strict rules? Why can't we be happy and act on our feelings?*

Sokha knew she had to be careful not to attract attention— she'd been warned. Yet the same harsh rules that frustrated her made her secret encounters feel all the more intense.

For weeks, Sokha's life pulsed with happiness. Every waking minute, she thought of Pong. Her imagination bloomed with images of him standing tall and handsome as a groom, his eyes radiating love as she walked to him dressed in a golden bridal costume, her hair swept up with flowers. She envisioned him lying next to her, wrapping her in a hug so secure she'd never want to move. She thought of him climbing the steps to their house on stilts, the house they would rebuild on her family's farm—the house they would fill with children.

In the clinic, Sokha's joy spread to others. She assisted a young physician named Dr. Mark, and one day he looked up from his medical charts. "You are the best assistant I've ever had here," he said. "You're always cheerful and never give up trying to understand English."

"Thank you," she said. "English hard. I think I learn more English here than school."

"You've been in the refugee camps a long time, Sokha. What's taking you so long to leave this country?" he asked.

Sokha continued rolling bandages and stocking supplies on the shelf. She concentrated on finding the right words and spoke slowly. "My brother-in-law, he try and try for papers for *all* my family to leave, but they not believe us—that my father was General in Royal Cambodian Army. We have *no* papers to prove it. And we all want to go together," she said.

"Do you have any photos of your father? Picture?" the doctor asked, pointing to a photo on the hut wall. "Because a picture of a general in your family —a Lon Nol general—would be an advantage with the Americans."

"Advantage?"

"*Advantage* means it could help. Having the picture could help with immigration."

"My sister bury his picture when Khmer Rouge come. Picture lost. House lost. Bomb or fire. No picture."

"I'm sorry to hear that," the doctor said. Sokha fought back tears as she tried to remember her father's face in the photo. "You are smart, and you work hard, Sokha. I hate to see you trapped in these camps for much longer. There's no life for you here. I'll do my best to help you and your family." He told her that he traveled to Bangkok often and had some connections at Immigration. "They might pull a few strings with my recommendation."

"Pull strings?" she asked.

"I did it again. Sorry. It means help. Help you get out of here."

When Sokha told Rotha and Mali her news at dinner, they both seemed pleased but not optimistic. "It's nice that he appreciates you, but I doubt this will get us anywhere," Rotha said. "I've been trying to get us out for years. But thanks, anyway."

Sokha's mood was not dampened. She had no desire to leave, and for the first time she felt she could be happy if she never left this place as long as she could see Pong every day. And Mali's baby was due to be born soon. She felt more hopeful and optimistic now that her sister held on to her pregnancy so long.

A week later, Sokha floated down the dirt road with another note tucked in her pocket when she felt the warning drops of a heavy rain pelt her head and broke into a sprint to arrive home before the deluge. She leapt over the small mud puddle that always formed near the door, then stopped short when she saw Rotha standing before her, a disgusted look twisting his face. Mali sat on the ground chopping a few vegetables for supper, but she, too, looked cross. Rotha pulled a letter out of his pocket and waved it in front of Sokha's face. "What is this? What have you been doing?" he asked.

Sokha stammered, "I...I...."

"Why? Why are you embarrassing the family? Why do you talk to this man in secret? Do you want people to think you are filthy?"

"No. No," Sokha said, finding her voice. "He cares for me. I care for him. I was going to tell you soon."

"What did we ask of you? Was it too much? We are trying to get everyone to another country. You will ruin this for everyone! You cannot do this. You are not to see this man again. Do you hear me?" With that, he tore Pong's letter in pieces. Sokha looked to Mali for understanding, but her face remained stern. Tears pooled in Sokha's eyes.

"Say it. Say it," Rotha repeated. "You will not see this man again! A decent man would have asked permission to see you. We know nothing about this person!"

Shrinking in shame, Sokha said, "I won't see him again." She curled up in the corner of the room. Rotha stomped outside, and Sokha heard only the sound of Mali's knife striking the cutting board.

Sokha intentionally avoided Pong for a while, but he sent her another letter through a friend. Then another. Each one professed his feelings for her, and his confusion.

Dear Sokha,

Are you angry at me? What have I done? Why won't you speak to me? I know you feel the same way. What's wrong?

Sokha never wrote back because she was afraid of Rotha and his anger, of being disowned by her family. Still, she could not stop herself from reading Pong's letters over and over again until her whole body felt too heavy to move. Finally, in a state of despair, she scrawled a note telling Pong what happened, and she asked him not to write back.

He would not give up. "Please try to change Rotha's mind. Tell him I am honorable. How could he refuse you?" he wrote.

"Mali, can't you talk to Rotha for me? Can't you do something to change his mind? Please help me," Sokha begged. But her words met a stoic, unflinching wall.

"Look at me. I am about to give birth. This is not the time," Mali said.

"Then when is the time? When is *my* time?"

"That boy is not right for you. We are trying so hard to leave this place, and you should avoid complications. Maybe you have forgotten what we have been taught, what has always been true: that a man is like gold—if he gets dirty, he can be washed clean, but a woman is like a white cloth that once soiled can never be clean again." Mali stared at Sokha. "You'll get over him."

"I won't!" Sokha cried until she could barely catch her breath. "I have never asked you for anything, yet you won't give me permission to love the only boy I cannot help loving."

"That's enough!" Mali said. "No more of this. See how he's upset you?"

Sokha's face turned purple. *You are upsetting me!* Her mind screamed the words she could not speak to her sister—the sister who always took care of everyone. She nodded and left for a walk to cry in private.

Mali gave birth to a baby girl a day later without any problems. Sokha watched as Mali adjusted to being a new mother for the third time. She wanted to be happy for her sister and Rotha, but she felt jealous watching them coo over the newborn—jealous and alone.

"Mali told me that we're moving back to Khao-I-Dang for six months to file for a special application," Chantou said to Sokha after work one evening.

While watching Mali set out a large bowl of soup and a small bowl of rice, Sokha asked, "We're being moved again?"

"Jah. We have no permanent home here. Look at my children, still not full after their meals, only enough fruit to want more, almost no meat. Once we are able to leave the refugee camp as a family, we can build a home and a life. See? This is for the good of the family." Sokha stood with her arms crossed, but her heart softened to see a hint of empathy in Mali's face.

"Come. Let's eat," Mali said as if tired of arguing. Rotha, Chantou, Kunthea, and Vibol sat cross-legged and ready for dinner.

"I'm not hungry," Sokha answered.

"Well come sit with us, anyway," Rotha huffed.

Sokha sat down reluctantly and picked at her rice. *I hate everything and everyone. I hate this place, this food, this disgusting crowded camp.* In spite of herself, she ate. Her stomach demanded food, even if it had no flavor and wasn't enough to fill her up.

A bus drove several families between camps, and Sokha sulked all the way to Khao-I-Dang, but Rotha wore a look of confidence. Mali nursed her infant and looked exhausted.

Once they were assigned to a dormitory-like shelter, Rotha said, "We are going to get out of Thailand. I've scheduled an interview with translators to help us find a sponsor. I'll let you know tomorrow where we all need to be. We have to give statements about our family."

Keo interrupted. "We don't want to be included." He looked at Ary, and she nodded in agreement.

"Why? After all this? What's here for you?" Rotha asked.

"Chhay," Keo said. The name on his lips carried all they needed to know. Ary nodded, her eyes filling up. "As long as we don't know what happened to him, we have hope that we may find him. Also, I am Kru Khmer. I can work in this part of the world, but not in America. We will stay with you until you leave, and then we will return to Battambang and wait."

"But the youns. What if the Vietnamese never leave Cambodia? How will you..."

Keo put up his palm to silence Rotha. "We have talked as a family, and this is our decision to make. Let us treasure our time together before you go." Keo nodded man to man.

Tears slid down Sokha's cheeks.

"But what about Aunt Ary!" Mali cried. "You will take her back there?"

"It is her wish," Keo said. Sokha could see Aunt Ary fighting to control her emotions.

"You have a new baby. This will make your journey easier.

You may find you can get into America with two less people on your list. We want what's best for everyone," Keo said. Ary's lip trembled, and he took her hand.

Water poured from Mali's eyes as Rotha flashed her a look to be quiet. Sokha had never seen her older sister so distraught and realized in that moment that she and Ary had been in the same camp throughout all of the Pol Pot years. *Maybe Ary felt like her mother, someone to look up to in the way that Uncle Keo is like a father to me. We have already lost one mother and father.* The thought filled her with grief.

"Then we wish you well," Rotha said. "But you must let us know where you are and that you are well from time to time."

Keo nodded his assent. All four of his nieces stood crying before him. Ary let go of Keo's hand and walked to them, her arms spread wide and drew them to her. "My girls," she said. "Davi's beautiful girls," she whispered.

Mali and Aunt Ary spent every day together. Ary was an expert cook, and she taught Mali a few ways to make appealing meals with few ingredients. When they didn't have the spices or vegetables that a dish required, she heard Mali repeating the recipes her Aunt recited, recipes that Davi once made on the farm, long before they only knew the taste of rice. Sokha lost herself in thought. *Other people come into my life, and then I don't see them anymore, like Na, but my sisters and Aunt Ary and Uncle Keo have always been there for me. Where is Chhay? If only we could find him, they would come to America with us.*

Several months passed, and the family fell into despair. Every day, Rotha checked for news. Finally, he received notice that no sponsors had accepted them. "Did they even look for us? Family after family has been sent to a better country, and we cannot get out of here! What is keeping them from accepting us? What do we have to do?"

Mali remained quiet, and Sokha grew despondent.

Keo suggested they all apply separately. "Maybe your family is too large for them to approve. Maybe you should go to separate countries and agree to be split up."

"No, Rotha insisted. We are family, and we'll stay together as a family." Mali shook her head in agreement. "But your idea gave me another idea. America is a large country. If we could be in the same country but not in the same city, should we consider that?"

Sokha, Chantou, and Kunthea looked fearful of the idea, but Mali looked pensive. "That might work. At least we could visit each other. But I'd want to be in a different city with one other family member if I had to be separated," she said. "Don't you think? If we have to split up, we should be sure two go together," Mali said. "Rotha, don't you have an aunt in Georgia? She got out last year, and she's on the east coast, so if we stay on one coast, we could visit each other," she said.

"But immigration said she could only sponsor one person because she has already taken her large family with her," he said.

Keo's brow furrowed. "All of you, don't rush ahead, we must take this day by day. We are no longer forced to work for no pay. We have a roof and food. I'm grateful that we can practice our religion again. We must be grateful for all these changes," he said.

"We've taken it day by day—hour by hour—for years now," Rotha said, and noticing his disrespectful tone, he sighed. "I'm sorry, Uncle. I wanted more than this when the war ended. We aren't able to live in our own country, and we can't get out of this wretched situation. I've applied for another interview, but we are now at the end of the list again." He kicked a stone.

Sokha watched the two men who made choices for her—the two men that changed the trajectory of her whole life by withholding permission or determining where she could live. She had no expectations of moving to another country. She couldn't even imagine what that would be like. *Why do they think life would be better somewhere else? We already left Cambodia for Thailand, and life is still hard. What do we know of America other than what people have told us—that it is paradise. Is there a paradise? Or is it the same as when we were told there will be shelter and food in Thailand only to find rice rations with a half-bucket of water and a stick house? Rotha has told me time and time again not to trust anyone, so why does he trust that America is so perfect?*

Rotha looked like he held a secret inside, news he could not wait to share, but he waited until everyone in the family was present.

"What's going on?" Mali asked.

"There's been a change of plans. We are to report to Kamput, a processing center for immigration to the U.S.," Rotha said. He held his head high and used his authoritative voice. "Upon receiving an excellent recommendation from Dr. Mark, we have been tentatively approved to leave Thailand."

Mali, Chantou, and Kunthea let out happy yelps. "Wait," said Rotha, looking at Sokha. "There is one condition. Since skilled help is hard to find, and Sokha speaks a little English, she must agree to work for three months as a translator at Chonburi Camp before we leave the country. Dr. Mark recommended her highly."

All eyes turned to Sokha. "Will you do this? For us?" he asked.

Sokha detected tenderness in Rotha's voice, and her

emotions roiled. She was tempted to say, *No, why should I?* But the glimmer of hope in Mali's face pulled her in.

"Will you?" he repeated.

Chantou and Kunthea's eager eyes cemented her decision.

"Jah. I will," she said.

Her family let out a collective cheer, and everyone chattered among themselves in excitement, but Sokha stood quietly, smiled weakly, and walked outside for a moment alone. She had heard talk of a new young man that recently arrived in Khao-I-Dang and thought it might be Pong. She kept expecting to stumble on him, but she hadn't. *Is he here? Maybe it's best I don't see him now that we are leaving. But....*

While walking down a muddy lane on an overcast afternoon, Sokha was sure she saw Pong from the back. Her heart skipped, and she turned quickly to hide because a torrent of unexpected tears poured down her face. *He's here! Maybe I can talk to him one more time before we leave!* She retraced her steps to the same spot the next day to see if she could bump into him—and there he was—with another girl.

Sokha ducked behind the corner of a hut and watched them. They walked at a leisurely pace, side-by-side, the girl's hair hiding most of her face as she turned to him. Sokha saw Pong's body lean in closer, and his flirtatious laughter filled Sokha's ears. *Has he forgotten me already? Who is this girl? What is going on?*

"Chantou," Sokha said after dinner. "Let's go for a walk." Once out the door, she said, "I must talk to you alone." The two sisters strolled a distance away from the housing area and along the boundary of the camp until they found a place to sit on a fallen tree limb. "I am miserable. Can you tell me anything about Pong? I feel sick and betrayed by everyone."

Chantou flinched. "There is not much I can tell you. I have given my word."

"Given your word? To who? Why?"

"Sokha, if I tell you what I know, you must promise me you will never repeat it, and you must promise to keep trying to forget about that boy."

"I promise. Just tell me!"

"Several months ago, Pong's adoptive parents visited Uncle Keo, and they said it was because he was the oldest male in your family. His parents asked for your hand in marriage for Pong."

Sokha looked confused. *Uncle Keo? He was part of this?* All of a sudden, it made sense. Of course Pong would go to Uncle Keo.

"He wanted to marry me?" Sokha asked.

Chantou nodded.

"What happened?"

"Uncle Keo asked if Pong would ever leave Cambodia for a foreign country to be with you. And..."

"And? ...What?"

"Pong's parents said they will wait here for peace to come to Cambodia and return home as soon as they can, and so will Pong. They will never leave Cambodia. So, Uncle Keo said Pong could not marry you."

Sokha gasped.

Chantou continued. "They tried to persuade Uncle Keo to let you stay in Cambodia. But he said, 'We love her, too. She is young, and we want her to have a good life without war. She will be going to another country, so he cannot marry her.'"

"How could he do that? I thought he respected me!"

"Uncle Keo loves you more than anyone!" Chantou said. "You know that! He wants you to have a better chance, to find a life without suffering. Cambodia will only see more misery in the coming days, Sokha, and Pong wants to stay here. We all want to get out. We *all* love you."

"But Uncle Keo is staying. I could have stayed with him! With Aunt Ary!"

"No, he is only staying to find Chhay. Their life will be very hard. He does not need another mouth to feed."

"But what about my happiness? I wanted Pong!" Sokha's face burned with anger.

"I know," Chantou said. "But is he worthy of you? He has been seen with other girls."

Sokha fell forward, knowing what her sister said was true. Chantou held her younger sister in her arms as her body convulsed in grief. When she finally stopped sobbing, Sokha let Chantou support her for the walk back home in the dark.

By morning, after a deep sleep, clarity formed in Sokha's mind. Something had opened up in her as she slept. She felt a wave of relief that the family would be moving to another camp, away from Pong and the sickness he made her feel.

While at Kamput, amid another endless row of huts full of people dressed in someone else's mismatched hand-me-downs, Sokha waited for a job to open up, and as the days wore on, she ruminated on her problems. *All this time I have been clinging to a grudge I could not name. I had wanted the family to stay together before I met Pong, but then I wanted only what I wanted—this young man's love, all for me. I was selfish again. It was not Rotha, but Keo who turned Pong away. He did it for me—he did it for all of us.*

While sulking, she saw Rotha leave the hut and decided to speak to him. She'd been avoiding him for many months, full of misplaced anger.

"I thought we were going to be able to get out of here fast

now that we've been approved," she said. Her tone sounded grumpy in spite of her effort to make amends.

"These things take time," he said. "There are many people ahead of us, so we must wait. At least we have a chance now."

"I'm just ready to start over," she said, in a conciliatory tone.

"We all are. Why don't you go help Mali with the children? She is tired of waiting, too." To her amazement, she saw Rotha from his point of view for the first time. She'd been nothing but trouble to him for months on end, pining over Pong, making Mali miserable, too. She'd been sour and defensive toward both of them. The realization did not please her. *Who am I lately?*

Sokha's sorrow slowly turned to anger. *Pong forgot me and found another girlfriend while I cried over him! What kind of man does that? Maybe he's not the man I thought he was!* Deciding not to wait a moment longer, she found the Mother Child HealthCare Center and asked if they had any openings for a daycare job. Once she stated her experience, she was assigned a supervisory position within two days.

Her new supervisor, an old Khmer woman with more lines on her face than Sokha had ever seen, explained, "There are about fifty babies cared for here—they come and go while their mothers work or receive medical attention. You will be responsible for making sure that all the helpers show up to care for these children, and some of the helpers are not very reliable. How old are you?"

"Nineteen," Sokha said.

"Good. You must also keep count of children and make sure we know who their parents are and what is going on with them. If someone does not report to work, you must find a replacement or work the hours yourself."

Sokha nodded her agreement but said nothing.

"This is a difficult job. Do you think you can handle it?"

"Jah. I'm sure of it. I'll do my best," she said, anxious to alleviate her boredom and forget her aching heart. When she found herself lonely at night, she signed up for evening training classes at the clinic to study hygiene and preventative medicine, including how to administer polio vaccinations.

As the pit latrines that lined the perimeter of the camp flooded during the rainy season, waves of sick people flowed into the health center with symptoms of malaria and dysentery, and more children filled the daycare center.

Depression spread through families as they were told that the U.S. would not be taking as many refugees as they had originally promised, and some refugees attempted suicide. More and more succeeded in their attempts, and Keo kept busy consoling families and helping them with his calming potions and prayers. Oddly, Sokha thrived on her busy schedule and found that work kept her mind off her sadness.

"Sokha! Help!" she heard across the room. Striding over, she saw a child of five convulsing in a seizure. "Don't touch him," she said. "It will stop in a minute. Go find his parents." Once the seizing stopped, she picked up the small boy. His body lay limp in her arms, but his eyes opened. "I'm taking him to the doctor," she said. She promptly put her helper in charge and walked over to the clinic.

"I've been told not to treat this boy because the parents think his seizures are caused by the unsettled spirits of relatives who died a violent death," the doctor said.

"I'll talk to the family for you. I know how they feel. They might listen to me."

"Thank you. You have done well," the doctor said.

When the boy's father and mother arrived, Sokha met them at the clinic's entrance. "Your boy had a seizure. Fits. May I come to your house and help you settle him?" she asked.

"Jah. Please," the mother said and took the boy in her arms. The father walked stiffly a few paces ahead of them.

Sitting cross-legged on the thin rug in the boy's hut, Sokha placed a thin blanket she had over the boy as he lay by his mother. "For now, he just needs rest," she said. "But it will happen again if he does not get medical help. The doctor at the clinic is wise and can stop these fits if you let her."

"No. We do not trust the white woman," the boy's father said. "She does not understand what has happened to us, to our family, to his sister."

"I understand," Sokha said, looking down at the boy. She paused, a shared grief crossed her face, and the parents listened. "But I also know that your son's attacks will only stop if you let her give him one small piece of medicine each day. I promise you—I will be there to make sure she gives him the right medicine. I will also have my Uncle Keo visit you. He is Kru Khmer. Your son will have all the medicine he needs to heal."

The boy's parents whispered to each other before they agreed to bring the boy directly to her the next day. "It must be you and only you who gives our boy this medicine."

"I will," she said.

On her way home, she thought about this family and the many losses her people had endured. She arrived back home, lost in thought, and sensed a buzz in the room. Right before dinner, Keo and Ary arrived, and Rotha asked everyone to step outside since they could not all fit in one room. Once assembled, he announced, "It's definite. We are leaving. All of our papers have been finalized for immigration to America!"

Sokha watched Rotha as he embraced Mali and cheered with Vibol, and her anger at him abated. *He is only guilty of trying to keep the family together. He has had to be a husband, father, and brother to us.* And though Pong never left her mind, she admitted to herself that he found another girl without trying harder to win her. *Perhaps Rotha was right all along.*

Sokha watched her sisters laughing with delight at the news

that they would soon be leaving Thailand and not have to live in these miserable camps anymore.

"Sokha, your doctor kept his word. Thank you for working so hard," Mali, said. Sokha hugged her sister. As she drew back, Rotha pressed his hands together and thanked her, too. The gesture of respect caught her off guard, and she forgave him.

Chantou grabbed Sokha in another excited hug. "I was afraid we'd be split up, and I would not want to leave Cambodia unless I could go with you," she whispered.

"We will return to Kao-I-Dang camp in February," Rotha announced once everyone grew quiet, "to sign more papers. The cost of our trip will be $450.00 for each person. Mali and I have signed a loan to the immigration department. The good news is that we can pay them back after we are in America and working, and I hear there are many jobs in America!"

Where in this world is America and what is it really like, Sokha wondered. Time froze as she watched her entire family experience joy together for the first time in years.

Next stop, Chonburi Camp. They were one step closer to getting out.

33

Chonburi Refugee Camp, Thailand

"I have so many new words to learn!" Sokha said. Pronunciation plagued her, especially the "th" and hard "t" sounds, and she kept belittling herself. "I can't say it right," she moaned. Thank you sounded like Sank you. Mother became mudder.

Her supervisor looked unfazed. "You are the best one here. As long as people understand you, that's what matters. Not perfect English," she said. "I certainly can't speak perfect Khmer." Sokha felt better but wanted to excel.

"You will improve with practice," the supervisor assured her. "Your sister is waiting. We are done for the day," she said with a smile. Chantou stood nearby with her hands folded in front of her.

"Okay. See you later," Sokha said to her supervisor with a wave.

While sitting with Chantou, Sokha said, "America is very different from Cambodia. They are teaching me all the rules we must know to live in that country."

"What are they? Tell me now," Chantou said. They were sitting under a lean-to as rain poured off the palm roof in sheets. Knees curled into chest, they talked.

"How to say hello, how to work machines—there are many new machines. I must even teach families how to use an American toilet!"

Chantou giggled and cupped her mouth with her hands.

"No squatting on the toilet!" Sokha said with authority, making Chantou laugh out loud.

After a week of daily lessons, Sokha began to translate what the instructor said to the Khmer families who would soon depart for America:

Do not throw trash all over the place. Use a trashcan. She showed several pictures of American trashcans. A few family members rolled their eyes.

"Are there trashcans everywhere?" a woman asked. Sokha looked at her supervisor with questioning eyes.

"Jah," the supervisor said. "If you don't see one, hold your trash and throw it away when you see the next one. Don't throw trash in your yard or in the street." Sokha nodded, translated, and filed away the information.

She continued with her list: *Do not urinate outside. Look for a restroom to use.* She held up pictures of a girl with a dress or a boy in pants to explain how Americans mark restrooms, and she showed how the spelled words looked: MEN for boys and men and WOMEN for girls and women. The women in class giggled, and some looked embarrassed.

Don't go to somebody's house unless they have asked you to come, and always knock before entering.

Learn rules of your city for yourself. Don't copy others.

Don't go with someone you don't know. Don't trust strangers. This rule frightened Sokha. She thought people would be friendlier in America. *Maybe it is just as dangerous over there,* she thought.

Do not take food or items from a store without paying before you leave or you might go to jail. This is stealing. Stores in America do not bargain or trade."

Sokha asked her supervisor, "What is *jail*? I need to explain."

The instructor said, "It's a place of punishment. Where they lock people in."

"Jail is Tuol Sleng," Sokha said to the families gathered around, and everyone gasped.

"No! No!" the instructor said. "Not Tuol Sleng. An American jail is not as bad. People get food there, no torture, they are just locked in, but in time, many get out." Sokha tried to clarify, but she was unsure about jail and certain that no one wanted to go there. The lesson continued.

This is how you greet Americans: "Hello. How are you?"

No need to bow. Americans don't perform the sampeah—they shake hands.

This is how you shake hands. Yes, you may hold and shake the hand of an elder or a male! Two teenage girls smiled. Some of the men in the room looked at their wives as if daring them to do such a thing.

This will soon be your new way of life. Touching hands and showing affection like a hug in public are acceptable practices in America.

Sokha pushed away a fleeting thought—the flash of a wish where she and Pong could walk hand in hand in America. When she looked out over the group of families, she saw two adult women clucking their tongues in distaste.

Day after day, she translated and learned how to use a stove, a refrigerator, an oven, and a flush toilet. Sitting on a toilet repulsed her, but she was told to teach this while wearing her clothes to show them the proper way to sit. *Who would sit on the same seat where others went to the bathroom? Squatting was so much cleaner!* Sokha taught this the way the barang wanted it taught, but she would do this her own way, she decided.

After class, Sokha walked toward her family's dormitory room, wondering if she was conveying the right information. She felt unsure about her language skills and ability to guide others, especially older men and women who sometimes flinched at American customs. She didn't want anyone to get in trouble in America on her account. As she approached her family's dormitory room, she heard Kunthea crying. Mali's soothing voice followed. Carefully, she entered.

"What happened? Has someone hurt you?" she asked. At sixteen, Kunthea had grown into a teenager, but Sokha would always see her as her little sister, as a little girl.

"We have heard more information about our trip to America," Mali said. "Kunthea will be sponsored by Rotha's aunt in Atlanta, Georgia, but we will be going to Richmond, Virginia as a group. Our sponsors insisted this was the only way. We were lucky to manage to get this arrangement," she said.

Sokha walked toward Kunthea and put her arm around her shoulder. "Oh, bong," she said.

"Kunthea has agreed, and she knows there is a young girl her age in the house, so that will be nice, but we won't be living together. It's close enough to drive for a visit. So once we get settled, we will be sure to visit her," Mali explained.

Over the next few months, Sokha spent more time with Kunthea when she wasn't translating. She was obligated to perform two translation sessions a day. Her head ached from all she had packed into her brain, from finding new ways to explain things to families with limited vocabulary. She sensed how anxious people were trying to understand all that would change in their lives, and she felt the same but tried to mask it and sound encouraging by repeating what her supervisor said: "It is a lot to learn now, but one day, we will feel normal in our new life."

Do I believe the words I'm speaking right now? What will it feel like to live in a land of white people who speak this language all the time? They will speak more quickly than I can understand. How will I keep up?

During one of her many late afternoon walks with Kunthea, Sokha asked, "Are you scared?"

"Not as scared as I was when the Khmer Rouge soldiers came. I'm not as scared as when they sent me away to work with the animals all day, away from the family. I think the scariest day I ever had was a day when I was working, and the sky grew black all around me. Clouds like black smoke suddenly lit up with flashes of lightening. The chickens I was feeding panicked, and the wind began to blow so hard that I thought I might blow away. Then I shook with fear thinking that the chickens would blow away and a soldier would shoot me for losing them. When the rain came like needles on my skin, I sank beneath a tree as the sky passed over me like an evil spirit that could press me into the ground."

Sokha knew primal fear. Her eyes filled up as she thought of her little sister alone and terrified. She was probably only eight years old when that happened. *At least I always had Chantou with me—until the punishment camp.*

"What happened? Did the animals get hurt?"

"No. The storm ended, and the soldiers were nowhere in sight. They had run off to a dry place. I was soaked and muddy, but I found all my chickens. I thought of you defending me at school. How silly, me defending chickens! I tried to be brave, but I cried and cried when it was over before I returned to my hut. I thought I was going to die that day."

Sokha nodded in understanding. Kunthea had already endured the worst kind of separation. "You will adjust to America. Mali says that Auntie is kind and generous. She is getting her house ready for you. I think you will grow fond of her."

"Jah. I will go to an American school. That scares me most."

"Why Bong? You are one of the kindest girls I know. You work hard, and American teachers will help you. If you could stand in a monsoon all alone when you were a child, you can live through an American school!"

Kunthea smiled. "I like American clothes. I want to have a dress with flowers like the one we saw the immigration barang wear."

"You will. I'll see that you have one someday," Sokha promised.

As they circled back toward the family, Chantou walked toward them with a look of excitement on her face. "See that plane? It draws a white line across the sky," she said and pointed to the chalky streak in the expanse of blue above them. "It doesn't seem possible we will be in one of those soon."

All three sisters looked up, and their eyes followed the plane until it disappeared and the line erased itself, as if it had never been there at all.

34

Promise

Each morning, Sokha's family of eight pressed against each other, jostling to read the list on the board outside the immigration office to see if their family name appeared. They had been checking every day for weeks, ever since the last papers were signed and they all passed their physicals.

"We did it! We're going to America," Rotha said, in a voice hushed with disbelief.

"Don't faint!" Sokha whispered to Mali, making fun of what happened to her at their final physical exam.

"So what if I fainted. I was not going to drop my sarong for that dirty immigration doctor all alone in a tent with him!" she huffed. Sokha snickered. Looking back at the long list of names posted, Mali's voice softened. "Is this really happening?"

"It is," Sokha said. "Our name is on the board." Her eyes misted with tears of relief and apprehension—tears for her lost childhood and the only boy she ever loved.

Chantou bumped Sokha's shoulder with her own and

flashed a broad grin. "No more scavenging for food," she said. "I hear there's lots of food in America. Buildings and buildings of food!"

"I will believe that when I see it with my own eyes!" Sokha said. "I no longer believe everything I'm told." Sokha took a deep breath to quiet her mind, but the silence lasted only a moment. Vibol tugged at his father's arm. He now stood as tall as Rotha's elbow. In a high-pitched voice, he released a waterfall of questions.

"What's it like in America? How far away? Will I like it there? Will I go to school? What will our house look like?"

"It's a place with no war," said Rotha. "It's very far away."

"How will we go? How long will it take?" Vibol asked.

"We'll fly, and it will take a long time. We must first travel to other countries."

"In a helicopter? A fighter jet?"

"No," Rotha said. "In a big airplane with many other families."

"Wait, hold on," said Mali. "I'll tell you all about it later, Vibol, but first we must pack and tell people we are leaving. The bus to Bangkok airport leaves in two days."

"Let's go. We can only bring a small amount with us. We must decide on the things we will carry," said Rotha.

"Someone told me each family is allowed no more than thirty-five pounds of belongings," added Chantou. "That's not a lot."

Sokha nudged Chantou and mimicked her, "Hey, bong, don't worry. We can buy *all new* things in America. There are buildings and building of new things over there!" She burst out laughing, and Chantou joined in.

Gray clouds formed low and heavy with rain, so the family quickened their pace. Mali handed her two-year-old to Sokha. "Can you hold her? My arms are tired."

"Jah." Sokha gathered the girl in her arms. It was May 1985, a little over ten years since the Khmer Rouge raged into her city and chased her family into the countryside. Those few days turned into nearly four years of forced hard labor, imposed starvation, and a death sentence for so many. Sokha and her family had now spent more time in refugee camps than they did under the Khmer Rouge regime. *We survived without our parents, but because of them.* In her mind's eye, she saw her mother and father smile at her and turn to stroll across the yard in Battambang.

"Sokha, are you alright?" Chantou asked as they hurried back to their dormitory. She couldn't find the words to answer. The tiny niece she held against her chest was born in the refugee camp, and she would never know the beauty of Cambodia that Sokha knew as a child. She would never smell the fresh farm air or walk to the temple with her family to hear the monks chant. She would never form clay toys and dry them in the blazing sun or watch the family pond burst with water lilies. Pol Pot destroyed Cambodia's beauty as surely as he tore away the flowing saffron robes from their beloved Buddhist traditions. A profound sense of finality seized Sokha as if the umbilical cord that tied her to this ancient land would soon be severed forever. She was not afraid of travel or the unknown, but fearful that she would lose her memories, the ones that bound her to her parents—that by flying overseas, her ability to walk across the border back home meant saying good-bye forever.

Days later, just before she boarded a bus bound for Bangkok airport, Sokha watched Mali bid farewell to Aunt Ary. In a flurry of hugs, long last looks, and tears, few good-byes were spoken, only gratitude and positive sentiments were exchanged.

"Sokha," Uncle Keo, said. "I know you will do well in America. Your father called you the bold one. He was right."

"I was bold but foolish," Sokha said. Against her will, her eyes filled up, and her throat choked. "I wanted so much to make it up to you. My selfishness could have gotten you killed, Uncle. I did steal that corn." She took a step backward as if pushed by the force of the confession that spilled out of her unexpectedly. "I was a bad comrade!" She looked up at Keo, and for the first time in her life, she saw a tear streak his face.

"Sokha, you did what you had to do. You were a child—a hungry child who needed food. I was ashamed that I had to tell the village chief that you were wrong. I had to tell him that *you* had made a mistake, so he would spare you, but everything I said was a lie. You were right. A child deserves food. A child deserves more than you were ever given in those camps." Keo enclosed Sokha in his arms, and his words washed away the guilt of all her silent years. The strength of his embrace took her by surprise as she inhaled his scent, a scent she would always recognize. Keo smelled like home—like fire, herbs, and incense —her muscles melted in relief.

When she stepped away, she bowed with her hands pressed together. "Uncle, how can I ever thank you for all you have given me? I will pray every day that you find Chhay, and I will try to return someday to see you."

Keo nodded and smiled through glassy eyes as she turned to finish her good-byes, boarded the bus, and watched him from the window, his right arm snug around Ary's shoulder.

After the bumpy bus ride, she and her family members each clutched a small bag of clothing and a toothbrush as they made their way through the airport. Mali carried a rice pot and a few dishes in a cloth sack gathered with a knot at the top, useful remnants of the past, and although she spoke calming words to her children, Sokha saw her sister's hand tremble.

Sokha had never seen an airport. She had never seen a plane up close before, and this one was immense. *How will it stay up in the air with all of us packed in here?* Hundreds of refugees filed onto the plane. The thought of takeoff was unimaginable. She pictured pelicans diving as if falling out of the sky, and she shivered.

Sokha felt a dreamlike sensation as she climbed the steps of the aircraft that would take her farther than she'd ever traveled in her life. Chantou grabbed her shoulder, "Bong! Sit with me!"

Mali and Rotha sat together with their two youngest children. Eleven-year-old Vibol sat next to Kunthea, while Chantou and Sokha sat side by side. Chatter and laughter followed as everyone struggled to fasten their safety belts, a contraption that most had never seen.

"No, this part goes here. No, I think it goes like this. Click! We did it." Women in uniforms spoke in Khmer, explaining emergency precautions that added to the nervous chatter.

Every voice stopped at the sound of the plane's engine starting. Hands gripped armrests as the giant metal bird began rolling. Sounds of amazement escaped from passengers as they gathered the courage to look out the window at the propellers spinning, at the scenery whizzing by. Children leaned over their parents for a better view, and suddenly, they were off the ground and rising into the clouds.

Sokha replayed a prayer in her mind to Buddha and all the Neak Ta of her country, to every spirit in every grain of Khmer earth, rock, and tree. *You will always be a part of me. I pray for peace, and I will come back. One day, I'll return to Srok Khmer to reunite with the family I left behind in huts, in urns, in ashes—I'll come home.*

THE STORY BEHIND THE STORY

Each one of us is inextricably affected by our birthplace, time in history, and environmental conditions, and how we remember our past is influenced by these variables. So it was with a close friend of mine. She grew up in Cambodia on a farm, and I grew up in America—two countries embroiled in a geopolitical war that would change the course of millions of lives. My parents lived into old age as I was educated, held white-collar jobs, married, and had children. She worked in forced labor camps and fled her birth country on foot to live in a refugee camp in Thailand before immigrating to America. I had many choices growing up; she had few. Most of her childhood and adolescence was dictated by circumstance or custom.

Years later, we met in a suburban hair salon. She was my hairdresser, and because she wishes to remain anonymous, I'll call her Sokha.

One day, as Sokha snipped my hair, I asked about her family and birth country. She hesitated. "If I tell you, will you write it down for my children?" she asked. "I've never told them any details about my past, and it's not a pretty story."

I agreed to do it, and we began a series of interviews in our homes, in coffee shops, and in the hair salon. Her children finally learned about her past through the discussions I documented, so the promise I made to her was fulfilled years ago, but I kept thinking about what people must have gone through during "the Pol Pot time." I once asked her how she remained so calm while telling her children and me about her experiences. "If I started crying, I might never stop," she said.

Before I met Sokha and her family, I knew almost nothing about the central role Cambodia played in the Vietnam War, and I wanted to know more. So over the course of five years, as our friendship continued through our children's graduations, through new jobs, and a period of family caregiving, I kept reading other stories about survivors of the Khmer Rouge, the Vietnam War, and America's involvement in Cambodia. And I kept visiting Sokha as a friend. We remained friends even after I moved from Richmond, VA to Nags Head, NC in 2015.

My breakthrough for this novel came in 2019 when she invited me on a trip to her ancestral homeland with her daughter where we toured the cities, countryside, and the Killing Fields. Finally, I was able to see, hear, smell, and taste the Cambodia of her childhood, and I was able to create a fictional story about a pivotal time in history. With the exception of historical figures and some of the experiences of Sokha, the characters in this book are fictional.

The title, *All My Silent Years*, actually refers to Sokha's decision to open up and tell her children about a past she kept hidden from them—to protect them—until they were of age and could fully comprehend and understand her traumatic history. Of course, in the novel, the book title has a different meaning altogether.

My friendship with Sokha has taught me that the human spirit is both fragile and unbreakable, and although the world is harsh, beauty remains. I also learned that when two strangers with different backgrounds and almost nothing in common listen to each other empathetically and open-mindedly, deep friendship is possible, and we grow in ways we never could if we had stayed in our comfortable corners.

ACKNOWLEDGMENTS

My admiration and appreciation overflow for the heroine of this book's inspiration, Sokha. Thank you for educating me in your culture and for opening my eyes to your beautiful birth country. Your resilience astounds me.

My heartfelt thanks extend to Sherita Grinter for the cover photo of the Wat Tahm Rai Saw. The White Elephant Temple is the actual site of Sokha's last Khmer New Year as a child, and it still stands. Sherita, I love you for all that you are and all that you give to so many.

An ocean of gratitude extends to fellow authors Jonathan Marcus (and Cyndi) and Tony Gentry for their careful reading and guidance and for helping me through the publication process.

I am thankful for the following relatives and friends for their careful reading, feedback, and recommendations: literary agent Barbara Clark, Terry Cleveland, Nellie Dixon, Cathie Feild, Tony Gentry, Sherita Grinter, Bryan Jones, Christian Lindstrom, Jonathan Marcus, Mary O'Brien, Susan Pfaff, Anna Rawlins, Hugh Rawlins, Mary Rawlins, Patty Smith, Jan Tarasovic, and Nancy Tomlinson.

Many thanks to my OBX writing group for helping me with the earliest versions of the book: Jarie Ebert, Marion Fritz, Martha Horst, Paige Kurtz, Barbara St. Amand, Paulette Cawthon Whitehurst, and Michele Young-Stone.

I would not be an author today if not for the James River Writers and all the skill-building fun they provide.

To my supportive Outer Banks book club, *Wine, Women, and Words,* thank you for always reading such relevant and thought-provoking books and discussing them with intelligence.

I have read many books in the course of my research, and I'm indebted to multiple authors, historians, and journalists for their outstanding books on the Khmer Rouge period in history:

David P. Chandler. *The Tragedy of Cambodian History.*

Ben Kiernan. *The Pol Pot Regime, Race, Power, and Genocide in Cambodia under the Khmer Rouge, 1975-1979.*

Locard, *Pol Pot's Little Red Book.*

Stephen J. Morris, *Why Vietnam Invaded Cambodia.*

Francois Ponchaud, *Cambodia Year Zero.*

Dith Pran, compilation. *Children of Cambodia's Killing Fields* by Roeun Sam.

I'm also grateful for the web sources that provided vital information about Cambodian culture and history:

Cambodia and the Khmer Rouge. https://alphahistory.com/vietnamwar/quotations-cambodia-khmer-rouge/ (Story of Comrade Ox)

Chbab-Srey: https://universelles.net/2017/07/25/chbab-srey-the-way-to-be-the-perfect-cambodian-woman/Henri

Nate Thayer, *The Night Pol Pot Died: A Journalist's First Hand Account,* nate-thayer.com.

Yale University Genocide Studies Program. *Bombs Over Cambodia*. https://gsp.yale.edu.

Deepest thanks to two dear friends who helped in numerous ways to make this book shine: Terry Cleveland and Susan Pfaff.

Anna and Mary Rawlins, my beloved girls, you inspire me in every way. Thank you for listening to my writing woes, for supporting my work, and celebrating each small success with exuberance.

To Hugh Rawlins, my husband, my heart. Thank you for your encouragement and making space for me to work in solitude for hours on end. Cheers! Here comes the fun part at Nags Head Pizza Company, our favorite place to visit with our author friends at the beach!

WRAP-UP NOTES ON HISTORY

One week before the Khmer Rouge took over and marched citizens out of Phnom Penh, Lon Nol's deputy wrote and left this note on a desk in the American Embassy.

April 12, 1975

To: John Gunther Dean, American Ambassador to Cambodia

Phnom Penh

Dear Excellency and Friend,

I thank you very sincerely for your letter and for your offer to transport me towards freedom. I cannot, alas, leave in such a cowardly fashion.

As for you, and in particular for your great country, I never believed for a moment that you would have this sentiment of abandoning a people, which has chosen liberty. You have refused us your protection, and we can do nothing about it. You leave, and my wish is that you and your country will find happiness under this sky. But, mark it well, that if I shall die here on the spot and in my country that I love, it is too bad, because we all are born and must die (one day). I have only committed this mistake of believing in you the Americans. Please accept, Excellency and dear friend, my faithful and friendly sentiments. (signed) Sirik Matak [1]

Shortly after leaving this note, Sirik Matak was brutally murdered; some accounts said his liver was cut out, mounted on a long stick, and paraded around the Capital for all to see. Three days later, on April 17th, two million people were forcibly marched out of the city and into the countryside. The new regime decided it was time to start a new civilization. They changed the calendar: 1975 was purged, and Year Zero began. Angkar's goal was to build a perfect agrarian society that did not depend on outsiders for help. They sealed off the country.

John Dean later lamented, "We'd accepted responsibility for Cambodia and then walked out without fulfilling our promise. That's the worst thing a country can do, and I cried because I knew what was going to happen."[2]

In Battambang, a short distance to the northwest, no one could imagine what had just occurred. Several days later, they were also marched into the countryside and placed in labor camps. Many workers starved to death. To understand what it meant to be starved of rice, one should know that rice is *so revered in Cambodian culture that the Khmer people have more than a hundred names for it, and the Khmer translation of "to eat" literally means "to eat rice."* [3]

Meanwhile, the Americans withdrew from the region after being defeated in the Vietnam War. (However, they still politically supported the Khmer Rouge throughout the 1980s because they wanted an anti-Vietnam leader in Cambodia).

From 1975-1978 there were escalating tensions and skirmishes between Cambodia and Vietnam. Pol Pot decided he wanted to try to retake the Mekong Delta, and his soldiers invaded the area a few times. Finally, in late 1978, the Vietnamese had had enough, and they attacked the Khmer Rouge, overthrowing them in a matter of weeks.

Once they secured the country, the Vietnamese occupied Cambodia and installed a puppet government.

Prince Sihanouk lived a long life, restored the monarchy, and served as King again for a time. He died in Beijing, China but was returned home for a lavish state funeral in Cambodia, where his son, the King, bestowed on him the title: "The King Who Lies in the Diamond Urn."

General Lon Nol fled to Indonesia when the Khmer Rouge took over Phnom Penh, and later lived in Hawaii and California with his wife and children. He died of a heart ailment in Fullerton, CA in 1985. Many described him as a "broken man."

A ceasefire agreement in 1991 ended hostilities between Vietnam and Cambodia, and the Khmer Rouge faded from power.

In 1997, Pol Pot was captured and placed under house arrest in Anlong Veng, northeast of Battambang, near the border of Thailand. Never punished for his crimes, he died on April 15, 1998, of apparent heart failure in his jungle hideout. Nate Thayer, a journalist who extensively studied the Khmer Rouge, believes that Pol Pot committed suicide because he learned that he was going to be turned over to the Americans. (See: natethayer.com.)

Pol Pot's cohorts were not brought to justice for decades. Only a few were charged for crimes against humanity, including Duch, the head of torture and execution from the infamous prison, Tuol Sleng where 12,000 Cambodians were killed. Total estimates of the number of people who died during the Khmer Rouge genocide ranges between 1.7- 3 million people, approximately a quarter of the total population of the country.

END NOTES

Chapter 10

1. Harris, Ian, *Cambodian Buddhism, History and Practice*. (Honolulu: University of Hawaii Press, 2005) 168

Chapter 14

1. Hinton, Alexander Laban. *Why Did They Kill? Cambodia in the Shadow of Genocide*. University of California Press. p. 222.

Wrap-Up Notes on History

1. Dean, John Gunter. "Danger Zones: A Diplomat's Fight for America's Interests"
2. *http://www.nydailynews.com/news/world/u-s-abandoned-cambodia-1975-pullout-ex-ambassador-article-1.2180529.*
3. Klindienst, Patricia. *The Earth Knows My Name: Food, Culture, and Sustainability in the Gardens of Ethnic Americans* (Beacon Press. Apr 1, 2007).

ABOUT THE AUTHOR

Rosemary Rawlins is the author of *Learning by Accident, a Caregiver's True Story of Fear, Family, and Hope.* Rosemary graduated from the University of Richmond, Virginia, and worked in the human resources field until a traumatic family incident spurred her to publish a memoir. A former editor of *BrainLine Blogs* for WETA, her work has been published in several medical journals, newspapers, and magazines. She finds the topic of resilience fascinating and loves reading, walking, and spending time on the beach with her husband in Nags Head, NC, where they now reside. This is her first work of historical fiction.

Rosemary's author website is https://rosemaryrawlins.com.

 twitter.com/@RoRawlins

 instagram.com/rawlinsrosemary

 facebook.com/RoRawlinsAuthor

READING GROUP GUIDE

1. At the beginning of the story, we learn that General Boran Sang retired early and moved his family to Battambang in the Northwestern part of Cambodia. Did you wonder about his decision? Why do you think he chose to live as a farmer instead of a General?

2. What do you infer about Boran and Davi's relationship? How do you imagine their marriage?

3. How did Davi and Boran shape Sokha's character? What role did she play in the family? What character traits does she retain from her parents after her short time with them?

4. How does losing a parent or both parents affect children of different ages? How did this loss affect Sokha and her sisters?

5. What do you perceive about issues of trust between citizens, government, and family members in Cambodia during and after the Civil War? What do

you think the average citizen of any country wants from their government and why?

6. What role do the monks play in Cambodia? Why do you think the Khmer Rouge abused the monks and defaced the temples? What effect did that have on the Khmer people?

7. Discuss the sisterhood of Sokha, Mali, Chantou, and Kunthea. Which sisters were close and why? How would their relationship have differed if there had been no war?

8. What role does Keo play in Sokha's life? How does their relationship develop and change throughout the story?

9. Sokha grows from a baby to a teen to a woman in the story. What experiences are pivotal in her personal growth? When does she gain insight as she grows?

10. How does the Khmer Rouge takeover change societal norms in Cambodia? Do any of these changes persist after the Vietnamese liberate Khmer workers from the communes? Do Sokha's ideas of what's expected of a woman change as she grows up in the refugee camp?

11. Personal identity usually follows us throughout our lives. What impact does the oppression under the Khmer Rouge have on individual identity in the communes? What effect did it have on Sokha?

12. How would you define Sokha's relationship with Rotha? Does it change and/or evolve as she grows up?

13. Can you name laws in your own country that you feel are worth breaking for ethical reasons?

14. Discuss Sokha's first love (with Pong.) What do you think about arranged marriage and her family's decision to reject Pong's marriage proposal?

15. The refugee camps in Thailand held hundreds of thousands of people. What stood out in your mind about life in the refugee camps? What is different about the immigration process today?

16. Sokha longs to return home. What does home mean to her? What does the word *home* evoke in you: a place or a feeling? Can you ever really return home?

17. Why do you think Sokha wishes to remain in war-torn Cambodia when her family is about to immigrate to the U.S.?

18. Does the book title, *All My Silent Years*, have more than one meaning in this story?

19. What does the color white symbolize in the book? (The color worn at funerals, the White Elephant Pagoda, the white-haired woman.) What might they all represent?